FAIRY LEGENDS AND TRADITIONS
OF THE SOUTH OF IRELAND

FAIRY LEGENDS AND TRADITIONS
OF THE SOUTH OF IRELAND

Thomas Crofton Croker

New Introduction by
Francesca Diano

THE COLLINS PRESS

Published by The Collins Press, West Link Park, Doughcloyne, Wilton, Cork, 1998

Fairy Legends of the South of Ireland was first published in Great Britain by John Murarry in 1825

Printed in Ireland by Colour Books Ltd., Dublin

Jacket design by Upper Case Ltd., Cornmarket Street, Cork

ISBN: 1-898256-53-5

ACKNOWLEDGEMENTS

I wish to thank Mrs Kitty Dillon, for her warm friendship, loving support and constant advice; Professor Patricia Lysaght, who has honoured me with her friendship and hospitality in Dublin; the friends from the Italian Department in University College Cork, Professor Eduardo Saccone, Dr Catherine O'Brien and Dr Ann Callaghan, who gave me the opportunity of coming to Ireland; Ms Aisling O'Leary, for her generous help and her friendship; Dr Gearoid O'Crowley and Dr Diarmaid O'Giolláin, from the Folklore Department in University College Cork, for their kindness and support; the people of Cork, for their warmth – they have made me feel at home.

Francesca Diano

To the memory of my son Carlo,
to my daughters Marged and Eurwen
and to Thomas Crofton Croker,
with love this work is dedicated

Francesca Diano

The following Tales are written in the style in which they are generally related by those who believe in them; and it is the object of the Compiler to illustrate, by their means, the Superstitions of the Irish Peasantry— Superstitions which the most casual observer cannot fail to remark powerfully influence their conduct and manner of thinking.

CONTENTS.

THE SHEFRO.

THE CLURICAUNE.

CONTENTS.

THE BANSHEE.

THE PHOOKA.

THIERNA NA OGE.

TO

LADY CHATTERTON,

CASTLE MAHON.

Thee, Lady, would I lead through Fairy land
  (Whence cold and doubting reasoners are exiled),
   A land of dreams, with air-built castles piled;
The moonlight SHEFROS there, in merry band
With artful CLURICAUNE, should ready stand
   To welcome thee—Imagination's child!
   Till on thine ear would burst so sadly wild
The BANSHEE's shriek—who points with wither'd hand
In the dim twilight should the PHOOKA come,
   Whose dusky form fades in the sunny light,
   That opens clear calm LAKES upon thy sight,
Where blessed spirits dwell in endless bloom.
I know thee, Lady—thou wilt not deride
Such Fairy Scenes.—Then onward with thy Guide.

INTRODUCTION

A long time ago, in London, on a late summer's afternoon, I met for the first time an Irishman without a name. I didn't know it at the time, but he would completely change the course of my life.

I met him in an antiquarian bookshop in Hornsey and the person who introduced us, the bookseller, had become a friend of mine. We shared a passion for old books, for things of the past, for the lovely smell of old dusty paper. His shop was a place where I could dig out the past – a past that proved to be my future.

Often, on my way back home from my work at the Courtauld Institute, I stopped there and he liked to show me his treasures – things that rarely I could afford, as he was well aware of the value of his merchandise and he wasn't very keen on parting with things he liked. Unless you got into his favour, that was.

I did. He knew very well of my love for books and old curiosities, so that afternoon, knowing I was leaving for Italy in a short time, he went into the back of his shop, from whence he emerged with a little book that was handed to me with the utmost care.

'This, I am sure, you will like very much,' he said to me with a mysterious smile.

It was a lovely little book, with beautiful engravings and a subject that, at the time, was totally unknown to me: Irish fairy tales.

No author's name on it.

Then I didn't know much about Ireland, or its folklore, but I have always been in love with stories, and tales, and mysteries and the invisible.

The price he aksed for it was ridiculous: £3. And he added, as a parting gift, a pencil sketch of an old village road, flooded with sunlight.

I didn't know how grateful I would be to this quite original man.

As soon as I read the book I was carried away and fascinated by it. How talented and cultivated, lively, humorous and passionate the anonymous author was! So, why had he chosen to remain anonymous? He surely was an authority on the subject. And who was he anyway?

Years went by. I was back in Italy and in a particularly difficult time of my life. I decided to translate that book for my children.

At bedtime, they were my first public and indeed they were enthusiastic! They stayed, open-mouthed, listening to the marvellous tales. But I knew that it wasn't meant to be a children's book. There was something more than that. A fine secret, a wider meaning. I just knew it.

Who was this anonymous Irishman whom I was beginning to love so dearly? And how, in 1825, he could have shown such a modern attitude towards folklore, to respect the storyteller so much?

The words flowed freely, like a mountain stream, gleaming and sparkling in all their beauty and richness. I was on my way to discover the very ancient Irish art of story-telling.

So I began to do some research and eventually, in Yeats' well-known collection, *Irish Fairy and Folk Tales*, I came across the legend of little Lusmore, that was included in my *Fairy Legends and Traditions of the South of Ireland* (the title of my book) and the name of its author: Thomas Crofton Croker. The name of my man at last!

But who was he?

He was born in Cork on 15 January 1798, near Buckingham Place, on George's Quay, from a protestant family. His father, Thomas Croker, was a major in the Army, who had distinguished himself in the American Wars and in the Rebellion of 1798. His mother, Maria, at her second marriage, was a Dillon from Baltidaniel.

Still very young, he revealed a strong interest in all things of the past, collecting and purchasing unusual objects, sketching old stones and inscriptions and roaming the whole of the Munster area in his thirsty research for traditions, superstitions and folklore.

He collected an impressive amount of material then, that formed the basis of his first book, *Researches in the South of Ireland* (1824), and for the *Fairy Legends* the following year.

His interests though were very versatile. Poet, painter, musician, engraver, he experimented a great deal with the recently discovered technique of lithography, which he introduced later in his work as a cartographer at the Admiralty in London.

Crofton Croker did not know the Irish language at the time (he learned that later), but his first dramatic impact with the Gaelic language and culture is linked to an event that took place on 23 June 1813 at the lake of Gougane Barra.

Following a very ancient tradition, each year, on that day, thousands of people gathered on the holy spot for a 'pattern', a pilgrimage to a Holy Well, possibly in honour of St Finbarr.

The pattern had a pagan origin and celebrated, like in many other European cultures, the crops and the gods of nature. With Christianity, the festivity was given a more acceptable connection with the Saint, but still retained its pagan and panic character. So much so, that in 1817, Bishop Murphy banned the celebration of the pattern, issuing a sentence of excommunication if anyone dared to attend.

What happened that night is better explained in Crofton Croker's own words:

'My attention was first attracted to the keen in 1813 by the following circumstance. In the summer of that year I visited in company with Mr Joseph Humphreys ... the lake of Gougane Barra, in the west of the county of Cork. The object of our little excursion was to witness what is called the pattern, held on St John's eve, when many thousands of the peasantry usually assembled there for the purposes of piety and mirth, penance and transgression. This combination of purposes may sound odd to the English, but it nevertheless correctly describes this and similar meetings in Ireland ... As night closed in, the tent became crowded almost to suffocation ... and a man, who, I learned, had served in the Kerry militia and had been flogged at Tralee about five years before as a White-boy, began to take a prominent part in entertaining the assembly, by singing Irish songs in a loud and effective voice ... Upon the conclusion of one of these songs, the old woman, who was a native of Bantry, observed to me: "Well, if God is just and good to us all, we may live to see the end of that schemer, Moriarty, and his *trason* songs, as we did of that poor boy, Flory Sullivan" ... Another old woman, who sat near us, confirmed this by nods of assent, looking at me and nodding expressively ... and she then began reciting, or rather murmuring, with a monotonous modulation of voice, about a dozen of Irish verses, clapping her hands and rocking her body backwards and forwards between each verse. I asked my translator to explain the meaning of what the older woman said. She told me that it was a keen which Flory Sullivan's mother had composed upon him; and from her dictation I noted a translation of three of the verses in my sketchbook, which I now accurately transcribe:

"Cold and silent is thy bed. Damp is the blessed dew of night."[1]

The attendance at this pattern was the event that focused Crofton Croker's interest on Irish folklore and proved to be the turning point of his life, an event that led him to become a folklore pioneer.

He versified the *caoine* and sent it to Richard Sainthill. Sainthill was thrilled and encouraged the young boy to improve the translation which, in 1815, was published in the *Morning Post* and in 1817 came to the attention of the poet Crabbe.

In 1813, with other young friends, Crofton Croker founded the Cork Scientific Society, that promoted research, studies and interest in art, music, poetry and antiquities.

In 1817, he distinguished himself at the annual exhibition of the Society of Fine Arts, set in the actual St Patrick Street Theatre (now the *Examiner* offices).

1. T. C. Croker, *The Keen of the South of Ireland*, London,1844, xviii-xxi.

Crofton Croker sent a collection of some forty musical airs to Thomas Moore, the most famous of Irish poets living in England, and Moore acknowledged Crofton Croker's name in his preface to the *Irish Melodies*.

In 1818, Crofton Croker's father suddenly died. At this point Crofton Croker felt that he had to leave Cork and try the much larger and more challenging world of London, where so many opportunities he knew would be offered to his volcanic talents.

His father's best friend was the Tory politician John Wilson Croker, not related to him in any way, but truly affectionate to the boy. He was Chief Secretary to the Admiralty in London and strongly interested in literature and art. Thanks to this powerful man, Crofton Croker was appointed junior clerk at the Admiralty and he remained there until he retired, at 50.

Due to the great influence that Wilson Croker enjoyed among London's most distinguished literary circles, Crofton Croker had the opportunity of meeting the most prominent men of his time.

His wit, his talent, his charming speech, opened many a door to him. In 1819, he was already working on the *Researches of the South of Ireland*, availing himself of the copious material he had collected during his extensive roaming of the Munster countryside. He received more material from his friends in Cork, but in the summer of 1821, he decided it was time for him to go back to Ireland, in order to collect more elements for his work in progress.

He was accompanied by Alfred and Marianne Nicholson (whom he married 9 years later), the children of the artist Francis Nicholson and painters themselves.

The journey provided Crofton Croker with more precious material, and back in London, he got in touch with the publisher, John Murray, regarding the publication of his book. Murray promptly agreed to publish and in 1824, 750 copies of the book were issued.

The work is a very pleasant and original mixture of a travel journal and an antiquarian and folklore description – a sort of sentimental journey, but endowed with a unique flavour, quite out of the ordinary. The work was unusual, new in its framework, contents and intent. Alfred and Marianne provided the delightful illustrations of the monuments, old ruins and everyday life sketches of this lovely and unusual 'traveller's companion'. Often the descriptions are intertwined with some very savoury dialogue with the occasional countryman. The wit that distinguishes these dialogues is completely Irish and devoid of any irreverent intention. There is a deep respect for the freshness, the humour and the ingenuity of the Irish people. It is clear that the author intended to show Ireland in all its aspects, its beauty, its many-fold realities.

Some chapters deal with folklore, traditions and superstitions, a part that would be developed in his following book, *Fairy Legends*.

The novelty of the book lies not only in its structure though, for there is something else. After all, the English reader had still a very confused and partial view of Ireland and of its inhabitants, seen, as they were, as a bunch of ragged, riotous people. Crofton Croker's aim is that of providing a fuller and deeper knowledge of this people – so different and yet so close, from a geographical point of view, to England. The rejection came from ignorance. By dissolving ignorance, you dissolve rejection. And this is the underlying leit-motiv of all Crofton Croker's work.

He has been accused by B.G. MacCarthy[2], of being dishonest, and of exploiting other people's work – of being Anglo-Irish, looking down on the 'superstition of the peasantry'.

Crofton Croker may have been Anglo-Irish and of protestant breed, but he was still the first to understand how important it was to spread the knowledge of Irish popular and oral culture among the English readers.

As Philip Hannon writes in his extensive and clever work on Thomas Crofton Croker: 'Scholarship has been less than

2. B.G. MacCarthy, 'Thomas Crofton Croker', *Studies*; 1943.

generous in the attention it has devoted to *Researches* and little or no treatment and exploration of its tone has been attempted. Though clearly not a novel, or within the realms of fiction, a close reading of *Researches* will reveal a barely concealed didactic purpose and political intent, not unlike many of the pre-Famine nineteenth-century Irish novels.' [3]

Although he condemns the riotous upbringing of Irish education and the revolutionary character of many aspects of Irish traditions and superstitions, Crofton Croker feels the urge to point out the danger resulting from the English colonial policy. He is deeply convinced that Ireland should be respected more for what it was in England and in Europe, and that a wiser handling of the Irish problem would result in a more peaceful future. His aim is to research, learn and inform. This is the underlying issue. Should the English reader know more about the beauty, the interest and the history of Irish tradition, much of the ignorance that fuelled the hatred (both sides), would be dissipated.

Crofton Croker is, of course, writing from a rational point of view. He doesn't actually believe in Irish superstitions and in the supernatural. But he is willing to analyse them and to understand them as a manifestation of a past greatness and spirituality.

This is his political intent. But most of all he realised, in the setting up of the *Researches*, that that beautiful and unique part of the Celtic tradition, the oral fairytale, should recieve more attention.

Spreading from Germany, the Romantic Movement had reached the British Isles. In Germany, Romantic artists and scholars stressed the importance of reaching back to the source, in order to disclose and bring back to life from the past the 'spirit of the folk'. It was a way of preserving the centuries old oral tradition when it was under threat, during the Industrial Revolution. Thousands were driven away from the fields to seek a better living in crowded towns and factories,

3. Philip Hannon, *Thomas Crofton Croker; from Antiquarian to Folklorist, 1813-1828* M.A. Thesis – UCC 1989 p.69.

coalmines and workhouses. They left behind their ancient knowledge, breaking the mouth to mouth, generation to generation handing down of the oral culture.

The oral tradition, not less noble and extended than the written literature, was a fundamental part of the rural culture tearing to pieces – an essential part of it indeed. The Industrial Revolution wasthe very core of that culture, with its delusions of progress and better standards of living.

In Germany, the Brothers Grimm were busy collecting as much lore as they could, producing their glorious book, *Kinder und Hausmärchen*, published in 1812.

Ireland, on the other hand, was still a part of Europe where the Industrial Revolution was a term unknown and everyday life was still imbued with magic, with the presence of the people of the *sidhe* . Irish soil was literally soaked in the supernatural. The Fairy People dwelt in every stream of water, in every glen, in every cairn , in every fairy ring, in every field and in the very soul of the ancient breed of Celtic origin. The children of the ancient Celtic gods, visible and invisible, were mingled in a dream-like reality, underlying every aspect of life.

'The branchy Irish, that so sweet and terse is,'[4] this poetic language, was their secret language and, when it pleased them, they disclosed themselves, from time to time, to the startled eye of the inhabitants of the Sacred Isle, their ancient abode.

Deeply rooted in the Celtic culture, the art of the *seanchaí*, had been the most powerful means of preserving the original identity against the rough and bloody cruelty of the Saxon invaders.

The ancient gods had not disappeared. They just hid themselves from the irreverent eye.

But only a very flimsy veil separated their existence from everyday life. A material woven with dreams and mist, through which one could sometimes step, like the looking-

4. David Murphy, To Crofton Croker, in *The Keen of the South of Ireland*, London, 1844.

glass through which Alice enters into 'the other room'. And men, sometimes, entered into 'the other room', the Other World. And they were lost, unable to find their way back, or came back still young and strong, after hundreds of years.

No conventional time, no conventional space in this Other World. Just a circular dimension, leading to the sacred world of the Heroes, of the immortal beings of the *sidhe*.

A soulful, spiritual dimension, that did not exist in Europe. So Crofton Croker understood that this was the new path he should follow and in 1825 he gave John Murray, the publisher, the new manuscript. The book was displayed in the London bookshops in March and sold out in a week.

But why was it anonymous? In the *Dublin University Magazine* (August 1849) the official reason is thus stated:

'The reason why the *Fairy Legends* had been published anonymously, when both names of the author and the publisher (in connection) were not unfavourably before the public, was the loss of Mr Crofton Croker's original manuscript and the necessity of immediately replacing it. To effect this, the late Doctor Maginn, Mr (now the Right Hon) David R. Pigot, "Friend Humphreys" and Mr Keightly tendered their assistance, and re-wrote some of the tales, with the view of enabling Mr Croker, who was obliged to work against time, to keep pace with the printer, writing in most instances from dictation. The tale of *Daniel O'Rourke*, as printed in the *Fairy Legends* was, we are assured, in the autograph of Mr Humphreys, touched up by Doctor Maginn and, finally, very much altered by Mr Croker – to all of whom it had been perfectly familiar. In consequence of some publisher having put Mr Keightley's name forward as the author of the *Irish Fairy Legends*, Mr Croker, in his preface to the third edition of the work, which appeared in the *Murray's Family Library* in 1834, says:

"Forty tales, descriptive of Irish superstitions, now appear instead of fifty. All superfluous annotations have been struck out, and a brief summary at the end of each section substituted ... It is therefore hoped that this curtailment will be regarded as an essential improvement ... although nothing which illustrates in the slightest degree the popular fairy creed in Ireland has been sacrificed. At the same time, the omission of the portion of the ten immaterial tales will sufficiently answer doubts idly raised as to the question of authorship."'

Crofton Croker's words reveal the persistence of a controversy on the issue of authorship that arose almost immediately after the unexpected success and about which he was still obviously very sensitive.

The book had certainly been the product of a collaboration and it was no mystery that some of his friends, back in Cork, like Keightly, Humphreys, Dodd, Maginn and Sainthill himself, had provided Crofton Croker with abundant material that he, then, adapted and elaborated. But Crofton Croker refers to himself as the 'Compiler', both in the first and in the second edition, and no attempt is made on his part to reclaim the paternity of the tales.

Actually, that was not Crofton Croker's intent. In the bitter critical turmoil that arose some years later around the question, one too easily forgets the kind of work involved in the compilation of *Kinder und Hausmarchen*, by the Brothers Grimm.

Although their proceedings were far more ambiguous, no one in Germany has ever accused them of exploiting other people's work – of course. Unlike Crofton Croker, they didn't roam the countryside, collecting tales and lore from the naive mouths of the peasantry, but gathered story-tellers at their home and wrote down on paper the tales that these well-educated young ladies (such were their informants) told aloud. More stories they transcribed directly from Dorothea Viehmann, a tailor's wife. But then they greatly altered and 'tailored' to measure the tales in a literary fashion, suitable for the well-educated public of nineteenth-century Germany. Their work is a masterpiece, a beautiful collection of fairy tales, traditions, stories, only a few of which have become universally popular. But, although at the beginning the tales were intended for an adult public, complete with footnotes etc., in the following editions they were adjusted to suit the taste of younger readers. And as such they are now known: childrens' fairytales. They had a moral and educational intent. They are paradigmatic.

The Brothers Grimm compiled appealing and sometimes disturbing material, polishing out the roughest parts into an acceptable book, which no bourgeois household could do without. The perfect product for the perfect modern society, for a perfect pedagogical aim.

Crofton Croker's idea is totally different. His stories, collected around the country, by himself or others, are altered just that much that enables them to be printed, but they retain the powerful presence of the people that told them.

We can still detect, under the surface, under the printed words, the lively wit of the peasants, like in *The Confessions of Tom Bourke* and in the famous *Daniel O'Rourke*, and the wild energies of nature. None of these stories bears the slightest moral, apart from the conclusion that it is better to avoid the Good People. But this is not Crofton Croker's moral. They inform us about the belief in the Good People. That's all. They still bear very strongly their ancient mythological character. They are what is left of the great mythological cycles of the Celts and probably of the people that dwelt on the island before them – a powerful landscape of the past that still speaks its presence. In every well, in every glen, in every stream, in every tree, in every old fort or cairn, in every stone and in every common object breathes a secret, magic life. The magic is there, everywhere around men and their lives are moulded according to nature's forces, energies and cycles.

Crofton Croker has created a method, whose effectiveness has been acknowledged only in this century. For, what else did the Irish Folklore Commission do, when Seamus O'Duilearga founded it in 1935? As Brid Mahon says: 'he told us we were the custodians of the soul of Ireland, that it was our duty to help gather the fragments of a once great civilisation before it was too late'.[5]

The Commission's method of research was not all that

5. Brid Mahon, *While Green Grass Grows*, Mercier Press; 1998

different from Crofton Croker's after all, a similarity that Kevin Danaher stresses in his introduction to the facsimile edition of *Researches*, (1981).

When the first edition made its appearance, the famous *Quarterly Review* highly praised the 'felicity of language' and the Irish spirit of the work. And the *Blackwood Magazine* thus wrote: 'This is a little book, about little people, by a little author, of the height of Tom Moore – full of little stories, pleasant to look at - a book, in short, all the persons and things connected with which are little, except the good humour and the research; both of which are great.'

The book sold out in a week, as we have already said and the Brothers Grimm translated it into German at the end of that same year, whereas a French translation, by P.A. Dufour, appeared in 1828.

Such incredible and unexpected success convinced Murray, and Crofton Croker's friends, that a second edition, richer in tales, should be produced; so Crofton Croker took the decision to leave for Ireland, in order to collect more material, and he did so in April of 1825.

He travelled alone and spent a lot of time with his friends Sainthill and Lady Chatterton, to whom the first edition of the *Legends* was dedicated. This time he did not go around much, choosing to stay for a while in Killarney, where he gathered enough material for a book that was to be published in 1829-31: *Legends of the Lakes or Sayings and Doings at Killarney*.

Unfortunately, Ireland was not good to him, as his health was affected by a rheumatic condition that got sharper and sharper for the rest of his life.

During this trip he met, in Cork, a young protegée of Richard Sainthill, the artist Daniel Maclise who, at the time, was at the beginning of a brilliant career and who would bring his Irish talent to London in later years.

Crofton Croker was greatly impressed by Maclise's talent and proposed to him to provide the illustrations for the second edition of the *Legends*.

But back in London the friendship with Murray began to fade. As it seems, both men had a strong character and this was probably at the origin of the problems that caused their further collaboration to be quite uneasy.

Crofton Croker even took on the task of seeking another publisher, but the contract he had signed with Murray bound him to the man still for a long time to come.

Anyway, the second edition, still anonymous, appeared in March 1826, and was dedicated to Sir Walter Scott, whose letter Crofton Croker included in his long preface, justly proud of Scott's appreciation.

This was slightly different from the first edition, containing one more story and made beautiful by Maclise's illustrations.

Although the book had an incredible success in England, Crofton Croker was hurt by some criticism that came from his native country:

'I have heard some objections from Ireland to the unpretending stories in this volume, such as their being too trite, and their being extremely common in that country. I confess that I look upon these objections as compliments. I make no pretension of originality and avow at once that there is no story in my book which has not been told by half the old women of the district in which the scene is laid. I give them as I found them – as indication of a particular superstition in the minds of a part, and an important part, of my countrymen – the peasantry.'[6]

This is the best proof of the innovative view of his work. Tales that everybody knew in Ireland, told exactly in that same way, as to be recognisable at once and, most of all, the acknowledgement of the fundamental role played by the peasantry in Irish society. This is exactly what he meant and this is the way the tales should be intended. Nothing more, nothing less.

And again, from the same preface to the second series:

'Deeply as I lament that such delusion should exist, these facts will sufficiently prove that I have not (as has been insinuated) conjured up forgotten tales, or attempted to

6. *Fairy Legends and Traditions of the South of Ireland*, London 1828

perpetuate a creed which has disappeared. On the contrary, my aim has been to bring the twilight tales of the peasantry before the view of the philosopher; as, if suffered to remain unnoticed, the latent belief in them may long have lingered among the inhabitants of the wild mountain and lonesome glen, to retard the progress of their civilization.'[7]

Words such as these could be obviously misunderstood and Crofton Croker gives us a hint of the different accusations he was made the object of, often contradictory, as we can easily detect. For some, the tales were 'too obvious', for others, 'forgotten tales'.

But Crofton Croker makes it very clear that, if a solution to the Irish situation is to be found, then it is in the spreading of knowledge. On the English side, getting to know the Irish culture more deeply and fully, would bring more understanding ('before the view of the philosopher'), enabling the rulers to move a step towards their unhappy subjects. On the Irish side, clearing away the old superstitions, would spread the light of modern civilisation and development, making possible a dialogue with the opposite part. That he was right would unfortunately too soon be evident.

Crofton Croker understood all too well the value of oral rural culture and knew that therein lay the identity of tradition. And even more precious is his work, if we think that the tragedy of the famine struck more sharply at that 'important part' of his countrymen, a part that Crofton Croker was the first to take notice of.

In 1828, the second series of *Legends* appeared, bearing Crofton Croker's name on the cover. But, by this time, the relationship with Murray had become particularly uneasy. Murray had criticised some of the new stories and Crofton Croker was so offended that he asked Murray to transfer the manuscript to the publisher Colburn. But Murray went on with the publication; he didn't intend to break the contract signed by Crofton Croker, who had sold the ownership of the

7. *Fairy Legends and Traditions of the South of Ireland*, London 1828

copyright to Murray.

This second series of the *Legends* contains fifty-one stories, each also followed by a commentary. The first edition, that is now reprinted in facsimile to celebrate Crofton Croker's bicentenary, remains the most appealing, elegant and balanced of all the ones that followed.

The third series, dedicated to the Brothers Grimm, to whom Crofton Croker was linked by an epistular friendship although they never met, is 'curious in the extreme', as Sainthill wrote to Crofton Croker, especially due to the introductory essay on European folklore. A large part of this introduction is dedicated to the translation of the *Irishe Elfenmärchen* by the Grimms and to the essay on Welsh folklore by Owen Pughe.

Interesting as these editions may be, they did not sell as well as the first one, but they gave Crofton Croker more fame and success – a success that was probably the reason for the 'authorship' polemic that has been brought into question over and over again by some obscure sources that we can easily dismiss.

None of these unpleasant arguments will diminish Crofton Croker's originality and intuition. No scholar of Irish folklore can ignore, or dismiss, Crofton Croker's work, even today. Nowadays we can criticise some of his statements or attitudes, but we musn't forget that he was a man of his time. Nevertheless, he was able to look back and ahead and to link the past to the future.

In the course of his life, Crofton Croker edited *Popular Songs of Ireland*, that appeared in 1839 and a miscellany entitled *The Christmas Box*, with contributions by Maria Edgeworth, Charles Lamb, Walter Scott and other well-known authors of his time. He was an active member of the Society of Antiquaries, of the Camden Society, of the Percy Society and of the British Archaeological Association, among others.

In 1844, he edited, for the Percy Society, the beautiful and interesting study, *The Keen of the South of Ireland*, the first extensive analysis ever attempted of this remarkable and extraordinary Irish tradition, containing some poetical translations of the most famous Irish keens. At the time, many still regarded this very ancient Indo-European tradition with contempt and horror, a sort of barbaric heritage, with nothing 'christian' in it. He was the first to understand the beauty, the poetic value, the nobility and the greatness of this expression of the Irish soul. The pages he wrote as an introduction to the keens are still among the most interesting studies on this subject, as are the descriptions of the pattern and of the keeners he met in the following years.

Deprived of their lives, the Irish people developed into art the only thing that was left to them: death. For the ancient Celts, death was just a threshold to the Other World; a world where death did not exist, where immortal beings dwelt for ever young and happy, among gods and heroes; a world that was a passage to other, innumerable states of being, in an eternal metamorphosis, with no end, no time. This vision of after-death made possible the rapid acceptance of the Christian faith; a unique example of conversion. The ancient Celts were rich in spirituality and they could be conquered by spirituality only. So, the passage rites that link life to death are among the greatest expressions of the Celtic soul, an expression that became the best way of preserving their values and their identity. This is why in Ireland the keening has been preserved for so long and has been developed to become a national form of poetic expression, the only example in the western world that has survived from the past.

During his quite short life Crofton Croker created a private museum, purchasing every object that appealed to his interests and fancy. He died a famous, but perhaps not a contented man, on 8 August 1854. His wife, Marianne, followed him to Tír na nÓg two months later.

In all his works Crofton Croker reveals a deep love for his country. His restless research on the past of his land led him to disclose hidden meanings and hidden beauties that for centuries were under the eyes of everybody, but that not many were able to see.

With all the limitations of his time, as he was alone, he has pointed out to Europe Ireland's soul. He has created a method, where no method existed, a method 'encompassing history and ethnology', as Henry Glassie says.

The golden key to the long and spiral-like path that has disclosed Ireland to me and has brought me to Cork, his native town, from London, where he left his book for me a long, long time ago, has been his work.

This little anonymous book has given a new direction to my life and my interests and I would never have thought that I would have the honour to write an introduction to its facsimile edition on the bicentenary of Crofton Croker's birth.

But life, as we all know, is very strange and often unexpected. So, this is but a very small homage that I can pay to Crofton Croker and to Ireland, a land that I feel to be my second country, but my first spiritual home.

And I would like to conclude by quoting the poem that David Murphy, Crofton Croker's friend, wrote for him and that appears in the *Keening of the South of Ireland*:

TO CROFTON CROKER
Translated from the Irish by Crofton Croker

Oh well fed scholar, of the cheerful face,
How neat your hand to plane and polish verse is!
To English turning, with a silken grace,
The branchy Irish, that so sweet and terse is.

Early and late, once proudly sung the bard,
The glowing strains his busy brain created;
And surely on such honied fame 'twas hard
That none his valued stores should have translated.

But Erin's long neglected minstrelsy,
Thy skill will save – nor shall it be neglected;
A merry champion has it found in thee,
Who seeks to make our country's name respected.

CEANGAL
Go on! and prosper, make a glorious gleaning,
I pray the Fays may aid you in your keening.

FRANCESCA DIANO
Padova/Cork, 1998

FAIRY LEGENDS.

THE SHEFRO.

—————— " Fairy Elves
Whose midnight revels, by a forest side
Or fountain, some belated peasant sees,
Or dreams he sees, while over head the moon
Sits arbitress, and nearer to the earth
Wheels her pale course."—

MILTON.

LEGENDS OF THE SHEFRO.

LEGEND OF KNOCKSHEOGOWNA.

In Tipperary is one of the most singularly shaped hills in the world. It has got a peak at the top like a conical nightcap thrown carelessly over your head as you awake in the morning. On the very point is built a sort of lodge, where in the summer the lady who built it and her friends used to go on parties of pleasure; but that was long after the days of the fairies, and it is, I believe, now deserted.

But before lodge was built, or acre sown, there was close to the head of the hill a large pasturage, where a herdsman spent his days and nights among the herd. The spot had been an old fairy ground, and the good people

B 2

were angry that the scene of their light and
airy gambols should be trampled by the rude
hoofs of bulls and cows. The lowing of the
cattle sounded sad in their ears, and the chief
of the fairies of the hill determined in person
to drive away the new comers, and the way
she thought of was this. When the harvest
nights came on, and the moon shone bright
and brilliant over the hill, and the cattle were
lying down hushed and quiet, and the herdsman wrapt in his mantle, was musing with his
heart gladdened by the glorious company of
the stars twinkling above him, bathed in the
flood of light bursting all over the sky, she
would come and dance before him,—now in
one shape—now in another,—but all ugly and
frightful to behold. One time she would be
a great horse, with the wings of an eagle, and
a tail like a dragon, hissing loud and spitting
fire. Then in a moment she would change
into a little man lame of a leg, with a bull's
head, and a lambent flame playing round it.
Then into a great ape, with duck's feet and
a turkeycock's tail. But I should be all day
about it were I to tell you all the shapes she
took. And then she would roar, or neigh, or

hiss, or bellow, or howl, or hoot, as never yet
was roaring, neighing, hissing, bellowing, howling, or hooting, heard in this world before or
since.   The poor herdsman would cover his
face, and call on all the saints for help, but it
was no use.   With one puff of her breath she
would blow away the fold of his great coat,
let him hold it never so tightly over his eyes,
and not a saint in heaven paid him the slightest
attention.   And to make matters worse, he
never could stir; no, nor even shut his eyes,
but there was obliged to stay, held by what
power he knew not, gazing at these terrible
sights until the hair of his head would lift his
hat half a foot over his crown, and his teeth
would be ready to fall out from chattering.
But the cattle would scamper about mad, as
if they were bitten by the fly; and this would
last until the sun rose over the hill.

The poor cattle from want of rest were
pining away, and food did them no good;
besides, they met with accidents without end.
Never a night passed that some of them did
not fall into a pit, and get maimed, or may
be, killed.   Some would tumble into a river
and be drowned: in a word, there seemed

never to be an end of the accidents. But
what made the matter worse, there could not
be a herdsman got to tend the cattle by night.
One visit from the fairy drove the stoutest-
hearted almost mad. The owner of the ground
did not know what to do. He offered double,
treble, quadruple wages, but not a man could
be found for the sake of money to go through
the horror of facing the fairy. She rejoiced
at the successful issue of her project, and
continued her pranks. The herd gradually
thinning, and no man daring to remain on
the ground, the fairies came back in numbers,
and gamboled as merrily as before, quaffing
dew-drops from acorns, and spreading their
feast on the head of capacious mushrooms.

What was to be done, the puzzled farmer
thought in vain. He found that his substance
was daily diminishing, his people terrified,
and his rent-day coming round. It is no
wonder that he looked gloomy, and walked
mournfully down the road. Now in that part
of the world dwelt a man of the name of
Larry Hoolahan, who played on the pipes
better than any other player within fifteen
parishes. A roving dashing blade was Larry,

and feared nothing.   Give him plenty of
liquor, and he would defy the devil.   He
would face a mad bull, or fight single-handed
against a fair.   In one of his gloomy walks
the farmer met him, and on Larry's asking
the cause of his down looks, he told him
all his misfortunes.   " If that is all ails you,"
said Larry, " make your mind easy.   Were
there as many fairies on Knocksheogowna as
there are potatoe blossoms in Eliogurty, I
would face them.   It would be a queer thing,
indeed, if I, who never was afraid of a proper
man, should turn my back upon a brat of a
fairy not the bigness of one's thumb." " Larry,"
said the farmer, " do not talk so bold, for you
know not who is hearing you; but, if you
make your words good, and watch my herds
for a week on the top of the mountain, your
hand shall be free of my dish till the sun has
burnt itself down to the bigness of a farthing
rushlight."

   The bargain was struck, and Larry went
to the hill-top, when the moon began to peep
over the brow.   He had been regaled at the
farmer's house, and was bold with the extract
of barleycorn.   So he took his seat on a big

stone under a hollow of the hill, with his back
to the wind, and pulled out his pipes.   He
had not played long when the voice of the
fairies was heard upon the blast, like a low
stream of music.   Presently they burst out
into a loud laugh, and Larry could plainly
hear one say, " What! another man upon
the fairies' ring ? Go to him, queen, and make
him repent his rashness ;" and they flew away.
Larry felt them pass by his face as they flew
like a swarm of midges; and, looking up hastily,
he saw between the moon and him a great
black cat, standing on the very tip of its
claws, with its back up, and mewing with a
voice of a water-mill.   Presently it swelled up
towards the sky, and, turning round on its
left hind leg, whirled till it fell on the ground,
from which it started in the shape of a salmon,
with a cravat round its neck, and a pair of
new top boots.   " Go on, jewel," said Larry ;
" if you dance, I 'll pipe ;" and he struck up.
So she turned into this, and that, and the
other, but still Larry played on, as he well
knew how.   At last she lost patience, as ladies
will do when you do not mind their scolding,
and changed herself into a calf, milk-white as

the cream of Cork, and with eyes as mild as those of the girl I love.　She came up gentle and fawning, in hopes to throw him off his guard by quietness, and then to work him some wrong.　But Larry was not so deceived; for when she came up, he, dropping his pipes, leaped upon her back.

Now from the top of Knocksheogowna, as you look westward to the broad Atlantic, you will see the Shannon, queen of rivers, "spreading like a sea," and running on in gentle course to mingle with the ocean through the fair city of Limerick.　It on this night shone under the moon, and looked beautiful from the distant hill.　Fifty boats were gliding up and down on the sweet current, and the song of the fishermen rose gaily from the shore. Larry, as I said before, leaped upon the back of the fairy, and she, rejoiced at the opportunity, sprung from the hill-top, and bounded clear, at one jump, over the Shannon, flowing as it was just ten miles from the mountain's base. It was done in a second, and when she alighted on the distant bank, kicking up her heels, she flung Larry on the soft turf.　No sooner was he thus planted, than he looked her straight in the face, and, scratching his head, cried out, " By my word, well done ! that was not a bad leap *for a calf!*"

She looked at him for a moment, and then assumed her own shape. " Laurence," said she, " you are a bold fellow ; will you come back the way you went ?" " And that 's what I will," said he, " if you let me." So changing to a calf again, again Larry got on her back, and at another bound they were again upon the top of Knocksheogowna. The fairy once more resuming her figure, addressed him : " You have shown so much courage, Laurence," said she, " that while you keep herds on this hill you never shall be molested by me or mine. The day dawns, go down to the farmer, and tell him this ; and if any thing I can do may be of service to you, ask and you shall have it." She vanished accordingly ; and kept her word in never visiting the hill during Larry's life : but he never troubled her with requests. He piped and drank at the farmer's expense, and roosted in his chimney corner, occasionally casting an eye to the flock. He died at last, and is buried in a green valley of pleasant Tippe-rary : but whether the fairies returned to the

hill of Knocksheogowna after his death is
more than I can say.

————————

    The hill of Knocksheogowna, the situation of which
is accurately enough described, either derives its name
from the foregoing legend, or the legend is derived
from it ; the literal translation of the name being,
" *The Hill of the Fairy Calf.*"

    Olaus Magnus (book iii. cap. 10,) tells us, that
" Travellers in the night, and such as watch their
flocks and herds, are wont to be compassed about with
many strange apparitions."

    The figure of " a salmon with a cravat round its
neck and a pair of new top boots," is perhaps rather
too absurd, but it has been judged best to give the
legend as received, particularly as it affords a fair specimen of the very extravagant imagery in which the
Irish are so fond of indulging :—of this many examples might be quoted, and among others, a popular
song attributed to a criminal, who, according to the
tradition, was offered his life, on condition of making
a song with as many verses as there were weeks in the
year, in which nothing possible or even probable
should be introduced. He had not, however, composed more than a dozen verses (still extant), when,
unfortunately for him, he introduced something about
a silly old owl, which was considered as an allegorical

sarcasm on the Judge (Crookshanks) by whom he was tried, and a halter terminated his further invention.

> " I saw the river Barrow
>   Running through the marrow
>   Bone of a Tom Tit"

is by no means the most improbable circumstance in this composition.

The song of Castle Hyde so well known in the south of Ireland may also be mentioned, in which a salmon appears engaged in as unfishlike an employment as that of dancing in a pair of new top boots.

> " The trout and salmon
>   Play at Backgammon
> All to adorn sweet Castle Hyde."

LEGEND OF KNOCKFIERNA.

I⊤ is a very good thing not to be any way in dread of the fairies, for without doubt they have then less power over a person ; but to make too free with them, or to disbelieve in them altogether, is as foolish a thing as man, woman, or child can do.

It has been truly said, that " good manners are no burthen," and that " civility costs nothing ;" but there are some people fool-hardy enough to disregard doing a civil thing, which, whatever they may think, can never harm themselves or any one else, and who at the same time will go out of their way for a bit of mischief, which never can serve them ; but sooner or later they will come to know better, as you shall hear of Carroll O'Daly, a strapping young fellow up out of Connaught, who

they used to call, in his own country, " Devil
Daly."

Carroll O'Daly used to go roving about from
one place to another, and the fear of nothing
stopped him ; he would as soon pass an old
churchyard or a regular fairy ground, at any
hour of the night, as go from one room into
another, without ever making the sign of the
cross, or saying " Good luck attend you, gentlemen."

It so happened that he was once journeying
in the county of Limerick, towards " the Bal-
bec of Ireland," the venerable town of Kilmallock ; and just at the foot of Knockfierna
he overtook a respectable-looking man jogging
along upon a white pony. The night was
coming on, and they rode side by side for
some time, without much conversation passing
between them, further than saluting each other
very kindly; at last, Carroll O'Daly asked his
companion how far he was going ?

" Not far your way," said the farmer, for
such his appearance bespoke him ; " I 'm only
going to the top of this hill here."

" And what might take you there," said
O'Daly, " at this time of the night ?"

" Why, then," replied the farmer, " if you want to know, 'tis the *good people*."

" The fairies, you mean," said O'Daly.

" Whist ! whist !" said his fellow-traveller, " or you may be sorry for it ;" and he turned his pony off the road they were going towards a little path that led up the side of the mountain, wishing Carroll O'Daly good night and a safe journey.

" That fellow," thought Carroll, " is about no good this blessed night, and I would have no fear of swearing wrong if I took my Bible oath, that it is something else beside the fairies, or the good people, as he calls them, that is taking him up the mountain at this hour— The fairies !" he repeated—" is it for a well-shaped man like him to be going after little chaps like the fairies ? to be sure some say there are such things, and more say not ; but I know this, that never afraid would I be of a dozen of them, ay, of two dozen, for that matter, if they are no bigger than what I hear tell of."

Carroll O'Daly, whilst these thoughts were passing in his mind, had fixed his eyes stedfastly on the mountain, behind which the full

moon was rising majestically.   Upon an elevated point that appeared darkly against the
moon's disk, he beheld the figure of a man
leading a pony, and he had no doubt it was
that of the farmer with whom he had just
parted company.

A sudden resolve to follow flashed across
the mind of O'Daly with the speed of lightning : both his courage and curiosity had been
worked up by his cogitations to a pitch of
chivalry ; and muttering "Here's after you,
old boy," he dismounted from his horse,
bound him to an old thorn-tree, and then
commenced vigorously ascending the mountain.

Following as well as he could the direction
taken by the figures of the man and pony,
he pursued his way, occasionally guided by
their partial appearance ; and after toiling
nearly three hours over a rugged and sometimes swampy path, came to a green spot on
the top of the mountain, where he saw the
white pony at full liberty grazing as quietly
as may be. O'Daly looked around for the
rider, but he was nowhere to be seen ; he
however soon discovered close to where the

pony stood an opening in the mountain like the mouth of a pit, and he remembered having heard, when a child, many a tale about the " Poul-duve," or Black Hole of Knockfierna ; how it was the entrance to the fairy castle which was within the mountain ; and how a man whose name was Ahern, a land surveyor in that part of the country, had once attempted to fathom it with a line, and had been drawn down into it and was never again heard of ; with many other tales of the like nature.

" But," thought O'Daly, " these are old women's stories ; and since I've come up so far, I'll just knock at the castle door, and see if the fairies are at home."

No sooner said than done ; for seizing a large stone as big, ay, bigger than his two hands, he flung it with all his strength down into the Poul-duve of Knockfierna. He heard it bounding and tumbling about from one rock to another with a terrible noise, and he leant his head over to try and hear if it would reach the bottom,—when what should the very stone he had thrown in do but come up again with as much force as it had gone down, and gave him such a blow full in the face, that it sent him rolling down the side of Knockfierna, head over heels, tumbling from one crag to another, much faster than he came up; and in the morning Carroll O'Daly was found lying beside his horse; the bridge of his nose broken, which disfigured him for life; his head all cut and bruised, and both his eyes closed up, and as black as if Sir Daniel Donnelly had painted them for him.

Carroll O'Daly was never bold again in riding alone near the haunts of the fairies after dusk; but small blame to him for that; and if ever he happened to be benighted in a lonesome place, he would make the best of his way to his journey's end, without asking questions, or turning to the right or to the left, to seek after the good people, or any who kept company with them.

———————

This legend has been briefly and in some parts inaccurately told in that excellent paper the *Literary Gazette* (Sept. 11, 1824), where Knock Fierna is translated, the Hill of *the Fairies:* this cannot be correct, as the compound, Fierna, is more probably derived from Firinne, the Irish for Truth; which conjecture is supported by an idiom, current in the county

Limerick, commonly used at the conclusion of an argument, when one party has failed to convince the other, " Go to Knockfierna, and you will see who is right."

Carroll O'Daly, the hero, is much celebrated both in Irish song and tradition.   The popular melody of *Ellen a Roon* is said to have been composed and sung by him when he carried off Miss Elinor Kavanagh after the manner of young Lochinvar.   This romantic anecdote is told in the life of Cormac Common, to be found in Walker's Memoirs of the Irish Bards.

An adventure of Carroll O'Daly's on the banks of Lough Lean (Killarney Lake), with a Sheban, or female spirit, forms the subject of a favourite Irish song.

In a note on the ballad of the Gay Goss Hawk, to be found in the 2d vol. of the Minstrelsy of the Scottish Border, reference is made to " a MS. translation of an Irish Fairy Tale, called the Adventures of Faravla, Princess of Scotland, and Carral O'Daly, son of Donogho More O'Daly, Chief Bard of Ireland." This tale, judging from the short extract and notice given of it, appears to be a fragment of the well-known adventures of the beautiful Deirdre and her unfortunate lover, Naoise, an analysis of which may be seen in Miss Brooke's Relics of Irish Poetry, (p. 13) : indeed the tale serves as the key-stone to a multitude of Irish verses in which the valour of Eogain and the vengeance of Cucullin are celebrated.

The family of O'Daly have been for many centuries

famous in Ireland for romantic courage and bardic acquirements.

Angus or Æneas O'Daly, better known by the names of Angus Na Naor (Angus of the satires), and Bard Ruadh or the Red Bard, who died in 1617, is said in a tradition, full of wild and singular incidents, to have been secretly employed by the Earl of Essex, and Sir George Carew, to satirize his own countrymen and the families of English descent, as the Fitzgeralds or Geraldines, who had from their long residence fallen into the habits of the " Irishry." This disreputable task, though his verses proved of little political importance, he performed with some skill, and was rewarded, according to the fashion of the times, with a grant of land.

Abuse and insult (much of which it is now, from a happy change in manners, difficult to understand correctly) are bestowed in the satires of Angus O'Daly, with the greatest liberality, on every one whom he has occasion to mention, always excepting with considerable ingenuity the Clan Daly : for instance,

" Da naoꞅuꞁꞇ claꞁ Aꞃoalaꞁꞡ,
Njoꞅ ꞇjoꞅ ꞇaꞃ ꞃjol ꞅeaꞅaꞇaꞁꞃ ;
£laꞅ Aꞃoalaꞁꞡ buꞇ ꞇjoꞅ ꞇaꞃ,
Aꞡuꞅ ꞃjol Aꞇoaꞁꞃ Ꞅaoꞅaꞇ."

" If I lampoon the clan Daly, no shield to me is the race of old Adam :—Let the clan Daly protect me, I may satirize all mankind."

A modern Kerry bard who has favoured the writer of this note with his MS. celebrates the ancient

power, fame, talent, and genealogy of the O'Dalys in
a song entitled " O'Sullivan's praises of Kilcrohan
Green," a place by the by which few other writers or
map makers have mentioned, unless it be a mountainous and barren parish of that name described by
Dr. Smith in his History of Kerry (p. 91 to 94) between the Kenmare river and Ballinskellig bay.

The poet recounts with great care the wonders of
this " charming" spot, " where Humphrey O'Daly
its monarch is seen," whose ancestor Owen O'Daly
(styled " the Tetrarch of Kilcrohan Green") had built
a castle ; and where " a renowned" college once stood,
in which " monarchs and sages divine," and

> " The brave and illustrious infant of Spain,
>   With his six noble brothers, did learning attain."

With becoming indignation he laments the rude
seizure of this castle and college by " Britain's
cursed Queen" (Elizabeth, it is presumed), and then
proceeds,

> " Brave Carroll O'Daly, so famed for each art,
>   Was here taught the best way to win woman's heart ;
>   Great Kavanagh's heiress, at the age of eighteen,
>   He brought from Killmainham to Kilcrohan green.

> " The name stands recorded for learning and love
>   On earth here below, and in heaven above ;
>   For musical numbers, no man there has been
>   A rival to Cormac of Kilcrohan green.

" His son, John O'Daly, a heart had of fire ;
    He travelled, and he too with skill touched the wire :
    No soldier so brave in the battle was seen
    As O'Daly, the hero of Kilcrohan green."

THE

LEGEND OF KNOCKGRAFTON.

THERE was once a poor man who lived in
the fertile glen of Aherlow, at the foot of the
gloomy Galtee mountains, and he had a great
hump on his back : he looked just as if his
body had been rolled up and placed upon his
shoulders ; and his head was pressed down
with the weight so much that his chin when
he was sitting used to rest upon his knees for
support. The country people were rather shy
of meeting him in any lonesome place, for
though, poor creature, he was as harmless and
as inoffensive as a new-born infant, yet his
deformity was so great, that he scarcely appeared to be a human creature, and some ill-
minded persons had set strange stories about
him afloat. He was said to have a great

knowledge of herbs and charms; but certain
it was that he had a mighty skilful hand in
plaiting straw and rushes into hats and bas-
kets, which was the way he made his live-
lihood.

Lusmore, for that was the nickname put
upon him by reason of his always wearing a
sprig of the fairy cap, or lusmore in his little
straw hat, would ever get a higher penny for
his plaited work than any one else, and perhaps that was the reason why some one, out of
envy, had circulated the strange stories about
him.   Be that as it may, it happened that he
was returning one evening from the pretty
town of Cahir towards Cappagh, and as little
Lusmore walked very slowly, on account of
the great hump upon his back, it was quite
dark when he came to the old moat of Knockgrafton, which stood on the right hand side
of his road.   Tired and weary was he, and no
way comfortable in his own mind at thinking how much further he had to travel, and
that he should be walking all the night; so he
sat down under the moat to rest himself, and
began looking mournfully enough upon the
moon, which

" Rising in clouded majesty, at length,
    Apparent Queen, unveil'd her peerless light,
    O'er the dark heaven her silver mantle threw,
    And in her pale dominion check'd the night."

Presently there rose a wild strain of un-earthly melody upon the ear of little Lusmore ; he listened, and he thought that he had never heard such ravishing music before. It was like the sound of many voices, each mingling and blending with the other so strangely, that they seemed to be one, though all singing dif-ferent strains, and the words of the song were these :

Da Luan, Da Mort, Da Luan, Da Mort, Da Luan, Da Mort, when there would be a moment's pause, and then the round of melody went on again.

Lusmore listened attentively, scarcely draw-ing his breath lest he might lose the slightest note. He now plainly perceived that the singing was within the moat, and though at first it had charmed him so much, he began to get tired of hearing the same round sung over and over so often without any change; so availing himself of the pause when the *Da Luan, Da Mort*, had been sung three times, he took up the tune and raised it with the words *augus Da Cadine*, and then went on singing with the voices inside of the moat, *Da Luan, Da Mort*, finishing the melody, when the pause again came, with *augus Da Cadine*.

The fairies within Knockgrafton, for the song was a fairy melody, when they heard this addition to their tune were so much delighted, that with instant resolve it was determined to bring the mortal among them, whose musical skill so far exceeded theirs, and little Lusmore was conveyed into their company with the eddying speed of a whirlwind.

Glorious to behold was the sight that burst upon him as he came down through the moat, twirling round and round and round with the lightness of a straw, to the sweetest music that kept time to his motion. The greatest honour was then paid him, for he was put up above all the musicians, and he had servants 'tending upon him, and every thing to his heart's content, and a hearty welcome to all; and in short he was made as much of as if he had been the first man in the land.

Presently Lusmore saw a great consultation

going forward among the fairies, and, notwithstanding all their civility, he felt very much
frightened, until one stepping out from the
rest came up to him and said,—

> " Lusmore ! Lusmore !
> Doubt not, nor deplore,
> For the hump which you bore
> On your back is no more;
> Look down on the floor,
> And view it, Lusmore !"

When these words were said, poor little Lusmore felt himself so light, and so happy, that
he thought he could have bounded at one jump
over the moon, like the cow in the history of
the cat and the fiddle; and he saw, with inex-
pressible pleasure, his hump tumble down
upon the ground from his shoulders.   He
then tried to lift up his head, and he did so
with becoming caution, fearing that he might
knock it against the ceiling of the grand hall,
where he was; he looked round and round
again with the greatest wonder and delight
upon every thing, which appeared more and
more beautiful; and overpowered at beholding
such a resplendent scene, his head grew dizzy,
and his eyesight became dim.   At last he fell

into a sound sleep, and when he awoke, he
found that it was broad day-light, the sun
shining brightly, the birds singing sweet;
and that he was lying just at the foot of the
moat of Knockgrafton, with the cows and
sheep grazing peaceably round about him.
The first thing Lusmore did, after saying his
prayers, was to put his hand behind to feel
for his hump, but no sign of one was there on
his back, and he looked at himself with great
pride, for he had now become a well-shaped
dapper little fellow; and more than that,
found himself in a full suit of new clothes,
which he concluded the fairies had made for
him.

Towards Cappagh he went, stepping out
as lightly, and springing up at every step as
if he had been all his life a dancing-master.
Not a creature who met Lusmore knew him
without his hump, and he had great work to
persuade every one that he was the same man
—in truth he was not, so far as outward appearance went.

Of course it was not long before the story
of Lusmore's hump got about, and a great
wonder was made of it. Through the coun-

try, for miles round, it was the talk of every one, high and low.

One morning as Lusmore was sitting contented enough at his cabin-door, up came an old woman to him, and asked if he could direct her to Cappagh?

" I need give you no directions, my good woman," said Lusmore, " for this is Cappagh ; and whom may you want here ?"

" I have come," said the woman, " out of Decie's country, in the county Waterford, looking after one Lusmore, who I have heard tell had his hump taken off by the fairies : for there is the son of a gossip of mine who has got a hump on him, that will be his death ; and may be, if he could use the same charm as Lusmore, the hump may be taken off him. And now I have told you the reason of my coming so far : 'tis to find out about this charm, if I can."

Lusmore, who was ever a good-natured little fellow, told the woman all the particulars, how he had raised the tune for the fairies at Knockgrafton, how his hump had been removed from his shoulders, and how he had got a new suit of clothes into the bargain.

The woman thanked him very much, and then went away quite happy and easy in her own mind.   When she came back to her gossip's house, in the county Waterford, she told her every thing that Lusmore had said, and they put the little hump-backed man, who was a peevish and cunning creature from his birth, upon a car, and took him all the way across the country.   It was a long journey, but they did not care for that, so the hump was taken from off him; and they brought him, just at night-fall, and left him under the old moat of Knockgrafton.

Jack Madden, for that was the humpy man's name, had not been sitting there long when he heard the tune going on within the moat much sweeter than before; for the fairies were singing it the way Lusmore had settled their music for them, and the song was going on: *Da Luan, Da Mort, Da Luan, Da Mort, Da Luan, Da Mort, augus Da Cadine,* without ever stopping.   Jack Madden, who was in a great hurry to get quit of his hump, never thought of waiting until the fairies had done, or watching for a fitting opportunity to raise the tune higher again than Lusmore had: so having heard them sing it over seven times without stopping, out he bawls, never minding the time, or the humour of the tune, or how he could bring his words in properly, *augus Da Dardine, augus Da Hena,* thinking that if one day was good, two were better; and that if Lusmore had one new suit of clothes given him, he should have two.

No sooner had the words passed his lips than he was taken up and whisked into the moat with prodigious force; and the fairies came crowding round about him with great anger, screeching, and screaming, and roaring out, " who spoiled our tune? who spoiled our tune?" and one stepped up to him above all the rest, and said—

> " Jack Madden! Jack Madden!
> Your words came so bad in
> The tune we feel glad in ;—
> This castle you're had in,
> That your life we may sadden :
> Here's two humps for Jack Madden."

And twenty of the strongest fairies brought Lusmore's hump and put it down upon poor

Jack's back, over his own, where it became fixed as firmly as if it was nailed on with twelvepenny nails, by the best carpenter that ever drove one. Out of their castle they then kicked him, and in the morning when Jack Madden's mother and her gossip came to look after their little man, they found him half dead, lying at the foot of the moat, with the other hump upon his back. Well to be sure, how they did look at each other! but they were afraid to say any thing, lest a hump might be put upon their own shoulders: home they brought the unlucky Jack Madden with them, as downcast in their hearts and their looks as ever two gossips were; and what through the weight of his other hump, and the long journey, he died soon after, leaving, they say, his heavy curse to any one who would go to listen to fairy tunes again.

————

It is almost needless to point out this legend as the foundation of Parnell's well-known fairy tale. " Parnell," says Miss Edgeworth, in a note on her admirable story of Castle Rackrent, " who showed himself so deeply ' skilled in faerie lore,' was an Irishman, and though he presented his fairies to the world in the ancient English dress of ' Britain's isle and Arthur's days,' it is probable that his first acquaintance with them began in his native country."

The name Knockgrafton should rather be Knock-graffan or Raffan,—see O'Brien's Irish Dictionary, where we are told that it was in ancient times a regal house of the kings of Munster, and that hither was the famous Cormac Mac Airt brought prisoner : " In after ages," adds Dr. O'Brien, " it was the estate together with its annexes of the O'Sullivans."

The popular voice has been followed in naming this legend the moat of Knockgrafton, as what is called the moat should be, correctly speaking, styled a barrow or tumulus ; the name of Knockgrafton is also written agreeably to the vulgar pronunciation ; and to render the words of the fairy song (signifying Monday, Tuesday, and Wednesday) suitable to the English reader, they are given according to their sound in preference to the correct spelling, which would be, " Dia Luain, Dia Mairt, agus Dia Ceadaoine."

In Irish the word dia', diê, or de, is prefixed before the proper names of the week days, agreeably to the Latin, but contrary to the custom of the languages of modern Europe, in which the common name, day, is subjoined to the proper name of the week day : thus, as in the Latin, Dies Solis, Dies Lunæ, Dies Martis, so in the Irish, Dia Sul, Dia Luain, Dia Mairt : the ancient name of Sunday has in modern times been changed into Dia Domhna (pronounced Dona), accord-

D

ing to the Christian Latin, most probably introduced by the clergy; but the derivation and comparison of names would lead into a digression much too long for this volume. From a curious circumstance, the writer is indebted to his friend, Mr. A. D. Roche (whose musical taste and knowledge must speedily give him eminence in his profession), for a notation of this unique specimen of fairy song :

Da Lu-an, da Mort, da Lu-an, da Mort, da Lu-an, da Mort, au - gus, da Ca - dine. Da Lu-an, da Mort, da Lu-an, da Mort, da Lu-an, da Mort, au-gus, da Ca - dine.

This rude melody, which is certainly, from its construction, very ancient, is commonly sung by every
skilful narrator of the tale, to render the recitation
more effective.   In different parts of the country, of
course various raths and mounds are assigned as the
scene of fairy revelry.   The writer's reason for select-
ing the moat of Knockgrafton was his having been
told the legend within view of the place in August
1816, and with little variation from the words of the
text.   It may perhaps be asked how the moat could
open and shut with such facility: but fairy historians
are privileged persons, who seldom trouble themselves
about the means by which effects are produced.   In
the legends of all countries, hill-sides are as moveable
as the door of the peasant's own habitation; and in
those of Scandinavia, not only does the hill-side open,
which is a matter of common and daily occurrence;
but on solemn festivals, such as New Year's night and
Saint John's eve, the whole hill itself is lifted up on
pillars and suspended like a canopy over the heads of
its inhabitants, who dance and revel beneath.

The verses used by the fairies in removing and
conferring humps are free translations from the Irish,
which should be given but for the necessity of termi-
nating this already long note; for the same reason, the
various localities must remain unnoticed: but it is
impossible to conclude without a few parting words
on little Lusmore, whose nickname is not perhaps
sufficiently explained by the word " Fairy Cap."
Lusmore, literally the *great herb*, is specifically ap-

plied to that graceful and hardy plant the " digitalis purpurea," usually called by the peasantry Fairy Cap, " from the supposed resemblance of its bells to this part of fairy dress. To the same plant many rustic superstitions are attached, particularly its salutation of supernatural beings, by bending its long stalks in token of recognition."

THE PRIEST'S SUPPER.

It is said by those who ought to understand such things, that the good people, or
the fairies, are some of the angels who were
turned out of heaven, and who landed on
their feet in this world, while the rest of their
companions, who had more sin to sink them,
went down further to a worse place. Be this as
it may, there was a merry troop of the fairies,
dancing and playing all manner of wild pranks
on a bright moonlight evening towards the
end of September. The scene of their merriment was not far distant from Inchegeela, in
the west of the county Cork—a poor village, although it had a barrack for soldiers;
but great mountains and barren rocks, like
those round about it, are enough to strike
poverty into any place : however, as the
fairies can have every thing they want for
wishing, poverty does not trouble them much,

and all their care is to seek out unfrequented
nooks and places where it is not likely any
one will come to spoil their sport.

On a nice green sod by the river's side were
the little fellows dancing in a ring as gaily as
may be, with their red caps wagging about at
every bound in the moonshine ; and so light
were these bounds, that the lobes of dew, although they trembled under their feet, were
not disturbed by their capering.   Thus did
they carry on their gambols, spinning round
and round, and twirling and bobbing, and
diving and 'going through all manner of
figures, until one of them chirped out,

> " Cease, cease, with your drumming,
>   Here's an end to our mumming ;
>   By my smell
>   I can tell
>   A priest this way is coming !"

And away every one of the fairies scampered
off as hard as they could, concealing themselves under the green leaves of the lusmore,
where if their little red caps should happen to
peep out, they would only look like its crimson bells ; and more hid themselves at the

shady side of stones, and brambles, and others under the bank of the river, and in holes and crannies of one kind or another.

The fairy speaker was not mistaken, for along the road, which was within view of the river, came Father Horrigan on his pony, thinking to himself that as it was so late he would make an end of his journey at the first cabin he came to, and according to this determination, he stopped at the dwelling of Dermod Leary, lifted the latch, and entered with " My blessing on all here."

I need not say that Father Horrigan was a welcome guest wherever he went, for no man was more pious or better beloved in the country. Now it was a great trouble to Dermod that he had nothing to offer his reverence for supper as a relish to the potatoes which " the old woman," for so Dermod called his wife, though she was not much past twenty, had down boiling in the pot over the fire ; he thought of the net which he had set in the river, but as it had been there only a short time, the chances were against his finding a fish in it. " No matter," thought Dermod, " there can be no harm in stepping down to try, and may be as I want the fish for the priest's supper that it will be there before me."

Down to the river side went Dermod, and he found in the net as fine a salmon as ever jumped in the bright waters of "the spreading Lee;" but as he was going to take it out, the net was pulled from him, he could not tell how or by whom, and away got the salmon, and went swimming along with the current as gaily as if nothing had happened.

Dermod looked sorrowfully at the wake which the fish had left upon the water, shining like a line of silver in the moonlight, and then with an angry motion of his right hand, and a stamp of his foot, gave vent to his feelings by muttering, " May bitter bad luck attend you night and day for a black-guard schemer of a salmon, wherever you go! You ought to be ashamed of yourself, if there's any shame in you, to give me the slip after this fashion! And I'm clear in my own mind you'll come to no good, for some kind of evil thing or other helped you—did I not feel it pull the net against me as strong as the devil himself?"

" That's not true for you," said one of the
little fairies, who had scampered off at the
approach of the priest, coming up to Dermod
Leary, with a whole throng of companions at
his heels; " there was only a dozen and a half
of us pulling against you."

Dermod gazed on the tiny speaker with
wonder, who continued, " Make yourself no
way uneasy about the priest's supper, for if
you will go back and ask him one question
from us, there will be as fine a supper as ever
was put on a table spread out before him in
less than no time."

" I 'll have nothing at all to do with you,"
replied Dermod, in a tone of determination;
and after a pause he added, " I'm much
obliged to you for your offer, sir, but I know
better than to sell myself to you or the like of
you for a supper; and more than that, I know
Father Horrigan has more regard for my
soul than to wish me to pledge it for ever,
out of regard to any thing you could put before him—so there's an end of the matter."

The little speaker, with a pertinacity not to
be repulsed by Dermod's manner, continued,
" Will you ask the priest one civil question
for us ?"

Dermod considered for some time, and he was right in doing so, but he thought that no one could come to harm out of asking a civil question. " I see no objection to do that same, gentlemen," said Dermod ; " but I will have nothing in life to do with your supper,— mind that."

" Then," said the little speaking fairy, whilst the rest came crowding after him from all parts, " go and ask Father Horrigan to tell us whether our souls will be saved at the last day, like the souls of good Christians ; and if you wish us well, bring back word what he says without delay."

Away went Dermod to his cabin, where he found the potatoes thrown out on the table, and his good woman handing the biggest of them all, a beautiful laughing red apple, smoking like a hard ridden horse on a frosty night, over to Father Horrigan.

" Please your reverence," said Dermod, after some hesitation, " may I make bold to ask your honour one question ?"

" What may that be?" said Father Horrigan.

" Why, then, begging your reverence's pardon for my freedom, it is, If the souls of the good people are to be saved at the last day?"

"Who bid you ask me that question, Leary?" said the priest, fixing his eyes upon him very sternly, which Dermod could not stand before at all.

"I'll tell no lies about the matter, and nothing in life but the truth," said Dermod. "It was the good people themselves who sent me to ask the question, and there they are in thousands down on the bank of the river waiting for me to go back with the answer."

"Go back by all means," said the priest, "and tell them, if they want to know, to come here to me themselves, and I'll answer that or any other question they are pleased to ask with the greatest pleasure in life."

Dermod accordingly returned to the fairies, who came swarming round about him to hear what the priest had said in reply; and Dermod spoke out among them like a bold man as he was: but when they heard that they must go to the priest, away they fled, some here and more there; and some this way and more that, whisking by poor Dermod so fast and in such numbers, that he was quite bewildered.

When he came to himself, which was not for a long time, back he went to his cabin and ate his dry potatoes along with Father Horrigan, who made quite light of the thing; but Dermod could not help thinking it a mighty hard case that his reverence, whose words had the power to banish the fairies at such a rate, should have no sort of relish to his supper, and that the fine salmon he had in the net should have been got away from him in such a manner.

———

It is curious to observe the similarity of legends, and of ideas concerning imaginary beings, among nations that for ages have had scarcely any communication. In the 4th vol. of the Danske Folkesagen, or Danish Popular Legends, lately collected by Mr. Thiele, the following story occurs, which has a great resemblance to the adventure of Dermod Leary: " A priest was going in a carriage one night from Kjeslunde to Roeskilde, in the island of Zealand, (Sjælland); and on his way passed by a hill, in which there was music and dancing, and other merry-making going on. Some dwarfs (Dærge) jumped suddenly out of the hill, stopped the carriage, and asked ' Hvor skall du hen?' (Where are you going?)—' Til Landemode,' (to the chapter-house), said the priest. They then asked him whether he thought they could be saved; to which he replied, that at present he could not tell: on which they begged of him to meet them with an answer that day twelvemonth. Notwithstanding, the next time the coachman drove that way, an accident befell him, for he was thrown on the level ground, and severely hurt. When the priest returned at the end of the year, they asked him the same question: to which he answered, ' Nei! I ere alle fordoemte,' (No! you are all damned); and scarcely had he spoken the word, when the whole hill was enveloped in a bright flame."

The hiding of the fairies in the bells of the lusmore may bring to the mind of the reader some playful stanzas in Drayton's very fanciful poem of Nymphidia. Queen Mab is with her gallant Pigwiggin, when Nymphidia brings tidings that Oberon had sent Puck in quest of her; there is a prodigious hurry and bustle among the fairy maids of honour to get concealed from the quick-sighted Puck.

> " At length one chanced to find a nut,
>   In th' end of which a hole was cut,
>   Which lay upon a hazel root,
>   There scatter'd by a squirrel,
>   Which out the kernel gotten had;
>   When quoth the fay, ' dear queen, be glad:
>   Let Oberon be ne'er so mad,
>   I 'll set you safe from peril.
>   Come all into this nut,' quoth she,
>   ' Come closely in; be ruled by me;
>   Each one may here a chooser be,
>   For room ye need not wrestle:

Nor need ye be together heaped.'
So one by one therein they crept,
And lying down they soundly slept,
    And safe as in a castle."

The notion of fairies, dwarfs, brownies, &c. being
excluded from salvation, and of their having formed
part of the crew that fell with Satan, seems to be
pretty general all over Europe.   In the text, we find
it in Ireland ; in the preceding part of this note, in
Denmark ; and in a sonnet of a celebrated Spanish
poet, the author observes—

" Disputase por hombres entendidos
    Si fue de los *caidos* este duende."

THE YOUNG PIPER.

THERE lived not long since, on the borders
of the county Tipperary, a decent honest couple, whose names were Mick Flanigan and Judy
Muldoon. These poor people were blessed,
as the saying is, with four children, all boys:
three of them were as fine, stout, healthy, good-
looking children as ever the sun shone upon;
and it was enough to make any Irishman proud
of the breed of his countrymen to see them about
one o'clock on a fine summer's day standing at
their father's cabin-door, with their beautiful
flaxen hair hanging in curls about their heads,
and their cheeks like two rosy apples, and a
big laughing potato smoking in their hand.
A proud man was Mick of these fine children,
and a proud woman, too, was Judy; and
reason enough they had to be so. But it was
far otherwise with the remaining one, which
was the third eldest: he was the most misera-

ble, ugly, ill-conditioned brat that ever God
put life into: he was so ill-thriven, that he
never was able to stand alone, or to leave his
cradle; he had long, shaggy, matted, curled
hair, as black as any raven; his face was
of a greenish yellow colour; his eyes were
like two burning coals, and were for ever
moving in his head, as if they had the perpe-
tual motion.   Before he was a twelvemonth
old, he had a mouth full of great teeth; his
hands were like kites' claws, and his legs were
no thicker than the handle of a whip, and
about as straight as a reaping-hook: to make
the matter worse, he had the gut of a cormo-
rant, and the whinge, and the yelp, and the
screech, and the yowl, was never out of his
mouth.   The neighbours all suspected that
he was something not right, particularly as it
was observed, when people, as they do in the
country, got about the fire, and began to talk
of religion and good things, the brat, as he
lay in the cradle, which his mother generally
put near the fire-place that he might be snug,
used to sit up, as they were in the middle of
their talk, and begin to bellow as if the devil
was in him in right earnest: this, as I said,

led the neighbours to think that all was not right, and there was a general consultation held one day about what would be best to do with him. Some advised to put him out on the shovel, but Judy's pride was up at that. A pretty thing indeed, that a child of hers should be put on a shovel and flung out on the dunghill, just like a dead kitten, or a poisoned rat! no, no, she would not hear to that at all. One old woman, who was considered very skilful and knowing in fairy matters, strongly recommended her to put the tongs in the fire, and heat them red hot, and to take his nose in them, and that that would, beyond all manner of doubt, make him tell what he was, and where he came from (for the general suspicion was, that he had been changed by the good people); but Judy was too soft-hearted, and too fond of the imp, so she would not give into this plan, though every body said she was wrong; and may be she was, but it's hard to blame a mother. Well, some advised one thing, and some another; at last one spoke of sending for the priest, who was a very holy and a very learned man, to see it; to this Judy of course

E

had no objection, but one thing or other always prevented her doing so; and the upshot of the business was, that the priest never saw him.

Things went on in the old way for some time longer. The brat continued yelping and yowling, and eating more than his three brothers put together, and playing all sorts of unlucky tricks, for he was mighty mischievously inclined; till it happened one day that Tim Carrol, the blind piper, going his rounds, called in and sat down by the fire to have a bit of chat with the woman of the house. So after some time, Tim, who was no churl of his music, yoked on the pipes, and began to bellows away in high style; when the instant he began, the young fellow, who had been lying as still as a mouse in his cradle, sat up, began to grin and twist his ugly face, to swing about his long tawny arms, and to kick out his crooked legs, and to show signs of great glee at the music. At last nothing would serve him but he should get the pipes into his own hands, and to humour him, his mother asked Tim to lend them to the child for a minute. Tim, who

was kind to children, readily consented ;
and as Tim had not his sight, Judy herself
brought them to the cradle, and went to put
them on him; but she had no occasion, for
the youth seemed quite up to the business. He
buckled on the pipes, set the bellows under
one arm, and the bag under the other, worked
them both as knowingly as if he had been
twenty years at the business, and lilted up
Sheela na guira, in the finest style imaginable.
All was in astonishment: the poor woman
crossed herself. Tim, who, as I said before,
was *dark*, and did not well know who was
playing, was in great delight; and when he
heard that it was a little *'prechan* not five
years old, that had never seen a set of pipes
in his life, he wished the mother joy of her
son ; offered to take him off her hands if she
would part with him, swore he was a *born*
piper, a natural *genus*, and declared that in a
little time more, with the help of a little good
instruction from himself, there would not be
his match in the whole country. The poor
woman was greatly delighted to hear all this,
particularly as what Tim said about natural
genus quieted some misgivings that were

rising in her mind, lest what the neighbours
said about his not being right might be too
true ; and it gratified her moreover to think
that her dear child (for she really loved the
whelp) would not be forced to turn out and
beg, but might earn decent bread for himself.
So when Mick came home in the evening from
his work, she up and told him all that had
happened, and all that Tim Carrol had said ;
and Mick, as was natural, was very glad to
hear it, for the helpless condition of the poor
creature was a great trouble to him ; so next
day he took the pig to the fair, and with what
it brought set off to Clonmel, and bespoke a
bran new set of pipes, of the proper size for
him. In about a fortnight the pipes came home,
and the moment the chap in his cradle laid
eyes on them, he squealed with delight, and
threw up his pretty legs, and bumped himself
in his cradle, and went on with a great many
comical tricks ; till at last, to quiet him, they
gave him the pipes, and he immediately set to
and pulled away at Jig Polthog, to the admiration of all that heard him. The fame of
his skill on the pipes soon spread far and
near, for there was not a piper in the six next

counties could come at all near him, in Old
Moderagh rue, or the Hare in the Corn, or
The Foxhunter Jig, or The Rakes of Cashel,
or the Piper's Maggot, or any of the fine
Irish jigs, which make people dance whether
they will or no; and it was surprising to hear
him rattle away " The Fox-hunt;" you'd
really think you heard the hounds giving
tongue, and the terriers yelping always behind,
and the huntsman and the whippers-in cheer-
ing or correcting the dogs; it was, in short,
the very next thing to seeing the hunt itself.
The best of him was, he was no ways stingy
of his music, and many a merry dance the
boys and girls of the neighbourhood used to
have in his father's cabin; and he would
play up music for them, that they said used as
it were to put quicksilver in their feet; and
they all declared they never moved so light
and so airy to any piper's playing that ever
they danced to.

But besides all his fine Irish music, he
had one queer tune of his own, the oddest
that ever was heard; for the moment he
began to play it, every thing in the house
seemed disposed to dance; the plates and

porringers used to jingle on the dresser, the
pots and pot-hooks used to rattle in the
chimney, and people used even to fancy they
felt the stools moving from under them ;
but, however it might be with the stools, it is
certain that no one could keep long sitting
on them, for both old and young always fell to
capering as hard as ever they could. The girls
complained that when he began this tune it
always threw them out in their dancing, and
that they never could handle their feet rightly,
for they felt the floor like ice under them,
and themselves every moment ready to come
sprawling on their backs or their faces ; the
young bachelors that wished to show off their
dancing and their new pumps, and their
bright red or green and yellow garters,
swore that it confused them so that they never
could go rightly through the *heel and toe*, or
cover the buckle, or any of their best steps,
but felt themselves always all bedizzied and
bewildered, and then old and young would go
jostling and knocking together in a frightful
manner ; and when the unlucky brat had them
all in this way whirligigging about the floor,
he'd grin and chuckle and chatter, for all the

world like Jacko the monkey when he has played off some of his roguery.

The older he grew the worse he grew, and by the time he was six years old there was no standing the house for him; he was always making his brothers burn or scald themselves, or break their shins over the pots and stools. One time in harvest, he was left at home by himself, and when his mother came in, she found the cat a horseback on the dog, with her face to the tail, and her legs tied round him, and the *urchin* playing his queer tune to them; so that the dog went barking and jumping about, and puss was mewing for the dear life, and slapping her tail backwards and forwards, which as it would hit against the dog's chaps, he'd snap at and bite, and then there was the philliloo. Another time, the farmer Mick worked with, a very decent respectable man, happened to call in, and Judy wiped a stool with her apron, and invited him to sit down and rest himself after his walk. He was sitting with his back to the cradle, and behind him was a pan of blood, for Judy was making pigs' puddings; the lad lay quite still in his nest, and watched his opportunity till he got ready a hook at the end of a piece of twine, which he contrived to fling so handily, that it caught in the bob of the man's nice new wig, and soused it in the pan of blood. Another time, his mother was coming in from milking the cow, with the pail on her head: the minute he saw her he lilted up his infernal tune, and the poor woman letting go the pail, clapped her hands aside, and began to dance a jig, and tumbled the milk all atop of her husband, who was bringing in some turf to boil the supper. In short there would be no end to telling all his pranks, and all the mischievous tricks he played.

Soon after, some mischances began to happen to the farmer's cattle; a horse took the staggers, a fine veal calf died of the black-leg, and some of his sheep of the red water; the cows began to grow vicious, and to kick down the milk-pails, and the roof of one end of the barn fell in; and the farmer took it into his head that Mick Flanigan's unlucky child was the cause of all the mischief. So one day he called Mick aside, and said to him, " Mick, you see things are not going on with me as they ought, and to be plain with you, Mick, I think that child of yours is the cause of it. I am really falling away to nothing with fretting, and I can hardly sleep on my bed at night for thinking of what may happen before the morning. So I'd be glad if you'd look out for work some where else; you're as good a man as any in the county, and there's no fear but you'll have your choice of work." To this Mick replied, " that he was sorry for his losses, and still sorrier that he or his should be thought to be the cause of them; that for his own part, he was not quite easy in his mind about that child, but he had him, and so must keep him;" and he promised to look out for another place immediately. Accordingly next Sunday at chapel, Mick gave out that he was about leaving the work at John Riordan's, and immediately a farmer, who lived a couple of miles off, and who wanted a ploughman (the last one having just left him), came up to Mick, and offered him a house and garden, and work all the year round. Mick, who knew him to be a good employer, immediately closed with him; so it was agreed that the farmer should send a

car* to take his little bit of furniture, and
that he should remove on the following
Thursday. When Thursday came, the car
came, according to promise, and Mick loaded
it, and put the cradle with the child and his
pipes on the top, and Judy sat beside it to
take care of him, lest he should tumble out
and be killed; they drove the cow before
them, the dog followed, but the cat was of
course left behind; and the other three children went along the road picking skeehories
(haws), and blackberries, for it was a fine
day towards the latter end of harvest.

They had to cross a river, but as it ran
through a bottom between two high banks,
you did not see it till you were close on it.
The young fellow was lying pretty quiet
in the bottom of his cradle, till they came
to the head of the bridge, when hearing
the roaring of the water (for there was a
great flood in the river, as it had rained
heavily for the last two or three days), he
sat up in his cradle and looked about him;
and the instant he got a sight of the water,

* Car,—a cart.

and found they were going to take him across
it, O how he did bellow and how he did
squeal!—no rat caught in a snap-trap ever
sang out equal to him. "Whisht! A lanna,"
said Judy, " there's no fear of you;" sure
its only over the stone-bridge we're going."
" Bad luck to you, you old rip!" cried he,
"what a pretty trick you've played me, to bring
me here!" and still went on yelling, and the
farther they got on the bridge the louder he
yelled; till at last Mick could hold out no
longer, so giving him a great skelp of the
whip he had in his hand, " Devil choke you,
you brat!" said he, " will you never stop bawl-
ing? a body can't hear their ears for you."
The moment he felt the thong of the whip, he
leaped up in the cradle, clapt the pipes under
his arm, gave a most wicked grin at Mick,
and jumped clean over the battlements of the
bridge down into the water. " O my child,
my child!" shouted Judy, " he's gone for
ever from me." Mick and the rest of the
children ran to the other side of the bridge,
and looking over, they saw him coming out
from under the arch of the bridge, sitting
cross-legged on the top of a white-headed wave,

and playing away on the pipes as merrily as
if nothing had happened. The river was
running very rapidly, so he was whirled away
at a great rate; but he played as fast, ay
and faster than the river ran; and though
they set off as hard as they could along the
bank, yet, as the river made a sudden turn
round the hill, about a hundred yards below
the bridge, by the time they got there he was
out of sight, and no one ever laid eyes on him
more; but the general opinion was, that he
went home with the pipes to his own relations,
the good people, to make music for them.

The circumstance with which the foregoing story
opens, of the young piper's father and mother bearing
different names, need cause no scandal, as it is a common custom, both in Ireland and Scotland, for a married woman to retain her maiden name.

Putting a child that is suspected of being a changeling out on a shovel, or tormenting it in any way, is
done with a view of inducing the fairies to restore the
stolen child. In Denmark, the mother heats the
oven, and places the changeling on the peel, pretending to put it in, or whips it severely with a rod, or

throws it into the water. In Sweden, they employ a method very similar to the Irish one, of putting on the shovel. "Tales," says Mr. J. Ihre, in his "Dissertatio de Superstitionibus hodiernis," when mentioning what are called Bythinga (changelings), " tales subinde morbosos infantes esse judicant ; quos si in fornacem ardentem se injicere velle simulaverint, aut si tribus dici Jovis vesperis *ad trivium deportentur* proprios se accepturos credunt." The change is always made before the child is christened, and the methods most approved of for preventing it are, good watching, keeping a light constantly burning, making a cross over the door or cradle, putting some pieces of iron, a needle, a nail, a knife, &c. in the cradle. In Thuringia, it is considered an infallible preventive to hang the father's breeches against the wall.

The Irish, like the Tuscans, as observed by Mr. Rose in his interesting "Letters from the North of Italy," are extremely picturesque in their language. Thus they constantly use the word *dark* as synonymous with *blind ;* and a blind beggar will implore you " to look down with pity on a poor *dark* man." It may be observed here that the Irish, like the Scotch (see Waverley), by a very beautiful and tender euphemism, call idiots *innocents.* A lady of rank in Ireland, in whose heart benevolence had fixed her seat, and who was the Lady Bountiful of her neighbourhood, was one day asking a man about a poor orphan : " Ah, my lady," said he, " the poor creature is sadly afflicted with *innocence.*" Another peculiarity in the phraseology of the Irish

is their fondness for using what Mr. Burke,—who
perhaps was thus led into his notion of terror being
the cause of the sublime,—would term *sublime adjec-
tives,* instead of the common English adverbs, very,
extremely, &c. ; and which, by sometimes unluckily
meeting with substantives expressing ideas of a totally opposite nature, produce very ludicrous combina-
tions. Thus they will very picturesquely say, " It's a
cruel cold morning ;" but at other times you may hear
that Mr. Such a one is " a *cruel* good man." A young
clergyman was once told by one of his parishioners
that the people all said he was most *horridly* improved
in his preaching.   And, describing female beauty, an
Irish peasant may perhaps say, that Peggy So and so
is a *shocking* pretty girl, or a *terrible* pretty girl.
These last, by the way, are quite classic, or perhaps
rather Oriental.   They correspond pretty exactly to
the δεινος and εκπαγλος of the Greeks ; and, in the " Song
of Songs," the wise son of David says of the Egyptian
princess, that " She is fair as the moon, clear as the
sun, and *terrible* as an army with banners." Mr. Pope
even says, " Now *awful* beauty puts on all her charms."
In the *bon ton* the word " *monstrous*" is often employed with as little propriety as the Hibernicisms
" *shocking and terrible*." There are, indeed, few Irish
idioms that are not the result of a lively imagination,
and which might not be justified in a similar manner.
Thus an Irishman will say, " There's a *power* of ivy
growing on the old church of such a place." What
is this but the " Est hederæ *vis*" of Horace ?

The " Fox-hunt" is a piece of music which every piper is expected to know. It, as described in the text, imitates the various sounds of the chase; and some pipers accompany their music with a very accurate topographical description of a hunt, the scene of which is the neighbourhood of the place where the piper is performing.

Es giebt sich ein Elfenkönigstück das zwar mancher geschichte Musicus spielen kann, aber nicht vorzutragen wagt; denn wenn es ertönt, wird Alt und Jung ja selbst das Leblose zum Tanzen getrieben und der Spieler kann nicht aufhören, wenn er nicht das Lied genau rückwärts spielen kann, oder ihm Jemand vom hinten die Saïten auf der Violine zerschneidet.

Die Edda von Fr. Rühs, p. 16.

The " Bold Dragoon," in Mr. Washington Irving's very entertaining " Tales of a Traveller," must have been familiar with the idea of this music, which had such power of communicating motion, as it seems to have been the stuff of which his dream or invention was composed.

Heel and toe and *cover the buckle* are Irish steps, which to be understood should be seen performed by some strapping Hibernian, on a barn-floor; or should the dance take place in a cabin, as the floor is seldom remarkably level, on a door which is taken off the hinges and laid down in the middle of the room; thus a fitting stage is formed for the dancer to go through his evolutions on. So the old song happily has it—

" But they couldn't keep time on the cold earthen
        floor,
    So, to humour the music, they danced on the
        door," &c.

It is possible that even D'Egville, eminent in his
art as he is, may never have heard of these steps.

Handle the feet may appear ludicrous, yet few
could have any great objection to *manage the feet*,
which is just the same thing.

It is a piece of superstition with the Irish never to
take a cat with them when they are removing, more
particularly when they have to cross a river.

The Irish terms which occur in this story are
merely the words 'Prechan and Alanna : the former is
an abbrevation of Leprechan (for which see following section), and is applied to ill-thriven children ;
the latter, properly ma leanbh, signifies my child.

THE

BREWERY OF EGG-SHELLS.

IT may be considered impertinent were I
to explain what is meant by a changeling;
both Shakespeare and Spenser have already
done so, and who is there unacquainted with
the Midsummer Night's Dream * and the
Fairy Queen † ?

Now Mrs. Sullivan fancied that her youngest
child had been changed by "fairies theft,"
and certainly appearances warranted such a

---

* " For Oberon is passing fell and wrath
    Because that she, as her attendant hath
    A lovely boy, stol'n from an Indian king:
    She never had so sweet a changeling."
          MIDSUMMER NIGHT'S DREAM, Act ii. s. 1.

† " ———A Fairy thee unweeting reft,
    There as thou slepst in tender swadling band,
    And her base elfin brood there for thee left,
    Such men do changelings call—so changed by
      fairies theft."
          FAIRY QUEEN, Book i. Canto 10.

F

conclusion; for in one night her healthy, blue-eyed boy had become shrivelled up into almost nothing, and never ceased squalling and crying.   This naturally made poor Mrs. Sullivan very unhappy; and all the neighbours, by way of comforting her, said, that her own child was, beyond any kind of doubt, with the good people, and that one of themselves was put in his place.

Mrs. Sullivan of course could not disbelieve what every one told her, but she did not wish to hurt the thing; for although its face was so withered, and its body wasted away to a mere skeleton, it had still a strong resemblance to her own boy: she therefore could not find it in her heart to roast it alive on the griddle, or to burn its nose off with the red hot tongs, or to throw it out in the snow on the road-side, notwithstanding these, and several like proceedings, were strongly recommended to her for the recovery of her child.

One day who should Mrs. Sullivan meet but a cunning woman, well known about the country by the name of Ellen Leah (or Grey Ellen).   She had the gift, however she got it, of telling where the dead were, and what was good for the rest of their souls; and could charm away warts and wens, and do a great many wonderful things of the same nature.

"You're in grief this morning, Mrs. Sullivan," were the first words of Ellen Leah to her.

"You may say that, Ellen," said Mrs. Sullivan, "and good cause I have to be in grief, for there was my own fine child whipped off from me out of his cradle, without as much as by your leave or ask your pardon, and an ugly dony bit of a shrivelled up fairy put in his place; no wonder then that you see me in grief, Ellen."

"Small blame to you, Mrs. Sullivan," said Ellen Leah; "but are you sure 'tis a fairy?"

"Sure!" echoed Mrs. Sullivan, "sure enough am I to my sorrow, and can I doubt my own two eyes? Every mother's soul must feel for me!"

"Will you take an old woman's advice?" said Ellen Leah, fixing her wild and mysterious gaze upon the unhappy mother; and, after a pause, she added, "but may be you'll call it foolish?"

"Can you get me back my child, my own

F 2

child, Ellen?" said Mrs. Sullivan with great energy.

"If you do as I bid you," returned Ellen Leah, "you'll know." Mrs. Sullivan was silent in expectation, and Ellen continued, "Put down the big pot, full of water, on the fire, and make it boil like mad; then get a dozen new laid eggs, break them, and keep the shells, but throw away the rest; when that is done, put the shells in the pot of boiling water, and you will soon know whether it is your own boy or a fairy. If you find that it is a fairy in the cradle, take the red hot poker and cram it down his ugly throat, and you will not have much trouble with him after that, I promise you."

Home went Mrs. Sullivan, and did as Ellen Leah desired. She put the pot on the fire, and plenty of turf under it, and set the water boiling at such a rate, that if ever water was red hot—it surely was.

The child was lying for a wonder quite easy and quiet in the cradle, every now and then cocking his eye, that would twinkle as keen as a star in a frosty night, over at the great fire, and the big pot upon it; and he looked

on with great attention at Mrs. Sullivan
breaking the eggs, and putting down the egg-
shells to boil. At last he asked, with the
voice of a very old man, " What are you
doing, mammy?"

Mrs. Sullivan's heart, as she said herself,
was up in her mouth ready to choke her, at
hearing the child speak. But she contrived
to put the poker in the fire, and to answer
without making any wonder at the words,
" I'm brewing *a vick*," (my son).

" And what are you brewing, mammy ?"
said the little imp, whose supernatural gift of
speech now proved beyond question that he
was a fairy substitute.

" I wish the poker was red," thought Mrs.
Sullivan ; but it was a large one, and took a
long time heating : so she determined to keep
him in talk until the poker was in a proper
state to thrust down his throat, and therefore
repeated the question.

" Is it what I'm brewing *a vick*," said she,
" you want to know ?"

" Yes, mammy : what are you brewing ?"
returned the fairy.

" Egg-shells *a vick*," said Mrs. Sullivan.

" Oh !" shrieked the imp, starting up in the cradle, and clapping his hands together, " I'm fifteen hundred years in the world, and I never saw a brewery of egg-shells before !" The poker was by this time quite red, and Mrs. Sullivan seizing it, ran furiously toward the cradle ; but somehow or other her foot slipped, and she fell flat on the floor, and the poker flew out of her hand to the other end of the house. However, she got up, without much loss of time, and went to the cradle intending to pitch the wicked thing that was in it into the pot of boiling water, when there she saw her own child in a sweet sleep, one of his soft round arms rested upon the pillow— his features were as placid as if their repose had never been disturbed, save the rosy mouth which moved with a gentle and regular breathing.

Who can tell the feelings of a mother when she looks upon her sleeping child ? Why should I therefore endeavour to describe those of Mrs. Sullivan at again beholding her long lost boy ? The fountains of her heart overflowed with the excess of joy—and she wept ! —tears trickled silently down her cheek, nor

did she strive to check them—they were tears
not of sorrow, but of happiness.

———————

The writer regrets that he is unable to retain the
rich vein of comic interest in the foregoing tale, as
related to him by Mrs. Philipps, to whose manner of
narration it may perhaps be ascribed.

The story has already been told, with some immaterial variations, in " Grose's Provincial Glossary,"
where it is quoted from " A Pleasant Treatise on
Witchcraft." For instance : Ellen Leah is there represented by an old man, and the mother of the
changeling, instead of brewing the egg-shells, breaks
a dozen eggs, and places the twenty-four half shells
before the child, who exclaims, " Seven years old was
I before I came to the nurse, and four years have I
lived since ; and never saw so many milk-pans before !"
The exposure of the fairy, and subsequent restitution
of the woman's child, form the sequel.

Ellen Leah (correctly written, Liath) is not an
ideal personage ; indeed, most of the characters introduced in these legends are sketched from nature.

The letter of a fair correspondent has furnished the
following extract.

" Of the superstition of the peasantry of Bantry, the
anecdotes concerning Aileen Leah, or Ellen of the Grey
Locks, to which they give the fullest credence, are
sufficient proof.

" This poor woman was said to belong to the fairies, or to have communication with the ' good people.' She was never known to sleep at home ; could foretell the death of any individual, even if personally unknown to her ; could describe every movement of those in the other world, and knew all their wants and wishes, which she would relate to the friends of the departed, and thereby enable them to supply those wants. A woman having two sons in the East Indies, and not hearing from them for a considerable time, applied to Aileen Leah ; who informed her without the least hesitation, that both her sons were dead, and she should receive a letter on that day fortnight with the intelligence : strange as it may seem, the event verified the prediction.

" Johanna Sullivan, a young woman who resided near us, had always lived on very bad terms with her brother-in-law, who had done her some injury, and when dying sent for her to obtain forgiveness, but she refused going, and he died without seeing her : the consequence was, she was never able to go out alone without being tormented by a supernatural appearance, which preyed so much upon her, that continued uneasiness of mind gradually undermined her health. In this unhappy situation she applied to Aileen Leah, who directed her to interrogate this spirit, and from her heart to forgive her brother-in-law, which until she did, the spirit would continue to haunt her incessantly, and Aileen Leah even named the exact place where it would again appear.

" Accordingly, summoning up all her courage, she determined to question the apparition; but when she beheld it, her resolution entirely forsook her; the blood chilled in her veins, and, with a violent shriek, she fell down senseless. In this state the poor young woman was found, and carried home; when she recovered, Aileen Leah was sent for, who on seeing her appeared very angry at her want of courage, and exhorted her most strenuously not to evince such weakness again; as the spirit would certainly appear to her once more, and should she not declare her forgiveness to it, the consequences to both would be dreadful.

" The apparition again stood before Johanna Sullivan; but, as at the former meeting, fear benumbed her faculties, and she fell down insensible without having uttered one word. In the fall she received several severe bruises, from the effect of which she never recovered.

" Aileen Leah was with her shortly after this happened, and with frightful contortions of feature, and signs of real misery, informed her that the wretched soul of her brother-in-law was now irrevocably doomed to endless torments, and that a few short hours would terminate her own existence. Johanna Sullivan died the following morning.

" These circumstances the lower orders relate with enthusiastic veneration, as proving the supernatural knowledge of Aileen Leah, and they receive with implicit credit all her revelations; looking with a degree of horror on any sceptic who may doubt them."

The comparison of the changeling's eye, at beholding the large pot of water on the fire, to "a star on a frosty night," is a familiar, though nevertheless beautiful simile. The reader will probably remember the description of the enchantress in Miss Brooke's spirited and faithful translation of the Chase. (Relics of Irish Poetry, p. 98.)

> " Gold gave its rich and radiant die,
>   And in her tresses flow'd;
> And like a freezing star, her eye
>   With Heaven's own splendour glow'd."

In the note on the preceding story, some remarks were made relative to the " picturesque phraseology" of the Irish peasant. Another example occurs in the present tale, in Mrs. Sullivan's expression, " Every mother's soul must feel for me." This would be considered among the higher classes in Ireland a decided vulgarism, and it is so; but will any one deny its poetical tenderness? In a former tale, also, the fairy's offer to provide supper for the priest " in less than no time" certainly surpasses all subtile subdivisions of time, even that made by Titania, in the Midsummer Night's Dream, Act ii. Sc. iii.

> " Come, now a roundel, and a fairy song.
>   Then, for the third part of a minute hence;"

and for rapidity, far exceeds the nimbleness of Robin
Goodfellow, in the old masquing song attributed to
Ben Jonson, where that sportive fairy tells us, he can

> " ———in a minute's space descrye
>   Each thing that's done belowe the moone."

Yet it must be granted, however suitable the phrase
" in less than no time" may be to fairy language, that
it is absurd enough to hear a stout " bog-trotter" offer
to " step over the mountain and be back again with
your honour in less than no time."

The word " Dony" in the text agrees exactly in
signification with " tiny," to which it is evidently related ; and is to be found in the Fairy Queen as the
name of Florimel's dwarf.

It is worthy of remark, that several words which
were in common use in the reign of Elizabeth, and
which are no longer to be met in English dictionaries
or conversation, should still exist in Ireland.   The
word "ho" may be given as an instance, which is used
as a substantive by Lord Berners, in his translation of
Froissart, as also by Laneham, in his letter describing
the festivities at Kenilworth, and is still so employed in
Ireland.   " As soon as he came into his fortune, there
was no *ho* to his dashing away money."   Another
word is " forenenst," which is always employed by the
Irish peasantry for " opposite," and which is used in
the same sense by Fairfax, in his " Godfrey of Bou-

logne." To return to the word "Dony;" there is a
village near Dublin named Donnybrook, situated on a
mountain stream, called the Dodder, over which there
is a handsome bridge with lofty arches. In dry weather the quantity of water is so inconsiderable, that a
stranger would be very apt to use the sarcastic observation of the Spaniard, who on viewing the magnificent bridge that spanned the contemptible Man-
zanares, near Madrid, exclaimed, "They ought to
sell the bridge and buy water;" but in a few hours
after a heavy fall of rain in the mountains, the Dodder
becomes a river indeed, and swells up to the very summit of the arches. This has been mentioned for the
sake of noticing a peculiarity in the name Donnybrook—little brook. It is curious that the word
"brook" hardly ever occurs in English speech or
writing, except in the sense defined by Johnson, "a
running water less than a river;" and is always asso-
ciated with the idea of flowery meads, &c. but in Ireland it appears to be employed in its true and original
sense. The streams, which in the county Wicklow
during rain burst or *break* from the hills, are always by the common people called *brooks*. Now the
Anglo-Saxon Bꞃoc, from whence it evidently comes,
signifies a torrent—torrens—Χειμαρρους; and it is clear
that it is derived from Bꞃocan, the participle of
Bꞃecan, to break.

THE CHANGELING.

A YOUNG woman, whose name was Mary
Scannell, lived with her husband not many
years ago at Castle Martyr. One day in harvest time she went with several more to help
in binding up the wheat, and left her child,
which she was nursing, in a corner of the field,
quite safe, as she thought, wrapped up in her
cloak. When she had finished her work, she
returned where the child was, but in place of
her own child she found a thing in the cloak
that was not half the size, and that kept up
such a crying you might have heard it a mile
off: so she guessed how the case was, and,
without stop or stay, away she took it in her
arms, pretending to be mighty fond of it all the
while, to a wise woman, who told her in a whis-
per not to give it enough to eat, and to beat
and pinch it without mercy, which Mary Scannell did; and just in one week after to the

day, when she awoke in the morning, she found her own child lying by her side in the bed! The fairy that had been put in its place did not like the usage it got from Mary Scannell, who understood how to treat it, like a sensible woman as she was, and away it went after the week's trial, and sent her own child back to her.

This story, with those preceding and the one subsequent, are illustrative of the popular opinion respecting the fairies stealing away children.

"The most formidable attribute of the Elves," says Sir Walter Scott, in his valuable Essay on Fairy Superstition in the second volume of the Minstrelsy of the Scottish Border," "was their practice of carrying away and exchanging children, and that of stealing human souls from their bodies."

Robin Goodfellow's song before mentioned thus describes the proceedings of a fairy troop :

> "When larks 'gin sing
>   Away we fling,
> And babes new borne steal as we go,
>   And elfe in bed
>   We leave instead,
> And wend us laughing.   Ho! Ho! Ho!"

And again from the Irish Hudibras (8vo. London, 1689, p. 122), we learn that fairies

" Drink dairies dry, and stroke the cattle ;
  Steal sucklings, and through key-holes sling
  Toping and dancing in a ring."

Mr. Anster has founded an exquisite ballad, printed in his Poems (8vo. Edinburgh, 1819, p. 157), on this point of fairy superstition, in which he applies the term "*weakling*" to the representative of the abstracted child.

Gay, in his fable of the Mother, Nurse, and Fairy, ridicules the superstitious idea of changelings ; but it is needless to multiply quotations on the subject.

Castle Martyr, formerly called Bally Martyr, is a pretty village, through which the high road from Cork to Youghall passes. It is chiefly remarkable as the residence of Lord Shannon.

Dr. Smith, in his History of Cork, mentions that " about a mile south-east of Castle Martyr, a river called the Dowr breaks out from a limestone rock, after taking a subterraneous course near half a mile, having its rise near Mogeely."

In an Irish keen, or funeral lamentation, some verses of which are translated in a subsequent note, the mother who sings it over the dead body of her son compares the cheerless feelings with which she must pass through life to the dark waters of the subterranean

Dowr.—A feeble attempt is made at giving this beautiful image in English verse :

> " Dark as flows the buried Dowr,
>   Where no ray can reach its tide,
>   So no bright beam has the power
>   Through my soul's cold stream to glide."

The original would seem to have suggested to Mr. Moore the notion of that touching song in his Irish Melodies—

> " As a beam o'er the face of the waters may glow,
>   While the tide runs in darkness and coldness
>   below," &c.

THE TWO GOSSIPS.

At Minane, near Tracton, there was a young couple whose name was Mac Daniel, and they had such a fine, wholesome-looking child, that the fairies determined on having it in their company, and putting a changeling in its place; but it so happened that Mrs. Mac Daniel had a gossip whose name was Norah Buckeley, and she was going by the house they lived in (it was a nice new slated one, by the same token) just coming on the dusk of the evening. She thought it too late to step in and ask how her gossip was, as she had above a mile and half further to go, and moreover she knew the fairies were abroad, for all along the road before her from Carrigaline, one eddy of dust would be followed by another, which was a plain sign that the good people were out taking their rounds; and she had

pains in her bones with dropping so many
curchies (courtesies). However, Norah Buckeley, when she came opposite her gossip's
house, stopped short, and made another, and
said almost under her breath, " God keep all
here from harm !"   No sooner had these words
been uttered than she saw one of the windows
lifted up, and her gossip's beautiful child without any more to do handed out ; she could not
tell, if her life depended on it, how, or by
whom : no matter for that, she went to the
window and took the child from whatever
handed it, and covered it well up in her cloak,
and carried it away home with her.

Next morning early she went over to see her
gossip, who began to make a great moan to
her, of how different her child was from what
it had ever been before, crying all the night,
and keeping her awake, and how nothing she
could think of would quiet it.

" I'll tell you what you'll do with the brat,"
said Norah Buckeley, looking as knowing as if
she knew more than all the rest of the world :
" whip it well first, and then bring it to the
cross-roads, and leave the fairy in the ditch
there for any one to take that pleases ; for I

have your own child at home safe and sound as he was handed out of the window last night to me."

Mrs. Mac Daniel on hearing this, when the surprise was over, stepped out to get a rod, and her gossip happening for one instant to look after her, on turning round again, found the fairy gone, and neither she nor the child's mother saw any more of it, nor could ever hear a word of tidings how it disappeared in so wonderful a manner.

Mrs. Mac Daniel went over with great speed to her gossip's house, and there she got her own child, and brought him back with her, and a stout young man he is at this day.

Tracton is situated about ten miles south of Cork, in a district usually called "Daunt's Country," from the residence of several families of that name. Tracton Abbey, now completely demolished, was formerly a place of some celebrity; see Archdale's Monasticon Hibernicum, and Dr. Smith's History of Cork.

In 1781, James Dennis, Chief Baron of the Exchequer, was created Baron Tracton, of Tracton Abbey; which title became extinct on his demise the following year. Lord Tracton was buried in the cathedral of Cork ; and, what is curious, a noble monument to his memory, possibly the largest and best piece of statuary in the south of Ireland, is placed in the parish church of St. Nicholas, the smallest in that city.

An eddy of dust, raised by the wind, is supposed by the superstitious peasantry to be occasioned by the journeying of a fairy troop from one of their haunts to another, and the same civilities are scrupulously observed towards the invisible riders as if the dust had been caused by a company of the most important persons in the country. In Scotland, the sound of bridles ringing through the air accompanies the whirlwind which marks the progress of a fairy journey.

The invisible agency by which the child was thrust out of the window will find a parallel in many stories, particularly in one related by Waldron, the Isle of Man chronicler.

At Minane, the scene of this tale, the finest specimens hitherto discovered of a rare mineral, called hydrargillite or wavellite, have been dug up.

LEGEND OF BOTTLE-HILL.

" Come, listen to a tale of times of old,
    Come, listen to me——."

I⊤ was in the good days when the little
people, most impudently called fairies, were
more frequently seen than they are in these
unbelieving times, that a farmer, named Mick
Purcell, rented a few acres of barren ground
in the neighbourhood of the once celebrated
preceptory of Mourne, situated about three
miles from Mallow, and thirteen from " the
beautiful city called Cork."   Mick had a wife
and family; they all did what they could,
and that was but little, for the poor man had
no child grown up big enough to help him in
his work; and all the poor woman could do
was to mind the children, and to milk the
one cow, and to boil the potatoes, and carry
the eggs to market to Mallow; but with all
they could do, 'twas hard enough on them to
pay the rent.   Well, they did manage it for

a good while; but at last came a bad year, and the little grain of oats was all spoiled, and the chickens died of the pip, and the pig got the measles—*she* was sold in Mallow and brought almost nothing; and poor Mick found that he hadn't enough to half pay his rent, and two gales were due.

"Why, then, Molly," says he, "what'll we do?"

"Wisha, then, mavournene, what would you do but take the cow to the fair of Cork and sell her," says she; "and Monday is fair day, and so you must go to-morrow, that the poor beast may be rested *again* the fair."

"And what'll we do when she's gone?" says Mick, sorrowfully.

"Never a know I know, Mick; but sure God won't leave us without him, Mick; and you know how good he was to us when poor little Billy was sick, and we had nothing at all for him to take, that good doctor gentleman at Ballydahin come riding and asking for a drink of milk; and how he gave us two shillings; and how he sent the things and the bottles for the child, and gave me my breakfast when I went over to ask a question,

so he did; and how he came to see Billy,
and never left off his goodness till he was
quite well."

"Oh! you are always that way, Molly, and
I believe you are right after all, so I won't
be sorry for selling the cow; but I'll go to-
morrow, and you must put a needle and thread
through my coat, for you know 'tis ripped
under the arm."

Molly told him he should have every thing
right; and about twelve o'clock next day he
left her, getting a charge not to sell his cow
except for the highest penny. Mick promised
to mind it, and went his way along the road.
He drove his cow slowly through the little
stream which crosses it, and runs under the
old walls of Mourne; as he passed he glanced
his eye upon the towers and one of the old
elder trees, which were only then little bits of
switches.

"Oh, then, if I only had half the money
that's buried in you, 'tisn't driving this poor
cow I'd be now! Why, then, isn't it too bad
that it should be there covered over with
earth, and many a one besides me wanting it?

Well, if it's God's will, I'll have some money myself coming back."

So saying, he moved on after his beast; 'twas a fine day, and the sun shone brightly on the walls of the old abbey as he passed under them; he then crossed an extensive mountain tract, and after six long miles he came to the top of that hill—Bottle-hill 'tis called now, but that was not the name of it then, and just there a man overtook him. " Good morrow," says he. " Good morrow, kindly," says Mick, looking at the stranger, who was a little man, you'd almost call him a dwarf, only he was'nt quite so little neither: he had a bit of an old, wrinkled, yellow face, for all the world like a dried cauliflower, only he had a sharp little nose, and red eyes, and white hair, and his lips were not red, but all his face was one colour, and his eyes never were quiet, but looking at every thing, and although they were red, they made Mick feel quite cold when he looked at them. In truth he did not much like the little man's company; and he couldn't see one bit of his legs nor his body, for though the day was warm,

he was all wrapped up in a big great coat.
Mick drove his cow something faster, but the
little man kept up with him. Mick didn't
know how he walked, for he was almost afraid
to look at him, and to cross himself, for fear
the old man would be angry. Yet he thought
his fellow-traveller did not seem to walk like
other men, nor to put one foot before the
other, but to glide over the rough road, and
rough enough it was, like a shadow, without
noise and without effort. Mick's heart trembled within him, and he said a prayer to himself, wishing he hadn't come out that day, or
that he was on Fair-hill, or that he hadn't the
cow to mind, that he might run away from
the bad thing—when, in the midst of his fears,
he was again addressed by his companion.

"Where are you going with the cow,
honest man?"

"To the fair of Cork then," says Mick,
trembling at the shrill and piercing tones of
the voice.

"Are you going to sell her?" said the
stranger.

"Why, then, what else am I going for but
to sell her?"

" Will you sell her to me ?"

Mick started—he was afraid to have any
thing to do with the little man, and he was
more afraid to say no.

" What 'll you give for her ?" at last says·he.

" I 'll tell you what, I 'll give you this
bottle," said the little one, pulling a bottle
from under his coat.

Mick looked at him and the bottle, and, in
spite of his terror, he could not help bursting
into a loud fit of laughter.

" Laugh if you will," said the little man,
" but I tell you this bottle is better for you
than all the money you will get for the cow
in Cork—ay, than ten thousand times as
much."

Mick laughed again. " Why, then," says
he, " do you think I am such a fool as to
give my good cow for a bottle—and an empty
one, too ? indeed, then, I won't."

" You had better give me the cow, and
take the bottle—you 'll not be sorry for it."

" Why, then, and what would Molly say ?
I 'd never hear the end of it ; and how would
I pay the rent ? and what would we all do
without a penny of money ?"

" I tell you this bottle is better to you than
money ; take it, and give me the cow.   I ask
you for the last time, Mick Purcell."

Mick started.

" How does he know my name?" thought
he.

The stranger proceeded : " Mick Purcell, I
know you, and I have a regard for you ; therefore do as I warn you, or you may be sorry for
it.   How do you know but your cow will die
before you go to Cork ?"

Mick was going to say " God forbid !" but
the little man went on (and he was too attentive
to say any thing to stop him ; for Mick was a
very civil man, and he knew better than to
interrupt a gentleman, and that's what many
people, that hold their heads higher, don't
mind now).

" And how do you know but there will be
much cattle at the fair, and you will get a
bad price, or may be you might be robbed
when you are coming home ? but what need I
talk more to you, when you are determined to
throw away your luck, Mick Purcell."

" Oh ! no, I would not throw away my
luck, sir," said Mick ; " and if I was sure the

bottle was as good as you say, though I never liked an empty bottle, although I had drank the contents of it, I'd give you the cow in the name——"

"Never mind names," said the stranger, "but give me the cow; I would not tell you a lie. Here, take the bottle, and when you go home do what I direct exactly."

Mick hesitated.

"Well, then, good bye, I can stay no longer: once more, take it, and be rich; refuse it, and beg for your life, and see your children in poverty, and your wife dying for want—that will happen to you, Mick Purcell!" said the little man with a malicious grin, which made him look ten times more ugly than ever.

"May be, 'tis true," said Mick, still hesitating: he did not know what to do—he could hardly help believing the old man, and at length, in a fit of desperation, he seized the bottle—" Take the cow," said he, " and if you are telling a lie, the curse of the poor will be on you."

"I care neither for your curses nor your blessings, but I have spoken truth, Mick Purcell, and that you will find to-night, if you do what I tell you."

"And what's that?" says Mick.

"When you go home, never mind if your wife is angry, but be quiet yourself, and make her sweep the room clean, set the table out right, and spread a clean cloth over it; then put the bottle on the ground, saying these words: "Bottle, do your duty," and you will see the end of it.

"And is this all?" says Mick.

"No more," said the stranger. "Good bye, Mick Purcell—you are a rich man."

"God grant it!" said Mick, as the old man moved after the cow, and Mick retraced the road towards his cabin; but he could not help turning back his head to look after the purchaser of his cow, who was nowhere to be seen.

"Lord between us and harm!" said Mick: "*He* can't belong to this earth; but where is the cow?" She too was gone, and Mick went homeward muttering prayers, and holding fast the bottle.

"And what would I do if it broke?" thought he. "Oh! but I'll take care of that;" so he put it into his bosom, and went on anxious to prove his bottle, and doubting of the reception he should meet from his wife; balancing his anxieties with his expectation, his fears with his hopes, he reached home in the evening, and surprised his wife, sitting over the turf fire in the big chimney.

" Oh ! Mick, are you come back ? Sure you weren't at Cork all the way ! What has happened to you ? Where is the cow ? Did you sell her ? How much money did you get for her ? What news have you ? Tell us every thing about it."

" Why, then, Molly, if you 'll give me time, I 'll tell you all about it. If you want to know where the cow is, 'tisn't Mick can tell you, for the never a know does he know where she is now."

" Oh ! then, you sold her ; and where 's the money ?"

" Arrah ! stop awhile, Molly, and I 'll tell you all about it."

" But what bottle is that under your waistcoat ?" said Molly, spying its neck sticking out.

" Why, then, be easy now, can't you," says

Mick, "till I tell it to you;" and putting the bottle on the table, "That's all I got for the cow."

His poor wife was thunderstruck. "All you got! and what good is that, Mick? Oh! I never thought you were such a fool; and what'll we do for the rent, and what ——"

"Now, Molly," says Mick, "can't you hearken to reason? Didn't I tell you how the old man, or whatsoever he was, met me—no, he did not meet me neither, but he was there with me—on the big hill, and how he made me sell him the cow, and told me the bottle was the only thing for me?"

"Yes, indeed, the only thing for you, you fool!" said Molly, seizing the bottle to hurl it at her poor husband's head; but Mick caught it, and quietly (for he minded the old man's advice) loosened his wife's grasp, and placed the bottle again in his bosom. Poor Molly sat down crying, while Mick told her his story, with many a crossing and blessing between him and harm. His wife could not help believing him, particularly as she had as much faith in fairies as she had in the priest, who indeed never discouraged her belief in the

fairies ; may be, he didn't know she believed in them, and may be he believed them
himself. She got up, however, without saying
one word, and began to sweep the earthen
floor with a bunch of heath ; then she tidied up
every thing, and put out the long table, and
spread the clean cloth, for she had only one,
upon it, and Mick placing the bottle on the
ground, looked at it and said, " Bottle, do
your duty."

" Look there! look there, mammy!" said
his chubby eldest son, a boy about five years
old—"look there! look there!" and he sprung
to his mother's side, as two tiny little fellows
rose like light from the bottle, and in an instant covered the table with dishes and plates
of gold and silver, full of the finest victuals
that ever were seen, and when all was done
went into the bottle again.   Mick and his
wife looked at every thing with astonishment ;
they had never seen such plates and dishes before, and didn't think they could ever admire
them enough, the very sight almost took away
their appetites ; but at length Molly said,
" Come and sit down, Mick, and try and eat
a bit : sure you ought to be hungry after such
a good day's work."

" Why, then, the man told no lie about the bottle."

Mick sat down, after putting the children to the table, and they made a hearty meal, though they couldn't taste half the dishes.

" Now," says Molly, " I wonder will those two good little gentlemen carry away these fine things again?" They waited, but no one came ; so Molly put up the dishes and plates very carefully, saying, " Why then, Mick, that was no lie sure enough : but you'll be a rich man yet, Mick Purcell."

Mick and his wife and children went to their bed, not to sleep, but to settle about selling the fine things they did not want, and to take more land.   Mick went to Cork and sold his plate, and bought a horse and cart, and began to show that he was making money ; and they did all they could to keep the bottle a secret ; but for all that, their landlord found it out, for he came to Mick one day and asked him where he got all his money—sure it was not by the farm ; and he bothered him so much, that at last Mick told him of the bottle. His landlord offered him a deal of money for it, but Mick would not give it, till at last he

H

offered to give him all his farm for ever: so
Mick, who was very rich, thought he'd never
want any more money, and gave him the bottle:
but Mick was mistaken—he and his family
spent money as if there was no end of it; and
to make the story short, they became poorer
and poorer, till at last they had nothing left
but one cow; and Mick once more drove his
cow before him to sell her at Cork fair, hoping
to meet the old man and get another bottle.
It was hardly daybreak when he left home,
and he walked on at a good pace till he
reached the big hill: the mists were sleeping
in the valleys and curling like smoke wreaths
upon the brown heath around him.   The sun
rose on his left, and just at his feet a lark
sprang from its grassy couch and poured forth
its joyous matin song, ascending into the clear
blue sky,

" Till its form like a speck in the airiness blending,
    And thrilling with music, was melting in light."

Mick crossed himself, listening as he advanced to the sweet song of the lark, but
thinking, notwithstanding, all the time of the
little old man ; when, just as he reached the

summit of the hill, and cast his eyes over the extensive prospect before and around him, he was startled and rejoiced by the same well-known voice: "Well, Mick Purcell, I told you, you would be a rich man."

"Indeed, then, sure enough I was, that's no lie for you, sir.   Good morning to you, but it is not rich I am now—but have you another bottle, for I want it now as much as I did long ago; so if you have it, sir, here is the cow for it."

"And here is the bottle," said the old man, smiling; "you know what to do with it."

"Oh! then, sure I do, as good right I have."

"Well, farewell for ever, Mick Purcell: I told you, you would be a rich man."

"And good bye to you, sir," said Mick, as he turned back; "and good luck to you, and good luck to the big hill—it wants a name—Bottle-hill.—Good bye, sir, good bye:" so Mick walked back as fast as he could, never looking after the white-faced little gentleman and the cow, so anxious was he to bring home the bottle.—Well, he arrived with it safely enough, and called out as soon as he saw Molly—" Oh! sure I've another bottle!"

"Arrah! then, have you? why, then, you're a lucky man, Mick Purcell, that's what you are."

In an instant she put every thing right; and Mick looking at his bottle, exultingly cried out, " Bottle, do your duty." In a twinkling, two great stout men with big cudgels issued from the bottle (I do not know how they got room in it), and belaboured poor Mick and his wife and all his family, till they lay on the floor, when in they went again. Mick, as soon as he recovered, got up and looked about him; he thought and thought, and at last he took up his wife and his children; and, leaving them to recover as well as they could, he took the bottle under his coat and went to his land-lord, who had a great company: he got a servant to tell him he wanted to speak to him, and at last he came out to Mick.

" Well, what do you want now ?"

" Nothing, sir, only I have another bottle."

" Oh! ho! is it as good as the first ?"

" Yes, sir, and better; if you like, I will

show it to you before all the ladies and gentlemen."

" Come along, then." So saying, Mick was brought into the great hall, where he saw his old bottle standing high up on a shelf: " Ah! ha!" says he to himself, " may be I won't have you by and by."

" Now," says his landlord, " show us your bottle." Mick set it on the floor, and uttered the words: in a moment the landlord was tumbled on the floor; ladies and gentlemen, servants and all, were running, and roaring, and sprawling, and kicking, and shrieking· Wine cups and salvers were knocked about in every direction, until the landlord called out " Stop those two devils, Mick Purcell, or I'll have you hanged."

" They never shall stop," said Mick, " till I get my own bottle that I see up there at top of that shelf."

" Give it down to him, give it down to him, before we are all killed!" says the landlord.

Mick put his bottle in his bosom: in jumped the two men into the new bottle, and he carried them home. I need not lengthen my story by telling how he got richer than ever, how

his son married his landlord's only daughter, how he and his wife died when they were
very old, and how some of the servants, fighting
at their wake, broke the bottles; but still the
hill has the name upon it; ay, and so 'twill
be always Bottle-hill to the end of the world,
and so it ought, for it is a strange story!

An excellent moral may be drawn from this story,
were the Irish a' moralizing people; not being so, the
omission is perhaps characteristic. A close resemblance
between the Legend of Bottle-hill, when allowance
is made for the difference of locality and manners, and
a well known eastern tale, will appear so evident,
that it is sufficient barely to point it out: a German
tale, called in English "The Bottle Imp," may also
be mentioned, as similar in some of the incidents to
this legend.

The comparison of the little man's face to a cauliflower will probably bring to the reader's recollection
the Ettrick shepherd's admirable ballad of the Witch
of Fife, in the "Queen's Wake."

> "Then up there raise ane wee wee man,
>   Franethe the moss-gray stane;
>   His fece was wan like the collifloure,
>   For he nouthir had blude nor bane."

The preceptory of Mourne is situated about four miles south of Mallow; the ruins still remain between the old and new roads from Cork to that town, both of which pass close under its walls. It was originally a foundation for knights templars; some particulars respecting it are given in Archdale's Monasticon Hibernicum and Smith's History of Cork; and much additional information may be found among the MSS. in the British Museum and the State Paper Office.

Mick Purcell's soliloquy respecting the buried treasure is in strict accordance with the popular belief of the Irish peasantry. There are few old ruins in and about which excavations have not been made in the expectation of discovering hidden wealth; in some instances the consequence is, the destruction of the building which had been actually undermined. About three miles south of Cork, near the village of Douglas, is a hill called Castle Treasure, where the writer has more than once witnessed the labours of an old woman "in search of the little crock of gold," which, according to tradition, is buried there. The discovery, a few years since, of a rudely-formed clay urn and two or three brazen implements, attracted' for some time, great crowds to the spot; and it is still a prevalent opinion, that "the little crock of gold" at Castle Treasure remains to reward some lucky person.

Bottle-hill, remarkable only (as unfortunately too many places in Ireland are) for a skirmish between the partisans of James and William, lies midway

between Cork and Mallow, and is a poorly cultivated
tract, along which the roofless walls of deserted
manufactories are thinly scattered.   These throw
an air of unspeakable melancholy over the barrenness
and desolation of the scene; and make it painful to
turn to the description given by Mr. Arthur Young,
in his Irish Tour, of the improvements effected here
by the enterprise of Mr. Gordon (Vol. i. p. 387).
The " very large house" which Mr. Young mentions
(in 1776) as building by Sir Robert Dean (afterwards
Lord Muskerry), even its site is only pointed out to
the inquisitive traveller by the remains of a pigeon-
house, which possibly may now exist no longer!

THE CONFESSIONS OF TOM BOURKE.

THE

CONFESSIONS OF TOM BOURKE.

Tom Bourke lives in a low long farm-house, resembling in outward appearance a large barn, placed at the bottom of the hill, just where the new road strikes off from the old one, leading from the town of Kilworth to that of Lismore. He is of a class of persons who are a sort of black swans in Ireland: he is a wealthy farmer. Tom's father had, in the good old times, when a hundred pounds were no inconsiderable treasure, either to lend or spend, accommodated his landlord with that sum, at interest; and obtained, as a return for the civility, a long lease, about half a dozen times more valuable than the loan which procured it. The old man died worth several hundred pounds, the greater part of which, with his farm, he bequeathed to his

son Tom. But besides all this, Tom received
from his father, upon his deathbed, another
gift, far more valuable than worldly riches,
greatly as he prized and is still known to prize
them. He was invested with the privilege,
enjoyed by few of the sons of men, of communicating with those mysterious beings,
called " the good people."

Tom Bourke is a little, stout, healthy,
active man, about fifty-five years of age. His
hair is perfectly white, short and bushy behind, but rising in front erect and thick above
his forehead, like a new clothes-brush. His
eyes are of that kind which I have often observed with persons of a quick, but limited
intellect—they are small, gray, and lively.
The large and projecting eyebrows under,
or rather within which they twinkle, give them
an expression of shrewdness and intelligence,
if not of cunning. And this is very much the
character of the man. If you want to make
a bargain with Tom Bourke, you must act as
if you were a general besieging a town, and
make your advances a long time before you
can hope to obtain possession ; if you march
up boldly, and tell him at once your object,

you are for the most part sure to have the
gates closed in your teeth. Tom does not
wish to part with what you wish to obtain,
or another person has been speaking to him
for the whole of the last week. Or, it may
be, your proposal seems to meet the most
favourable reception. " Very well, sir;"
" That's true, sir;" " I'm very thankful to
your honour," and other expressions of kindness and confidence, greet you in reply to
every sentence; and you part from him wondering how he can have obtained the character
which he universally bears, of being a man
whom no one can make any thing of in a
bargain. But when you next meet him, the
flattering illusion is dissolved : you find you
are a great deal farther from your object than
you were when you thought you had almost
succeeded ; his eye and his tongue express a
total forgetfulness of what the mind within
never lost sight of for an instant ; and you
have to begin operations afresh, with the dis-
advantage of having put your adversary completely upon his guard.

Yet, although Tom Bourke is, whether
from supernatural revealings, or (as many

will think more probable) from the tell-truth, experience, so distrustful of mankind and so close in his dealings with them, he is no misanthrope. No man loves better the pleasures of the genial board. The love of money, indeed, which is with him (and who will blame him?) a very ruling propensity, and the gratification which it has received from habits of industry, sustained throughout a pretty long and successful life, have taught him the value of sobriety, during those seasons, at least, when a man's business requires him to keep possession of his senses. He has therefore a general rule, never to get drunk but on Sundays. But in order that it should be a general one to all intents and purposes, he takes a method which, according to better logicians than he is, always proves the rule. He has many exceptions; among these, of course, are the evenings of all the fair and market-days that happen in his neighbourhood; so also all the days on which funerals, marriages, and christenings take place among his friends within many miles of him. As to this last class of exceptions, it may appear at first very singular, that he is much more punctual in his attendance at the funerals than at the baptisms or weddings of his friends. This may be construed as an instance of disinterested affection for departed worth, very uncommon in this selfish world. But I am afraid that the motives which lead Tom Bourke to pay more court to the dead than the living are precisely those which lead to the opposite conduct in the generality of mankind—a hope of future benefit, and a fear of future evil. For the good people, who are a race as powerful as they are capricious, have their favourites among those who inhabit this world; often show their affection, by easing the objects of it from the load of this burdensome life; and frequently reward or punish the living, according to the degree of reverence paid to the obsequies and the memory of the elected dead.

Some may attribute to the same cause the apparently humane and charitable actions which Tom, and indeed the other members of his family, are known frequently to perform. A beggar has seldom left their farm-yard with an empty wallet, or without obtaining a night's lodging, if required, with a sufficiency of po-

tatoes and milk to satisfy even an Irish beggar's appetite; in appeasing which, account
must usually be taken of the auxiliary jaws
of a hungry dog, and of two or three still
more hungry children, who line themselves
well within, to atone for their nakedness without. If one of the neighbouring poor be
seized with a fever, Tom will often supply
the sick wretch with some untenanted hut
upon one of his two large farms (for he has
added one to his patrimony), or will send his
labourers to construct a shed at a hedge-side,
and supply straw for a bed while the disorder
continues. His wife, remarkable for the large-
ness of her dairy, and the goodness of every
thing it contains, will furnish milk for whey;
and their good offices are frequently extended
to the family of the patient, who are, perhaps,
reduced to the extremity of wretchedness, by
even the temporary suspension of a father's or
a husband's labour.

If much of this arises from the hopes and
fears to which I above alluded, I believe
much of it flows from a mingled sense of compassion and of duty, which is sometimes seen
to break from an Irish peasant's heart, even

where it happens to be enveloped in an habitual covering of avarice and fraud; and which I once heard speak in terms not to be misunderstood, " when we get a deal, 'tis only fair we should give back a little of it."

It is not easy to prevail on Tom to speak of those good people, with whom he is said to hold frequent and intimate communications. To the faithful, who believe in their power, and their occasional delegation of it to him, he seldom refuses, if properly asked, to exercise his high prerogative, when any unfortunate being is *struck* in his neighbourhood. Still, he will not be won unsued : he is at first difficult of persuasion, and must be overcome by a little gentle violence. On these occasions, he is unusually solemn and mysterious, and if one word of reward be mentioned, he at once abandons the unhappy patient, such a proposition being a direct insult to his supernatural superiors. It is true, that as the labourer is worthy of his hire, most persons, gifted as he is, do not scruple to receive a token of gratitude from the patients or their friends *after* their recovery. It is recorded that a very handsome gratuity was once given to a female practitioner in this occult science, who deserves to be mentioned, not only because she was a neighbour and a rival of Tom's, but from the singularity of a mother deriving her name from her son. Her son's name was Owen, and she was always called *Owen sa vauher* (Owen's mother). This person was, on the occasion to which I have alluded, *persuaded* to give her assistance to a young girl who had lost the use of her right leg: *Owen sa vauher* found the cure a difficult one. A journey of about eighteen miles was essential for the purpose, probably to visit one of the good people who resided at that distance; and this journey could only be performed by *Owen sa vauher* travelling upon the back of a white hen. The visit, however, was accomplished; and at a particular hour, according to the prediction of this extraordinary woman, when the hen and her rider were to reach their journey's end, the patient was seized with an irresistible desire to dance, which she gratified with the most perfect freedom of the diseased leg, much to the joy of her anxious family. The gratuity in this case was, as it surely ought to have been, unusually large, from the difficulty of procuring a hen willing to go so long a journey with such a rider.

To do Tom Bourke justice, he is on these occasions, as I have heard from many competent authorities, perfectly disinterested. Not many months since, he recovered a young woman (the sister of a tradesman living near him), who had been struck speechless after returning from a funeral, and had continued so for several days. He steadfastly refused receiving any compensation; saying, that even if he had not as much as would buy him his supper, he could take nothing in this case, because the girl had offended at the funeral one of the *good people* belonging to his own family, and though he would do her a kindness, he could take none from her.

About the time this last remarkable affair took place, my friend Mr. Martin, who is a neighbour of Tom's, had some business to transact with him, which it was exceedingly difficult to bring to a conclusion. At last, Mr. Martin having tried all quiet means, had recourse to a legal process, which brought Tom to reason, and the matter was arranged

I

to their mutual satisfaction, and with perfect good-humour between the parties. The accommodation took place after dinner at Mr. Martin's house, and he invited Tom to walk into the parlour, and take a glass of punch, made of some excellent *potteen*, which was on the table: he had long wished to draw out his highly-endowed neighbour on the subject of his supernatural powers, and as Mrs. Martin, who was in the room, was rather a favourite of Tom's, this seemed a good opportunity.

" Well, Tom," said Mr. Martin, " that was a curious business of Molly Dwyer's, who recovered her speech so suddenly the other day."

" You may say that, sir," replied Tom Bourke; " but I had to travel far for it: no matter for that, now. Your health, ma'am," said he, turning to Mrs. Martin.

" Thank you, Tom. But I am told you had some trouble once in that way in your own family," said Mrs. Martin.

" So I had, ma'am; trouble enough: but you were only a child at that time."

" Come, Tom," said the hospitable Mr.

Martin, interrupting him, " take another tumbler;" and he then added, " I wish you would tell us something of the manner in which so many of your children died. I am told they dropped off, one after another, by the same disorder, and that your eldest son was cured in a most extraordinary way, when the physicians had given him over."

" 'Tis true for you, sir," returned Tom; " your father, the doctor (God be good to him, I won't bely him in his grave), told me, when my fourth little boy was a week sick, that himself and Doctor Barry did all that man could do for him; but they could not keep him from going after the rest. No more they could, if the people that took away the rest wished to take him too. But they left him; and sorry to the heart I am I did not know before why they were taking my boys from me; if I did, I would not be left trusting to two of 'em now."

" And how did you find it out, Tom?" inquired Mr. Martin.

" Why, then, I 'll tell you, sir," said Burke. " When your father said what I told you, I did not know very well what to do. I walked

down the little *bohereen* you know, sir, that goes
to the river side near Dick Heafy's ground ; for
'twas a lonesome place, and I wanted to think
of myself. I was heavy, sir, and my heart
got weak in me, when I thought I was to
lose my little boy ; and I did not know well
how to face his mother with the news, for she
doted down upon him. Beside, she never
got the better of all she cried at his brother's
berrin * the week before. As I was going
down the bohereen, I met an old *bocough*,
that used to come about the place once or
twice a year, and used always sleep in our
barn while he staid in the neighbourhood.
So he asked me how I was. ' Bad enough,
Shamous†,' says I. ' I 'm sorry for your
trouble,' says he ; ' but you 're a foolish man,
Mr. Bourke. Your son would be well enough
if you would only do what you ought with
him.' ' What more can I do with him,
Shamous ?' says I : ' the doctors give him
over.' ' The doctors know no more what
ails him than they do what ails a cow when
she stops her milk,' says Shamous : ' but go

* Berrin—burying.   † Shamous—James.

to such a one,' telling me his name, 'and try what he 'll say to you.'"

"And who was that, Tom?" asked Mr. Martin.

"I could not tell you that, sir," said Bourke, with a mysterious look: "howsoever, you often saw him, and he does not live far from this. But I had a trial of him before; and if I went to him at first, may be I'd have now some of them that's gone, and so Shamous often told me. Well, sir, I went to this man, and he came with me to the house. By course, I did every thing as he bid me. According to his order, I took the little boy out of the dwelling-house immediately, sick as he was, and made a bed for him and myself in the cow-house. Well, sir, I lay down by his side, in the bed, between two of the cows, and he fell asleep. He got into a perspiration, saving your presence, as if he was drawn through the river, and breathed hard, with a great *impression* on his chest, and was very bad—very bad entirely through the night. I thought about 12 o'clock he was going at last, and I was just getting up to go call the man I told you of; but there was no

occasion. My friends were getting the better
of them that wanted to take him away from
me. There was nobody in the cow-house
but the child and myself. There was only
one halfpenny candle lighting, and that was
stuck in the wall at the far end of the house.
I had just enough of light where we were
laying to see a person walking or standing
near us; and there was no more noise than if
it was a churchyard, except the cows chewing
the fodder in the stalls. Just as I was thinking of getting up, as I told you—I won't bely
my father, sir—he was a good father to me—
I saw him standing at the bedside, holding
out his right hand to me, and leaning his
other hand on the stick he used to carry when
he was alive, and looking pleasant and smiling
at me, all as if he was telling me not to be
afeard, for I would not lose the child. ' Is
that you, father?' says I. He said nothing.
' If that's you,' says I again, ' for the love of
them that's gone let me catch your hand.'
And so he did, sir; and his hand was as soft
as a child's. He stayed about as long as
you'd be going from this to the gate below at
the end of the avenue, and then went away.

In less than a week the child was as well as if
nothing ever ailed him; and there isn't to-
night a healthier boy of nineteen, from this
blessed house to the town of Ballyporeen,
across the Kilworth mountains."

"But I think, Tom," said Mr. Martin,
"it appears as if you are more indebted to
your father than to the man recommended to
you by Shamous; or do you suppose it was he
who made favour with your enemies among the
good people, and that then your father——"

"I beg your pardon, sir," said Bourke, interrupting him; "but don't call them my
enemies. 'Twould not be wishing to me for
a good deal to sit by when they are called so.
No offence to you, sir.—Here's wishing you a
good health and long life."

"I assure you," returned Mr. Martin,
"I meant no offence, Tom; but was it not as
I say?"

"I can't tell you that, sir," said Bourke;
"I'm bound down, sir. Howsoever, you may
be sure the man I spoke of, and my father, and
those they know, settled it between them."

There was a pause, of which Mrs. Martin
took advantage to inquire of Tom; whether

something remarkable had not happened about
a goat and a pair of pigeons, at the time of his
son's illness—circumstances often mysteriously
hinted at by Tom.

"See that, now," said he, turning to Mr.
Martin, "how well she remembers it! True
for you, ma'am. The goat I gave the mistress,
your mother, when the doctors ordered her
goats' whey?"

Mrs. Martin nodded assent, and Tom
Bourke continued—"Why, then, I'll tell
you how that was. The goat was as well
as e'er a goat ever was, for a month after
she was sent to Killaan to your father's. The
morning after the night I just told you of, before the child woke, his mother was standing
at the gap, leading out of the barn-yard into
the road, and she saw two pigeons flying from
the town of Kilworth, off the church, down
towards her. Well, they never stopped, you
see, till they came to the house on the hill at
the other side of the river, facing our farm.
They pitched upon the chimney of that house,
and after looking about them for a minute or
two, they flew straight across the river, and
stopped on the ridge of the cow-house where

the child and I were lying. Do you think they came there for nothing, sir?"

"Certainly not, Tom," returned Mr. Martin.

"Well, the woman came in to me, frightened, and told me. She began to cry.— 'Whisht, you fool!' says I: ''tis all for the better.' 'Twas true for me. What do you think, ma'am? the goat that I gave your mother, that was seen feeding at sunrise that morning by Jack Cronin, as merry as a bee, dropped down dead, without any body knowing why, before Jack's face; and at that very moment, he saw two pigeons fly from the top of the house, out of the town, towards the Lismore road. 'Twas at the same time my woman saw them, as I just told you."

"'Twas very strange indeed, Tom," said Mr. Martin; "I wish you could give us some explanation of it."

"I wish I could, sir," was Tom Bourke's answer; "but I'm bound down. I can't tell but what I'm allowed to tell, any more than a sentry is let walk more than his rounds."

"I think you said something of having had some former knowledge of the man that assisted in the cure of your son," said Mr. Martin.

"So I had, sir," returned Bourke. "I had a trial of that man. But that's neither here nor there. I can't tell you any thing about that, sir. But would you like to know how he got his skill?"

"Oh! very much, indeed," said Mr. Martin.

"But you can tell us his christian name, that we may know him the better through the story," added Mrs. Martin. Tom Bourke paused for a minute to consider this proposition.

"Well, I believe I may tell you that, any how: his name is Patrick. He was always a smart, active, 'cute* boy, and would be a great clerk if he stuck to it. The first time I knew him, sir, was at my mother's wake. I was in great trouble, for I did not know where to bury her. Her people and my father's people—I mean their friends, sir, among the *good people*, had the greatest battle that was known for many a year, at Dunmanway-cross,

* 'Cute—acute.

to see to whose churchyard she'd be taken. They fought for three nights, one after another, without being able to settle it. The neighbours wondered how long I was before I buried my mother; but I had my reasons, though I could not tell them at that time. Well, sir, to make my story short, Patrick came on the fourth morning and told me he settled the business, and that day we buried her in Kilcrumper churchyard, with my father's people."

"He was a valuable friend, Tom," said Mrs. Martin, with difficulty suppressing a smile. "But you were about to tell how he became so skilful."

"So I will and welcome," replied Bourke. "Your health, ma'am—I'm drinking too much of this punch, sir; but to tell the truth, I never tasted the like of it: it goes down one's throat like sweet oil. But what was I going to say?—Yes—well—Patrick, many a long year ago, was coming home from a *berrin* late in the evening, and walking by the side of the river, opposite the big inch *,

* Inch—low meadow ground near a river.

near Ballyhefaan ford. He had taken a drop,
to be sure; but he was only a little merry, as
you may say, and knew very well what he was
doing. The moon was shining, for it was in
the month of August, and the river was as
smooth and as bright as a looking-glass. He
heard nothing for a long time but the fall
of the water at the mill weir about a mile
down the river, and now and then the crying
of the lambs on the other side of the river.
All at once, there was a noise of a great number of people, laughing as if they'd break
their hearts, and of a piper playing among
them. It came from the inch at the other side
of the ford, and he saw, through the mist that
hung over the river, a whole crowd of people
dancing on the inch. Patrick was as fond of
a dance as he was of a glass, and that's saying
enough for him; so he whipped off his shoes
and stockings, and away with him across the
ford. After putting on his shoes and stockings
at the other side of the river, he walked over
to the crowd, and mixed with them for some
time without being minded. He thought, sir,
that he'd show them better dancing than any of
themselves, for he was proud of his feet, sir,

and good right he had, for there was not a
boy in the same parish could foot a double
or treble with him. But pwah !—his dancing
was no more to theirs than mine would be to
the mistress there. They did not seem as if
they had a bone in their bodies, and they kept
it up as if nothing could tire them. Patrick
was 'shamed within himself, for he thought he
had not his fellow in all the country round ;
and was going away, when a little old man,
that was looking at the company for some
time bitterly, as if he did not like what was
going on, came up to him. ' Patrick,' says
he. Patrick started, for he did not think
any body there knew him. ' Patrick,' says
he, ' you're discouraged, and no wonder for
you. ·But you have a friend near you. I'm
your friend, and your father's friend, and I
think worse* of your little finger than I do of
all that are here, though they think no one is
as good as themselves. Go into the ring and
call for a lilt. Don't be afeard. I tell you
the best of them did not do as well as you
shall, if you will do as I bid you.' Patrick
felt something within him as if he ought not
to gainsay the old man. He went into the

* Worse—more.

ring, and called the piper to play up the best double he had. And, sure enough, all that the others were able for was nothing to him! He bounded like an eel, now here and now there, as light as a feather, although the people could hear the music answered by his steps, that beat time to every turn of it, like the left foot of the piper. He first danced a hornpipe on the ground. Then they got a table, and he danced a treble on it that drew down shouts from the whole company. At last he called for a trencher; and when they saw him, all as if he was spinning on it like a top, they did not know what to make of him. Some praised him for the best dancer that ever entered a ring; others hated him because he was better than themselves; although they had good right to think themselves better than him or any other man that never went the long journey."

"And what was the cause of his great success?" inquired Mr. Martin.

"He could not help it, sir," replied Tom Bourke. "They that could make him do more than that made him do it. Howsomever, when he had done, they wanted him to dance again, but he was tired, and they could not persuade him. At last he got angry, and swore a big oath, saving your presence, that he would not dance a step more; and the word was hardly out of his mouth, when he found himself all alone, with nothing but a white cow grazing by his side."

" Did he ever discover why he was gifted with these extraordinary powers in the dance, Tom ?" said Mr. Martin.

" I'll tell you that too, sir," answered Bourke, " when I come to it. When he went home, sir, he was taken with a shivering, and went to bed; and the next day they found he got the fever, or something like it, for he raved like as if he was mad. But they couldn't make out what it was he was saying, though he talked constant. The doctors gave him over. But it's little they know what ailed him. When he was, as you may say, about ten days sick, and every body thought he was going, one of the neighbours came in to him with a man, a friend of his, from Ballinlacken, that was keeping with him some time before. I can't tell you his name either, only it was Darby. The minute Darby saw

Patrick, he took a little bottle, with the juice
of herbs in it, out of his pocket, and gave
Patrick a drink of it.   He did the same every
day for three weeks, and then Patrick was able
to walk about, as stout and as hearty as ever
he was in his life.   But he was a long time before he came to himself; and he used to walk
the whole day sometimes by the ditch side,
talking to himself, like as if there was some
one along with him.   And so there was, surely,
or he wouldn't be the man he is to-day."

   "I suppose it was from some such companion he learned his skill," said Mr. Martin.

   "You have it all now, sir," replied Bourke.
"Darby told him his friends were satisfied
with what he did the night of the dance; and
though they couldn't hinder the fever, they'd
bring him over it, and teach him more than
many knew beside him.   And so they did.
For you see all the people he met on the inch
that night were friends of a different faction;
only the old man that spoke to him; he was
a friend of Patrick's family, and it went again
his heart, you see, that the others were so
light and active, and he was bitter in himself
to hear 'em boasting how they'd dance with

any set in the whole country round. So he gave Patrick the gift that night, and afterwards gave him the skill that makes him the wonder of all that know him. And to be sure it was only learning he was that time when he was wandering in his mind after the fever."

" I have heard many strange stories about that inch near Ballyhefaan ford," said Mr. Martin. " 'Tis a great place for the good people, isn't it, Tom ?"

" You may say that, sir," returned Bourke. " I could tell you a great deal about it. Many a time I sat for as good as two hours by moonlight, at th' other side of the river, looking at 'em playing goal as if they'd break their hearts over it ; with their coats and waistcoats off, and white handkerchiefs on the heads of one party, and red ones on th' other, just as you'd see on a Sunday in Mr. Simmings's big field. I saw 'em one night play till the moon set, without one party being able to take the ball from th' other. I'm sure they were going to fight, only 'twas near morning. I'm told your grandfather, ma'am, used to see 'em there, too," said Bourke, turning to Mrs. Martin.

" So I have been told, Tom," replied Mrs.

K

Martin. " But don't they say that the churchyard of Kilcrumper is just as favourite a place
with the good people, as Ballyhefaan inch ?"

" Why, then, may be, you never heard,
ma'am, what happened to Davy Roche in
that same churchyard," said Bourke; and
turning to Mr. Martin, added, " 'Twas a
long time before he went into your service, sir.
He was walking home, of an evening, from the
fair of Kilcummer, a little merry, to be sure,
after the day, and he came up with a berrin.
So he walked along with it, and he thought it
very queer, that he did not know a mother's
soul in the crowd, but one man, and he was
sure that man was dead many years afore.
Howsomever, he went on with the berrin, till
they came to Kilcrumper churchyard; and
faith he went in and staid with the rest, to see
the corpse buried.   As soon as the grave was
covered, what should they do but gather about
a piper that *come* along with 'em, and fall to
dancing, as if it was a wedding.   Davy longed
to be among 'em (for he hadn't a bad foot of
his own, that time, whatever he may now);
but he was loath to begin, because they all
seemed strange to him, only the man I told

you that he thought was dead. Well, at last
this man saw what Davy wanted, and came up
to him. ' Davy,' says he, ' take out a partner, and show what you can do, but take care
and don't offer to kiss her.' 'That I won't,'
says Davy, ' although her lips were made of
honey.' And with that he made his bow to
the *purtiest* girl in the ring, and he and she
began to dance. 'Twas a jig they danced, and
they did it to th' admiration, do you see, of all
that were there. 'Twas all very well till the
jig was over; but just as they had done, Davy,
for he had a drop in, and was warm with the
dancing, forgot himself, and kissed his partner,
according to custom. The smack was no
sooner off of his lips, you see, than he was left
alone in the churchyard, without a creature
near him, and all he could see was the tall
tombstones. Davy said they seemed as if
they were dancing too, but I suppose that was
only the wonder that happened him, and he
being a little in drink. Howsomever, he
found it was a great many hours later than he
thought it; 'twas near morning when he came
home; but they couldn't get a word out of

him till the next day, when he woke out of
a dead sleep about 12 o'clock."

When Tom had finished the account of
Davy Roche and the berrin, it became quite
evident that spirits, of some sort, were working too strong within him to admit of his
telling many more tales of the good people.
Tom seemed conscious of this.—He muttered
for a few minutes broken sentences concerning churchyards, riversides, leprechans, and
dina magh, which were quite unintelligible,
perhaps to himself, certainly to Mr. Martin
and his lady. At length he made a slight
motion of the head upwards, as if he would
say, " I can talk no more;" stretched his
arm to the table, upon which he placed the
empty tumbler slowly, and with the most
knowing and cautious air ; and rising from his
chair, walked, or rather rolled, to the parlour
door. Here he turned round to face his host
and hostess ; but after various ineffectual attempts to bid them good night, the words, as
they rose, being always choked by a violent
hiccup, while the door, which he held by the
handle, swung to and fro, carrying his un-

yielding body along with it, he was obliged to depart in silence. The cow-boy, sent by Tom's wife, who knew well what sort of allurement detained him, when he remained out after a certain hour, was in attendance to conduct his master home. I have no doubt that he returned without meeting any material injury, as I know that within the last month, he was, to use his own words, " As stout and hearty a man as any of his age in the county Cork."

The character of Tom Bourke is accurately copied from nature, and it has been thought better to preserve the scene entire, rather than derive two or three tales from his confessions. It affords an illustration of the difficulty with which an acknowledgment of supernatural skill is extorted from the gifted possessor, of the credulity of the peasantry, and of some national superstitions.

" Don't call them my enemies," exclaims Tom Bourke, on hearing Mr. Martin apply the term enemy to an adverse fairy faction ; and throughout it will be observed that he calls the fairies, as all Irish in his class of life would do, " *Good People.*" (*Dina Magh,* correctly written *Daoine Maith.*)

In some parts of Wales, the fairies are termed

tylwyth teg, or the fair family ; in others *y teulu,* the family : also, *bendith eu mamau,* or the blessings of their mothers ; and *gwreigedh anwyl,* or dear wives.

A similar desire of propitiating superior beings of malignant nature, or a wish to avoid words of ill omen, characterizes people of higher civilization. The Greeks denominated the furies by the name of Ευμενιδες, the benevolent, and gave to one of them the title of Μεγαιρα, the merciful. On similar principles, without having recourse to grammatical quiddities, may possibly be explained the name of Charon, " the *grim* ferryman that poets write of," which if it be of Greek origin signifies " the rejoicing ;" and why *Lucus,* the gloomy and appalling grove, should be derived from *luceo,* to shine with light : other instances will immediately occur to the scholar, as *Maleventum* changed to *Beneventum* ; πονῖος αξεγος, the sea unfriendly to strangers to πονῖος ευξεγος, the friendly, &c. We see it in more modern days in the alteration of " the Cape of Storms" into the " Cape of Good Hope." In one of the Waverley novels, Sir W. Scott, if Sir Walter it be, mentions that the Highlanders call the gallows, by which so many of their countrymen suffered, the *kind* gallows, and address it with uncovered head. Sir W. cannot account for this, but it is evidently propitiatory.

The term " fairy-struck" is applied to paralytic affections, which are supposed to proceed from a blow given by the invisible hand of an offended fairy ; this belief, of course, creates fairy doctors, who by means of charms and mysterious journeys profess to cure the afflicted. It is only fair to add, that the term has also a convivial acceptation, the fairies being not unfrequently made to bear the blame of the effects arising from too copious a sacrifice to the jolly god.

Bocough or Buckaugh is the name given to a singular class of Irish mendicants, whose character bears some resemblance to that of the Gaberlunzie man of Scotland, and their adventures, perhaps, are sometimes not unlike those recorded in the verses of James Vth.

The importance attached to the manner and place of burial by the peasantry is almost incredible : it is always a matter of consideration and often of dispute whether the deceased shall be buried with his or her " own people."

Ballyhefaan was a ford of the river Funcheon (the Fanchin of Spenser), on the road leading from Fermoy along the banks of the Blackwater, through Isle-clash (called also Liclash), Ballydera-own and Mocrony to Araglin, a wild district of the county Cork, situated where that county joins those of Waterford and Tipperary ; the road terminates at a place called " The Furnace," in the angle of the junction of the three counties where some years since an iron foundery was established, which is understood to have failed from the want of fuel, perhaps of capital. This road, which has lately been put into excellent order, crosses the highway leading from Kilworth to Lismore, about a mile east of the former town, and about half a mile north from the ford of Ballyhefaan, over which a bridge has been recently built.

The " big Inch," on which the " good people" were so fond of playing goal or hurling, a game illiberally explained by Mr. Arthur Young, as " the Cricket of Savages," is an extensive, flat, and very rich piece of ground, bounded by the Funcheon on the south, and the Blackwater on the east.

Kilcrumper churchyard, the scene of Davy Roche's dance, lies about two hundred yards off the Dublin mail-coach road, about half way between Kilworth and Fermoy.

FAIRIES OR NO FAIRIES.

JOHN MULLIGAN was as fine an old fellow
as ever threw a Carlow spur into the sides of
a horse. He was, besides, as jolly a boon
companion over a jug of punch as you would
meet from Carnsore Point to Bloody Farland.
And a good horse he used to ride; and a
stiffer jug of punch than his was not in nineteen baronies. May be he stuck more to it
than he ought to have done—but that is nothing whatever to the story I am going to
tell.

John believed devoutly in fairies; and an
angry man was he if you doubted them. He
had more fairy stories than would make, if
properly printed in a rivulet of print running
down a meadow of margin, two thick quartos
for Mr. John Murray, of Albemarle-street;
all of which he used to tell on all occasions
that he could find listeners. Many believed

his stories—many more did not believe them
—but nobody, in process of time, used to
contradict the old gentleman, for it was a pity
to vex him.   But he had a couple of young
neighbours who were just come down from
their first vacation in Trinity College to spend
the summer months with an uncle of theirs,
Mr. Whaley, an old Cromwellian, who lived
at Ballybegmullinahone, and they were too
full of logic to let the old man have his own
way undisputed.

Every story he told they laughed at, and
said that it was impossible—that it was merely
old woman's gabble, and other such things.
When he would insist that all his stories were
derived from the most credible sources—nay,
that some of them had been told him by his
own grandmother, a very respectable old lady,
but slightly affected in her faculties, as things
that came under her own knowledge—they cut
the matter short by declaring that she was in
her dotage, and at the best of times had a
strong propensity to pulling a long bow.

" But," said they, " Jack Mulligan, did
you ever see a fairy yourself ?"

" Never," was the reply.

" Well, then," they answered, " until you do, do not be bothering us with any more tales of my grandmother."

Jack was particularly nettled at this, and took up the cudgels for his grandmother ; but the younkers were too sharp for him, and finally he got into a passion, as people generally do who have the worst of an argument. This evening—it was at their uncle's, an old crony of his with whom he had dined —he had taken a large portion of his usual beverage, and was quite riotous. He at last got up in a passion, ordered his horse, and, in spite of his host's entreaties, galloped off, although he had intended to have slept there, declaring that he would not have any thing more to do with a pair of jackanapes puppies, who, because they had learned how to read good-for-nothing books in cramp writing, and were taught by a parcel of wiggy, red-snouted, prating prigs, (" not," added he, " however, that I say a man may not be a good man and have a red nose,") they imagined they knew more than a man who has held buckle and tongue together facing the wind of the world for five dozen years.

He rode off in a fret, and galloped as hard
as his horse Shaunbuie could powder away
over the limestone. " Damn it !" hiccuped
he, " Lord pardon me for swearing ! the brats
had me in one thing—I never did see a fairy ;
and I would give up five as good acres as
ever grew apple-potatoes to get a glimpse of
one—and, by the powers ! what is that ?"

He looked and saw a gallant spectacle.
His road lay by a noble demesne, gracefully
sprinkled with trees, not thickly planted as in
a dark forest, but disposed, now in clumps of
five or six, now standing singly, towering over
the plain of verdure around them, as a beautiful promontory arising out of the sea.   He
had come right opposite the glory of the
wood.   It was an oak, which in the oldest
title-deeds of the county, and they were at
least five hundred years old, was called the
old oak of Ballinhassig.   Age had hollowed
its centre, but its massy boughs still waved
with their dark serrated foliage.   The moon
was shining on it bright.   If I were a poet,
like Mr. Wordsworth, I should tell you how
the beautiful light was broken into a thousand
different fragments—and how it filled the

entire tree with a glorious flood, bathing every
particular leaf, and showing forth every particular bough; but, as I am not a poet, I shall
go on with my story. By this light Jack saw
a brilliant company of lovely little forms
dancing under the oak with an unsteady and
rolling motion. The company was large.
Some spread out far beyond the farthest boundary of the shadow of the oak's branches —
some were seen glancing through the flashes of
light shining through its leaves—some were
barely visible, nestling under the trunk—some
no doubt were entirely concealed from his
eyes. Never did man see any thing more
beautiful. They were not three inches in
height, but they were white as the driven
snow, and beyond number numberless. Jack
threw his bridle over his horse's neck, and
drew up to the low wall which bounded the
demesne, and leaning over it, surveyed, with
infinite delight, their diversified gambols. By
looking long at them, he soon saw objects
which had not struck him at first; in particular that in the middle was a chief of superior stature, round whom the group appeared
to move. He gazed so long that he was quite

overcome with joy, and could not help shouting
out. " Bravo ! little fellow," said he, " well
kicked and strong." But the instant he uttered the words the night was darkened, and
the fairies vanished with the speed of lightning.

" I wish," said Jack, " I had held my
tongue ; but no matter now. I shall just
turn bridle about and go back to Ballybegmullinahone Castle, and beat the young
Master Whaleys, fine reasoners as they think
themselves, out of the field clean."

No sooner said than done ; and Jack was
back again as if upon the wings of the wind.
He rapped fiercely at the door, and called
aloud for the two collegians.

" Halloo !" said he, " young Flatcaps, come
down now, if you dare. Come down, if you
dare, and I shall give you ocular demonstration
of the truth of what I was saying."

Old Whaley put his head out of the window,
and said, " Jack Mulligan, what brings you
back so soon ?"

" The fairies !" shouted Jack ; " the fairies !"

" I am afraid," muttered the Lord of Ballybegmullinahone, " the last glass you took

was too little watered : but, no matter—come in and cool yourself over a tumbler of punch."

He came in and sat down again at table. In great spirits he told his story :—how he had seen thousands and tens of thousands of fairies dancing about the old oak of Ballin-hassig ; he described their beautiful dresses of shining silver ; their flat-crowned hats, glittering in the moonbeams ; and the princely stature and demeanour of the central figure. He added, that he heard them singing, and playing the most enchanting music ; but this was merely imagination. The young men laughed, but Jack held his ground. "Suppose," said one of the lads, "we join company with you on the road, and ride along to the place where you saw that fine company of fairies ?"

"Done !" cried Jack ; "but I will not promise that you will find them there, for I saw them scudding up in the sky like a flight of bees, and heard their wings whizzing through the air." This, you know, was a bounce, for Jack had heard no such thing.

Off rode the three, and came to the demesne of Oakwood. They arrived at the wall flanking the field where stood the great oak ; and the moon, by this time, having again emerged from the clouds, shone bright as when Jack had passed. " Look there," he cried, exultingly ; for the same spectacle again caught his eyes, and he pointed to it with his horsewhip ; " look, and deny if you can."

" Why," said one of the lads, pausing, " true it is that we do see a company of white creatures ; but were they fairies ten times over, I shall go among them ;" and he dismounted to climb over the wall.

" Ah, Tom ! Tom !" cried Jack, " stop, man, stop ! what are you doing ? The fairies —the good people, I mean—hate to be meddled with. You will be pinched or blinded ; or your horse will cast its shoe ; or—look ! a wilful man will have his way. Oh ! oh ! he is almost at the oak—God help him ! for he is past the help of man."

By this time Tom was under the tree, and burst out laughing. " Jack," said he, " keep your prayers to yourself. Your fairies are not bad at all. Believe they will make tolerably good catsup."

" Catsup," said Jack, who, when he found

that the two lads (for the second had followed
his brother) were both laughing in the middle
of the fairies, had dismounted and advanced
slowly—" What do you mean by catsup ?"

" Nothing," replied Tom, " but that they
are mushrooms (as indeed they were) ; and
your Oberon is merely this overgrown puff-
ball."

Poor Mulligan gave a long whistle of
amazement, staggered back to his horse
without saying a word, and rode home in a
hard gallop, never looking behind him. Many
a long day was it before he ventured to face
the laughers at Ballybegmullinahone ; and to
the day of his death the people of the parish,
ay, and five parishes round, called him nothing
but Musharoon Jack, such being their pronunciation of mushroom.

I should be sorry if all my fairy stories
ended with so little dignity ; but—

> " ———— These our actors,
>   As I foretold you, were all spirits, and
>   Are melted into air—into thin air."

L

In concluding this section, it has been judged right
to present the reader with the account of the origin
of the fairies given by Addison in his Latin poem of
the Πυγμαιογερανομαχια, where, after mentioning the ex-
termination of the pygmy race by the victorious cranes,
and showing how, as the Assyrian, the Persian, and
the Roman empires had yielded to fate, so had that of
the pygmies; and saying, that the souls of the pygmy
warriors now roamed through the vallies of elysium,
he thus proceeds:—

" ——— Aut si quid fidei mereatur anilis
　　Fabula, pastores per noctis opaca pusillas
　　Sæpe vident umbras, pygmæos corpore cassos,
　　Dum secura gruum, et veteres oblita labores,
　　Lætitiæ penitus vacat, indulgetque choreis,
　　Angustosque terit calles, viridesque per orbes
　　Turba levis salit, et lemurum cognomine gaudet."

FAIRY LEGENDS.

THE CLURICAUNE.

"——————— That sottish elf
Who quaffs with swollen lips the ruby wine,
Draining the cellar with as free a hand
As if it were his purse which ne'er lack'd coin ;—
And then, with feign'd contrition ruminates
Upon his wasteful pranks, and revelry,
In some secluded dell or lonely grove
Tinsel'd by twilight."—

Δ.

LEGENDS

OF

THE CLURICAUNE.

_____

THE HAUNTED CELLAR.

THERE are few people who have not heard
of the Mac Carthies—one of the real old
Irish families, with the true Milesian blood
running in their veins as thick as butter-
milk. Many were the clans of this family in
the south ; as the Mac Carthy-more—and
the Mac Carthy-reagh—and the Mac Carthy
of Muskerry ; and all of them were noted
for their hospitality to strangers, gentle and
simple.

But not one of the name, or of any other,
exceeded Justin Mac Carthy, of Ballinacarthy,
at putting plenty to eat and drink upon his
table ; and there was a right hearty welcome
for every one who would share it with him.

Many a wine-cellar would be ashamed of the name if that at Ballinacarthy was the proper pattern for one; large as that cellar was, it was crowded with bins of wine, and long rows of pipes, and hogsheads and casks, that it would take more time to count than any sober man could spare in such a place, with plenty to drink about him, and a hearty welcome to do so.

There are many, no doubt, who will think that the butler would have little to complain of in such a house; and the whole country round would have agreed with them if a man could be found to remain as Mr. Mac Carthy's butler for any length of time worth speaking of; yet not one who had been in his service gave him a bad word.

" We have no fault," they would say, " to find with the master; and if he could but get any one to fetch his wine from the cellar, we might every one of us have grown gray in the house, and have lived quiet and contented enough in his service until the end of our days."

" 'Tis a queer thing that, surely," thought young Jack Leary, a lad who had been

brought up from a mere child in the stables
at Ballinacarthy to assist in taking care of the
horses, and had occasionally lent a hand in
the butler's pantry—" 'tis a mighty queer
thing, surely, that one man after another cannot content himself with the best place in the
house of a good master, but that every one of
them must quit, all through the means, as
they say, of the wine-cellar. If the master,
long life to him! would but make me his
butler, I warrant never the word more would
be heard of grumbling at his bidding to go to
the wine-cellar."

Young Leary accordingly watched for what
he conceived to be a favourable opportunity
of presenting himself to the notice of his
master.

A few mornings after, Mr. Mac Carthy went
into his stable-yard rather earlier than usual,
and called loudly for the groom to saddle his
horse, as he intended going out with the
hounds. But there was no groom to answer,
and young Jack Leary led Rainbow out of
the stable.

" Where is William?" inquired Mr. Mac
Carthy.

" Sir ?" said Jack ; and Mr. Mac Carthy
repeated the question.

" Is it William, please your honour ?" returned Jack ; " why, then, to tell the truth,
he had just *one* drop too much last night."

" Where did he get it ?" said Mr. Mac
Carthy ; " for since Thomas went away, the
key of the wine-cellar has been in my pocket,
and I have been obliged to fetch what was
drank myself."

" Sorrow a know I know," said Leary,
" unless the cook might have given him the
least taste in life of whiskey. But," continued
he, performing a low bow by seizing with his
right hand a lock of hair, and pulling down his
head by it, whilst his left leg, which had
been put forward, was scraped back against
the ground, " may I make so bold as just to
ask your honour one question ?"

" Speak out, Jack," said Mr. Mac Carthy.

" Why, then, does your honour want a
butler ?"

" Can you recommend me one," returned
his master, with the smile of good-humour
upon his countenance, " and one who will not
be afraid of going to my wine-cellar ?"

" Is the wine-cellar all the matter ?" said young Leary ; " devil a doubt I have of myself then for that."

" So you mean to offer me your services in the capacity of butler ?" said Mr. Mac Carthy, with some surprise.

" Exactly so," returned young Leary, now for the first time looking up from the ground.

" Well, I believe you to be a good lad, and have no objection to give you a trial."

" Long may your honour reign over us, and the Lord spare you to us !" ejaculated Leary, with another national bow, as his master rode off ; and he continued for some time to gaze after him with a vacant stare, which slowly and gradually assumed a look of importance.

" Jack Leary," said he at length, " Jack— is it Jack ?" in a tone of wonder ; " faith, 'tis not Jack now, but Mr. John, the butler ;" and with an air of becoming consequence, he strided out of the stable-yard towards the kitchen.

It is of little purport to my story, although it may afford an instructive lesson to the reader, to depict the sudden transition of nobody into somebody. Jack's former stable companion, a poor superannuated hound named Bran, who had been accustomed to receive many an affectionate pat on the head, was spurned from him with a kick and an " Out of the way, sirrah." Indeed, poor Jack's memory seemed sadly affected by his sudden change of situation. What established the point beyond all doubt was his almost forgetting the pretty face of Peggy, the kitchen wench, whose heart he had assailed but the preceding week by the offer of purchasing a gold ring for the fourth finger of her right hand, and a lusty imprint of good-will upon her lips.

When Mr. Mac Carthy returned from hunting, he sent for Jack Leary—so he still continued to call his new butler. " Jack," said he, " I believe you are a trustworthy lad, and here are the keys of my cellar. I have asked the gentlemen with whom I hunted to-day to dine with me, and I hope they may be satisfied at the way in which you will wait on them at table; but above all, let there be no want of wine after dinner."

Mr. John having a tolerably quick eye for

such things, and being naturally a handy lad, spread his cloth accordingly, laid his plates and knives and forks in the same manner he had seen his predecessors in office perform these mysteries, and really, for the first time, got through attendance on dinner very well.

It must not be forgotten, however, that it was at the house of an Irish country squire, who was entertaining a company of booted and spurred fox-hunters, not very particular about what are considered matters of infinite importance under other circumstances and in other societies.

For instance, few of Mr. Mac Carthy's guests, though all excellent and worthy men in their way, cared much whether the punch produced after soup was made of Jamaica or Antigua rum; some even would not have been inclined to question the correctness of good old Irish whiskey; and, with the exception of their liberal host himself, every one in company preferred the port which Mr. Mac Carthy put on his table to the less ardent flavour of claret,—a choice rather at variance with modern sentiment.

It was waxing near midnight, when Mr.

Mac Carthy rung the bell three times. This
was a signal for more wine; and Jack proceeded to the cellar to procure a fresh supply,
but it must be confessed not without some
little hesitation.

The luxury of ice was then unknown in the
south of Ireland; but the superiority of cool
wine had been acknowledged by all men of
sound judgment and true taste.

The grandfather of Mr. Mac Carthy, who
had built the mansion of Ballinacarthy upon
the site of an old castle which had belonged
to his ancestors, was fully aware of this important fact; and in the construction of his
magnificent wine-cellar had availed himself of
a deep vault, excavated out of the solid rock
in former times as a place of retreat and se-
curity. The descent to this vault was by a
flight of steep stone stairs, and here and there
in the wall were narrow passages—I ought
rather call them crevices; and also certain
projections, which cast deep shadows, and
looked very frightful when any one went
down the cellar stairs with a single light:
indeed, two lights did not much improve the
matter, for though the breadth of the shadows

became less, the narrow crevices remained as dark and darker than ever.

Summoning up all his resolution, down went the new butler, bearing in his right hand a lantern and the key of the cellar, and in his left a basket, which he considered sufficiently capacious to contain an adequate stock for the remainder of the evening : he arrived at the door without any interruption whatever ; but when he put the key, which was of an ancient and clumsy kind—for it was before the days of Bramah's patent—and turned it in the lock, he thought he heard a strange kind of laughing within the cellar, to which some empty bottles that stood upon the floor outside vibrated so violently, that they struck against each other : in this he could not be mistaken, although he may have been deceived in the laugh, for the bottles were just at his feet, and he saw them in motion.

Leary paused for a moment, and looked about him with becoming caution. He then boldly seized the handle of the key, and turned it with all his strength in the lock, as if he doubted his own power of doing so ; and the door flew open with a most tremendous crash, that, if the house had not been built upon the solid rock, would have shook it from the foundation.

To recount what the poor fellow saw would be impossible, for he seems not to know very clearly himself; but what he told the cook the next morning was, that he heard a roaring and bellowing like a mad bull, and that all the pipes and hogsheads and casks in the cellar went rocking backwards and forwards with so much force that he thought every one would have been staved in, and that he should have been drowned or smothered in wine.

When Leary recovered, he made his way back as well as he could to the dining-room, where he found his master and the company very impatient for his return.

" What kept you ?" said Mr. Mac Carthy in an angry voice; " and where is the wine? I rung for it half an hour since."

" The wine is in the cellar, I hope, sir," said Jack, trembling violently; " I hope 'tis not all lost."

" What do you mean, fool ?" exclaimed Mr. Mac Carthy in a still more angry tone: " why did you not fetch some with you ?"

Jack looked wildly about him, and only uttered a deep groan.

" Gentlemen," said Mr. Mac Carthy to his guests, " this is too much. When I next see you to dinner, I hope it will be another house, for it is impossible I can remain longer in this, where a man has no command over his own wine-cellar, and cannot get a butler to do his duty. I have long thought of moving from Ballinacarthy; and I am now determined, with the blessing of God, to leave it to-morrow. But wine shall you have were I to go myself to the cellar for it." So saying, he rose from table, took the key and lantern from his half-stupified servant, who regarded him with a look of vacancy, and descended the narrow stairs, already described, which led to his cellar.

When he arrived at the door, which he found open, he thought he heard a noise, as if of rats or mice scrambling over the casks, and on advancing perceived a little figure, about six inches in height, seated astride upon the pipe of the oldest port in the place, and bearing a spigot upon his shoulder. Raising the lantern, Mr. Mac Carthy contemplated the little fellow with wonder: he wore a red night-cap on his head; before him was a short leather apron, which now, from his attitude, fell rather on one side; and he had stockings of a light blue colour, so long as nearly to cover the entire of his leg; with shoes, having huge silver buckles in them, and with high heels (perhaps out of vanity to make him appear taller). His face was like a withered winter apple; and his nose, which was of a bright crimson colour, about the tip wore a delicate purple bloom, like that of a plum; yet his eyes twinkled

—————————— " like those mites
Of candid dew in moony nights—"

and his mouth twitched up at one side with an arch grin.

" Ha, scoundrel!" exclaimed Mr. Mac Carthy, " have I found you at last? disturber of my cellar—what are you doing there?"

" Sure, and master," returned the little fellow, looking up at him with one eye, and with the other throwing a sly glance towards the spigot on his shoulder, " a'n't we going to move to-morrow? and sure you would not leave your own little Cluricaune Naggeneen behind you ?"

" Oh !" thought Mr. Mac Carthy, " if you are to follow me, master Naggeneen, I don't see much use in quitting Ballinacarthy." So filling with wine the basket which young Leary in his fright had left behind him, and locking the cellar door, he rejoined his guests.

For some years after Mr. Mac Carthy had always to fetch the wine for his table himself, as the little Cluricaune Naggeneen seemed to feel a personal respect towards him. Notwithstanding the labour of these journeys, the worthy lord of Ballinacarthy lived in his paternal mansion to a good round age, and was famous to the last for the excellence of his wine, and the conviviality of his company ; but at the time of his death, that same conviviality had nearly emptied his wine-cellar ; and as it was never so well filled again, nor so often visited, the revels of master Naggeneen became less celebrated, and are now only spoken of amongst the legendary lore of the country. It is even said that the poor little fellow took the declension of the cellar so to

M

heart, that he became negligent and careless of himself, and that he has been sometimes seen going about with hardly a *skreed* to cover him.

The Cluricaune of the southern counties of Ireland appears to be the same as the Leprechan of Leinster; and both words are probably provincialisms of Luacharma'n, the Irish for a pigmy. The peculiarities of this extraordinary spirit will be sufficiently illustrated in the following legends; but the main point of distinction between the Cluricaune and the Shefro arises from the sottish and solitary habits of the former, who are never found in troops or communities.

Having been favoured (by letter from Cork) with another version of this tale, which contains some additional traits of Irish fairy character, not unlike those of the Scotch brownie, it is annexed for the purpose of comparison. It is singular, however, that the Cluricaune should become attached to a peaceful quaker family.

"Mr. Harris, a quaker, had a Cluricaune in his family: it was very diminutive in form. If any of the servants, as they sometimes do through negligence, left the beer-barrel running, little Wildbeam (for that was his name) would wedge himself into the cock and stop it at the risk of being smothered, until some one came to turn the key. In return for such services, the cook was in the habit, by her master's orders, of leaving

a good dinner in the cellar for little Wildbeam.
One Friday it so happened that she had nothing to
leave but part of a herring and some cold potatoes,
when just at midnight something pulled her out of
bed, and, having brought her with irresistible force to
the top of the cellar stairs, she was seized by the heels
and dragged down them; at every knock her head
received against the stairs, the Cluricaune, who was
standing at the door, would shout out—

> ' Potatoe skins and herring bones !—
> I 'll knock your head against the stones !'

" The poor cook was so much bruised by that night's
adventure, she was confined to her bed for three weeks
after. In consequence of this piece of violent conduct,
Mr. Harris wished much to get rid of his fairy attendant; and being told if he removed to any house
beyond a running stream, that the Cluricaune could
not follow him, he took a house, and had all his furniture packed on carts for the purpose of removing :
the last articles brought out were the cellar furniture ;
and when the cart was completely loaded with casks
and barrels, the Cluricaune was seen to jump into
the car, and fixing himself in the bung-hole of an
empty cask, cried out to Mr. Harris, ' Here, master !
here we go, all together !'

" ' What !' said Mr. Harris, ' dost thou go also ?'

" ' Yes, to be sure, master,' replied little Wildbeam ;
' here we go, all together.'

M 2

" ' In that case, friend,' said Mr. Harris, ' let the cars be unpacked; we are just as well where we are.' Mr. Harris died soon after, but it is said the Cluricaune still attends the Harris family."

In the Danske Folkesagen, a work before alluded to, a Nis, a being that answers to the Scotch brownie, was exceedingly troublesome in the family of a farmer. The farmer, like Mr. Harris, thought his best way to secure peace and quietness would be to leave the Nis and house to take care of each other, and for himself and family to decamp. Accordingly a new house was taken, and all was removed but the last cart-load, composed of empty tubs, barrels, &c. when the farmer having occasion to go behind the cart, espied master Nis peeping out of one of the tubs. Nis burst out laughing, and cried out " See, idag flytter vi" (see, we 're moving to-day). The story does not say how the farmer acted, but it is probable, that, like Mr. Harris, he staid where he was.

In that most amusing scene, in the Dama Duende of Calderon, when the lady's maid has put out the light, which Don Manuel's man Cosimo held, and afterwards escaped by leaving a bundle of clothes in the hands of Don Manuel himself while Cosimo is gone for a light; Cosimo on his return describes the Duende, for which description he draws on his imagination or his invention, as he had not in reality seen any thing, any more than his countryman Sancho Panza, when he describes so minutely the seven nanny goats.

C. Vive Dios, que yo le vi
    A los ultimos reflexos
    Que la pavesa dexò
    De la luz que me avia muerto.
Don M. Que forma tenia?
    C. Era un Frayle
    Tamañito y tenia puesto
    Un cucurucho temaño
    Que por estas senas creo
    Que era duende Capuchino.

The following definition of the word Duende is given in the dictionary of the Spanish Academy. "Duende, a species of demon or spirit, so called from its usually haunting houses. It may be derived from the Arabic duar, which signifies a house."

Naggeneen, the name given to the Cluricaune, implies something even less than the smallest measure of drink; naggin or noggin being about the same as an English gill. *Een* is the Irish diminutive, and like the Italian *ino,* which it closely resembles in form and signification, is often applied as a term of endearment : thus a snug covering for the head is called a *fodaheen,* or little hood, which carries with it a notion of comfort ; and a mother will speak of her infant by the pet term, *ma coliheen,* or my little woman. *Potheen* is the name given to illicit whiskey, because secretly manufactured in small quantities, which can be brewed in " a little pot." Again, *boher* is a road, therefore *bohereen* signifies " a little road," or narrow by-way between two hedges. So the English word buck or dandy forms the ludicrous compound *buckeen*, a little buck, or would-be dandy. As these examples are intended for the English reader, the Irish words have been spelled here, as in other places, according to sound, in preference to their correct orthography.

The writer has ventured to retain the Irish name of Naggeneen, in opposition to the advice of a critical English friend, who recommended that of Flip-nip, as conveying something the same idea, and being in better accordance with fairy nomenclature. The latter part of this remark was enforced by a quotation from Poole's English Parnassus (8vo. 1677), where the Fairy Court, founded on Drayton's Nymphidia, is arranged as follows :

OBERON, *the Emperor.*   MAB, *the Empress.*

Periwiggin, Periwinckle, Puck, Hobgoblin, Tomalin, Tom Thumb —*Courtiers.*

Hop, Mop, Drop, Pip, Trip, Skip, Fib, Tib, Tick, Pink, Pin, Quick, Gill, Jin, Tit, Wap, Win, Nit— *The Maids of Honour.*

Nymphidia—*Mother of the Maids.*

Herrick also, in a poem entitled " the Fairie Temple," an exuberantly fanciful satire on the rites of the Romish church, thus playfully recounts the fairy saints.

" Saint *Tit*, Saint *Nit*, Saint *Is*, Saint *Itis*,
   Who 'gainst *Mab's State* plac't here right is,
   Saint *Will o' th' Wispe* (of no great bignes)
   But *alias* call'd here *Fatuus ignis.*

Saint *Frip*, Saint *Trip*, Saint *Fill*, Saint *Fillie*.
Neither those other saintships will I
Here goe about for to recite,
Their number almost infinite;
Which, one by one, here set down are,
In this most curious calendar."

Common consent seems to have nominated Herrick the laureat of the fairies; and it must be acknowledged that the quaint beauty of his verses well merited for their author the distinction. Herrick evidently took delight in fairy-sounding monosyllabic names. Those which occur in his epigrams furnish no inconsiderable list, as we find in them alone the following formidable muster-roll.

Prigg.	Pratt.	Bush.
Batt.	Crabb.	Grubbs.
Luggs.	Bice.	Doll.
Gubbs.	Chubb.	Tuck.
Bunce.	Trigg.	Flinn.
Lulls.	Tugg.	Parke.
Nis.	Sibb.	Guesse.
Blinks.	Tubbs.	Pink.
Tap.	Deb.	Brock.
Hanch.	Bran.	Sneape.
Burr.	Cob.	Leech.
Megg.	Crot.	Larr.
Mudge.	Slouch.	Mease.

The circumstance of old English words, which are lost in England, having been still retained in Ireland, has been already remarked on more than one occasion. The word *skreed*, which is found in the concluding sentence of the tale, presents an opportunity of once more pointing it out.   It is a word that probably will not be met with in any dictionary or glossary ; but the Anglo-Saxon ꞃcꞃýꝺan, from which it is plainly derived, signifies " to clothe;" and in the Danish, ꞇꞏ ꞃæꝺꞃ is " a tailor," and ꞇꞏꞃæꝺꞓ " to clothe."

SEEING IS BELIEVING.

THERE's a sort of people whom every one must have met with some time or other; people that pretend to disbelieve what, in their hearts, they believe and are afraid of. Now Felix O'Driscoll was one of these. Felix was a rattling, rollicking, harum-scarum, devil-may-care sort of fellow, like—but that's neither here nor there: he was always talking one nonsense or another; and among the rest of his foolery, he pretended not to believe in the fairies, the cluricaunes, and the phoocas; and he even sometimes had the impudence to affect to doubt of ghosts, that every body believes in, at any rate. Yet some people used to wink and look knowing when Felix was *gostering*, for it was observed that he was very shy of passing the ford of Ahnamoe after nightfall; and that when he was once riding past the old church of Grenaugh in the dark, even though he had got enough of *potheen* into him to make any man stout, he made the horse trot so that there was no keeping up with him; and every now and then he would throw a sharp look out over his left shoulder.

One night there was a parcel of people sitting drinking and talking together at Larry Reilly's *public* *, and Felix was one of the party. He was, as usual, getting on with his *bletherumskite* about the fairies, and swearing that he did not believe there were any *live* things, barring men and beasts, and birds and fish, and such things as a body could see, and he went on talking in so profane a way of the "*good people*," that some of the company grew timid, and began to cross themselves, not knowing what might happen, when an old woman called Moirna Hogaune, with a long blue cloak about her, who had been sitting in the chimney corner smoking her pipe without taking any share in the conversation, took the pipe out of her mouth, threw the ashes out of it, spit in the fire, and, turning round, looked Felix straight in the face.

" And so you don't believe there are such things as Cluricaunes, don't you ?" said she.

---

* *Public*—Public house.

Felix looked rather daunted, but he said nothing.

" Upon my troth, it well becomes the like o' you, that's nothing but a bit of a *gossoon*, to take upon you to pretend not to believe what your father and your father's father, and his father before him, never made the least doubt of! But to make the matter short, seeing's believing, they say; and I that might be your grandmother tell you there are such things as Cluricaunes, and I myself saw one— there's for you, now !"

All the people in the room looked quite surprised at this, and crowded up to the fireplace to listen to her. Felix tried to laugh, but it wouldn't do; nobody minded him.

" I remember," said she, " some time after I married my honest man, who's now dead and gone, it was by the same token just a little afore I lay in of my first child (and that's many a long day ago), I was sitting out in our bit of garden with my knitting in my hand, watching some bees that we had that were going to swarm. It was a fine sunshiny day about the middle of June, and the bees were humming and flying backwards and forwards

from the hives, and the birds were chirping
and hopping on the bushes, and the butter-
flies were flying about and sitting on the
flowers, and every thing smelt so fresh, and
so sweet, and I felt so happy, that I hardly
knew where I was. When all of a sudden
I heard, among some rows of beans that we
had in a corner of the garden, a noise that
went tick-tack, tick-tack, just for all the world
as if a brogue-maker was putting on the heel
of a pump. ' Lord preserve us!' said I to
myself: ' what in the world can that be?' So
I laid down my knitting, and got up and
stole softly over to the beans, and never
believe me if I did not see sitting there before
me, in the middle of them, a bit of an old
man not a quarter so big as a new-born child,
with a little cocked hat on his head, and a
dudeen in his mouth smoking away, and a
plain old-fashioned drab-coloured coat with big
buttons upon it on his back, and a pair of massy
silver buckles in his shoes, that almost covered
his feet, they were so big; and he working away
as hard as ever he could, heeling a little pair
of brogues. As soon as I clapt my two eyes
upon him, I knew him to be a Cluricaune; and

as I was stout and fool-hardy, says I to him,
' God save you, honest man ! that 's hard
work you're at this hot day.' He looked up
in my face quite vexed like ; so with that I
made a run at him, caught a hold of him in
my hand, and asked him where was his purse
of money. ' Money ?' said he, ' money, indeed ! and where would a poor little old
creature like me get money ?'—' Come, come,'
said I, ' none of your tricks : doesn't every
body know that Cluricaunes, like you, are as
rich as the devil himself ?' So I pulled out
a knife I had in my pocket, and put on as
wicked a face as ever I could (and, in troth,
that was no easy matter for me then, for I was
as comely and good-humoured a looking girl
as you'd see from this to Carrignavar),—and
swore if he didn't instantly give me his purse,
or show me a pot of gold, I'd cut the nose off
his face. Well, to be sure, the little man did
look so frightened at hearing these words,
that I almost found it in my heart to pity the
poor little creature. ' Then,' said he, ' come
with me just a couple of fields off, and I'll
show you where I keep my money.' So I
went, still holding him in my hand and

keeping my eyes fixed upon him, when all
of a sudden I heard a *whiz-z* behind me.
' There ! there !' cried he, ' there's your
bees all swarming and going off with themselves.' I, like a fool as I was, turned my head
round, and when I saw nothing at all, and
looked back at the Cluricaune, I found nothing at all at all in my hand, for when I had
the ill luck to take my eyes off him, he slipped
out of my hand just as if he was made of fog
or smoke, and the sorrow the foot he ever came
nigh my garden again."

The popular voice assigns shoe-making as the occu-
pation of the Cluricaune, and his recreations smoking
and drinking. His characteristic traits are those
which create little sympathy or regard, and it is always the vulgar endeavour to outwit a Cluricaune, who
however generally contrives to turn the tables upon
the self-sufficient mortal. This fairy is represented
as avaricious and cunning, and when surprised by a
peasant, fearful of his superior strength, although
gifted with the power of disappearing if by any stra-
tagem, for which he is seldom at a loss, he can unfix
the eye which has discovered him.

In the Irish Melodies this point of superstition is
thus happily explained—

" Her smile when beauty granted,
   I hung with gaze enchanted,
      Like him the sprite,
      Whom maids by night,
   Oft meet in glen that's haunted.
   Like him too beauty won me ;
   But while her eyes were on me,
      If once their ray
      Was turn'd away,
   O ! winds could not outrun me."

Mr. Moore, in a note on these words, apparently
with more of gallantry than skill in " fairie lore,"
doubts his own knowledge of the Leprechan or Cluricaune, in consequence of the account given by Lady
Morgan, which though unquestionably her ladyship
is " a high authority on such subjects," it will be seen
can be reconciled without much difficulty, as it is but
the tricking sequel of a Cluricaune adventure, should
his endeavour to avert the eye prove unsuccessful.

The Cluricaune is supposed to have a knowledge of
buried treasure, and is reported to be the possessor of
a little leather purse, containing a shilling, which,
no matter how often expended, is always to be found
within it.   This is called Sprè na Skillenagh, or, the
Shilling Fortune.   Sprè, literally meaning cattle, is
used to signify a dower or fortune, from the marriage
portion or fortune being paid by the Irish, not in
money, but in cattle.   Sometimes the Cluricaune carries two purses, the one containing this magic shilling,

the other filled with brass coin; and, if compelled to deliver, has recourse to the subterfuge of giving the latter, the weight of which appears satisfactory, until the examination of its contents, when the eye being averted, the giver of course disappears.

"Gostering," which occurs in the text, may be explained as boasting talk. The reader is referred to the edition published by Galignani (Paris, 1819), of Mr. Moore's Works, for an illustration, vol. iv. p. 270.

> "Poh, Dermot! go along with your *goster*,
>   You might as well pray at a jig,
>   Or teach an old cow pater noster,
>   Or whistle Moll Row to a pig!"

Dudeen signifies a little stump of a pipe. Small tobacco-pipes, of an ancient form, are frequently found in Ireland, on digging or ploughing up the ground, particularly in the vicinity of those circular entrenchments, called Danish forts, which were more probably the villages or settlements of the native Irish. These pipes are believed by the peasantry to belong to the Cluricaunes, and when discovered are broken, or otherwise treated with indignity, as a kind of retort for the tricks which their supposed owners had played off. A sketch of one of these pipes is annexed. In the Anthologia Hi-bernica, Vol. i. p. 352 (Dublin, 1793), there is also a print of one, which was found at Brannockstown, county Kildare, sticking between the teeth of a human skull; and it is accompanied by a paper, which, on the authority of Herodotus (lib. 1. sec. 36), Strabo (lib. vii. 296), Pomponius Mela (2), and Solinus (c. 15), goes to prove that the northern nations of Europe were acquainted with tobacco, or an herb of similar properties, and that they smoked it through small tubes—of course, long before the existence of America was known.

These arguments, in favour of the antiquity of smoking, receive additional support from the discovery of several small clay pipes in the hull of a ship, found somewhere about ten years since, when excavating under the city of Dantzig. Like those interesting remains of ancient vessels, one of which (discovered the same year in a bog in the north of Ireland) was so barbarously destroyed by the peasantry, and like that dug out from an old branch of the river Rother in Kent, and recently exhibited in London, the vessel at Dantzig must, from its situation, have lain undisturbed for many centuries.

Should the reader feel inclined to doubt any part of Moirna Hogaune, *anglice*, Mary Hogan's relation, it will not be difficult to obtain an account of her adventure with the Cluricaune, and many other even more wonderful tales from her own lips; as Moirna is well known, and is, or at least was living within the last six months, not far from the ford of Ahnamoe, alluded to in the text, which is considered to be a favourite haunt of the fairies. This information may perhaps be acceptable to Mr. Ellis, the able and ju-

N

dicious editor of Brand's Popular Antiquities ; for in one of his notes on that valuable work, he says, " I made strict inquiries after fairies in the unculti- vated wilds of Northumberland, but even there I could only meet with a man who said that he had seen *one that had seen fairies*.   Truth is hard to come at in most cases ; none, I believe, ever came nearer to it in this than I have."

Ahnamoe, correctly written Ath na bo, signifies " the ford of the cow."   It is a little clear stream, which, crossing the Carrignavar road, divides two farms, situated about seven miles north-east of Cork.

Grenaugh, or Greenagh, is a ruined church, seven or eight miles north-west of Cork, concerning which, and that of Garrycloyne, not far distant, marvellous tales of the Tam o' Shanter class are told without end. From the autograph of a respectable farmer, named Rilehan, who resides in this neighbourhood, and who attests the veracity of the story, the following is copied verbatim.

" There did eight men, and one of them is a tenant of mine now, go to the churchyard of Garrycloyne, which was wrongful of them, thinking to cut sticks to tresh oats with, and the young osier they began to cut the first, showed that it was all on fire, like the burning bush ; and all the trees about them in the churchyard were the same, and in the road from the church ; so being frightened, they went back without ever the stick or the switch.   But they set to the work again, in the latter end of the next night, at the coming on of the morning, and they cut a tree out of the churchyard, and brought it away with them; it was all on fire, until they came to the river, and then it went up in the sky from them roaring like a mad bull! They never got such a fright or shock; and they were not the better of that night's work for two months after."

———————

Some particulars respecting the ancient vessels, mentioned in the above note at page 177, are worth preservation, as this remarkable series of discoveries seems not to be generally known.

Of the ancient vessel found in Kent, an account has been preserved in a little pamphlet sold at the place of exhibition; and a beautiful lithographic print by Mr. J. D. Harding of the excavation was published by Messrs. Rodwell and Martin.

In August 1813, the remains of a vessel were discovered in Ballywilliam Bog, about a mile from Portrush, in the liberties of Colerain. From the examination of the size and form of the ribs and planks, it was supposed that she carried from forty to fifty tons. Notwithstanding the injuries of time, the outside planks measured an inch and a quarter in thickness; of them, however, only small pieces could be traced. Some of the ribs were eight inches broad, five deep, and seven or eight feet long, and many of them exceeded this measurement considerably;—neither keel nor mast could be discovered.

N 2

These remains were torn up and carried off before the particulars were fully investigated. The timber was all oak, and several car loads of it were drawn away.

This ship was found in a moat about forty feet in diameter, composed of stones and clay, but chiefly of moss, fifteen perches from the shore of the bog; the bog has been all cut away round this mount, which was between six and eight feet in height;—some silver coins of Edward III. were also found in it, and several bones, which crumbled on being exposed to the air.

On the 8th December following, in digging a new sluiceway at the upper end of the Fairwater, at Dantzig, a ship was found buried in the ground, at the depth of about twenty feet. She measured from stem to stern, in the inside, fifty-four feet, and in breadth near twenty feet. A box of tobacco-pipes was found, all whole, with heads about the size of a thimble, and tubes from four to six inches in length.—The ship was built of oak; her planks about twenty inches broad, full of tree-nails, and no iron about her, except her rudder bands. A boat was found near, which had fallen to pieces. Many human bones were in the hold, both fore and aft; and it is supposed that the vessel had been lost in some convulsion of nature, before the foundation of the city, upwards of five hundred years ago, as the place had been so long built over.

MASTER AND MAN.

BILLY MAC DANIEL was once as likely a young man as ever shook his brogue at a patron, emptied a quart, or handled a shillelagh; fearing for nothing but the want of drink; caring for nothing but who should pay for it; and thinking of nothing but how to make fun over it: drunk or sober, a word and a blow was ever the way with Billy Mac Daniel; and a mighty easy way it is of either getting into, or of ending a dispute. More is the pity that, through the means of his thinking, and fearing, and caring for nothing, this same Billy Mac Daniel fell into bad company; for surely the good people are the worst of all company any one could come across.

It so happened, that Billy was going home one clear frosty night not long after Christmas ; the moon was round and bright ; but although it was as fine a night as heart could wish for, he felt pinched with the cold. " By my word," chattered Billy, " a drop of good liquor would be no bad thing to keep a man's soul from freezing in him ; and I wish I had a full measure of the best."

" Never wish it twice, Billy," said a little man in a three-cornered hat, bound all about with gold lace, and with great silver buckles in his shoes, so big that it was a wonder how he could carry them ; and he held out a glass as big as himself, filled with as good liquor as ever eye looked on or lip tasted.

" Success, my little fellow," said Billy Mac Daniel, nothing daunted, though well he knew the little man to belong to the *good people ;* " here's your health, any way, and thank you kindly ; no matter who pays for the drink ;" and he took the glass and drained it to the very bottom, without ever taking a second breath to it.

" Success," said the little man ; " and you're heartily welcome, Billy ; but don't think to cheat me as you have done others,—

out with your purse and pay me like a gentleman."

" Is it I pay you?" said Billy : " could I
not just take you up and put you in my
pocket as easily as a blackberry ?"

" Billy Mac Daniel," said the little man,
getting very angry, " you shall be my servant
for seven years and a day, and that is the way
I will be paid ; so make ready to follow me."

When Billy heard this, he began to be very
sorry for having used such bold words towards
the little man ; and he felt himself, yet could
not tell how, obliged to follow the little man
the livelong night about the country, up and
down, and over hedge and ditch, and through
bog and brake without any rest.

When morning began to dawn, the little
man turned round to him and said, " You
may now go home, Billy, but on your peril
don't fail to meet me in the Fort-field to-night ;
or if you do, it may be the worse for you in
the long run.   If I find you a good servant,
you will find me an indulgent master."

Home went Billy Mac Daniel ; and though
he was tired and weary enough, never a wink

of sleep could he get for thinking of the little man ; but he was afraid not to do his bidding, so up he got in the evening, and away he went to the Fort-field. He was not long there before the little man came towards him and said, " Billy, I want to go a long journey to-night ; so saddle one of my horses, and you may saddle another for yourself, as you are to go along with me, and may be tired after your walk last night."

Billy thought this very considerate of his master, and thanked him accordingly : " But," said he, " if I may be so bold, sir, I would ask which is the way to your stable, for never a thing do I see but the Fort here, and the old thorn-tree in the corner of the field, and the stream running at the bottom of the hill, with the bit of bog over against us."

" Ask no questions, Billy," said the little man, " but go over to that bit of bog, and bring me two of the strongest rushes you can find."

Billy did accordingly, wondering what the little man would be at ; and he picked out two of the stoutest rushes he could find, with a little bunch of .brown blossom stuck at the side of each, and brought them back to his master.

" Get up, Billy," said the little man, taking one of the rushes from him, and striding across it.

" Where shall I get up, please your honour ?" said Billy.

" Why, upon horseback, like me, to be sure," said the little man.

" Is it after making a fool of me you'd be," said Billy, " bidding me get a-horseback upon that bit of a rush ? May be you want to persuade me that the rush I pulled but while ago out of the bog over there is a horse ?"

" Up ! up ! and no words," said the little man, looking very angry ; " the best horse you ever rode was but a fool to it." So Billy, thinking all this was in joke, and fearing to vex his master, straddled across the rush : " Borram ! Borram ! Borram !" cried the little man three times (which, in English, means to become great), and Billy did the same after him : presently the rushes swelled up into fine horses, and away they went full speed ; but Billy, who had put the rush be-

tween his legs, without much minding how he
did it, found himself sitting on horseback the
wrong way, which was rather awkward, with
his face to the horse's tail; and so quickly
had his steed started off with him, that he
had no power to turn round, and there was
therefore nothing for it but to hold on by the
tail.

At last they came to their journey's end,
and stopped at the gate of a fine house : " Now,
Billy," said the little man, " do as you see me
do, and follow me close ; but as you did not
know your horse's head from his tail, mind
that your own head does not spin round until
you can't tell whether you are standing on it
or on your heels : for remember that old liquor,
though able to make a cat speak, can make a
man dumb."

The little man then said some queer kind
of words, out of which Billy could make no
meaning ; but he contrived to say them after
him for all that ; and in they both went
through the key-hole of the door, and through
one key-hole after another, until they got into
the wine-cellar, which was well stored with all
kinds of wine.

The little man fell to drinking as hard as he could, and Billy, nowise disliking the example, did the same. "The best of masters are you, surely," said Billy to him; "no matter who is the next; and well pleased will I be with your service if you continue to give me plenty to drink."

"I have made no bargain with you," said the little man, "and will make none; but up and follow me." Away they went, through key-hole after key-hole; and each mounting upon the rush which he left at the hall door, scampered off, kicking the clouds before them like snow-balls, as soon as the words, "Borram, Borram, Borram," had passed their lips.

When they came back to the Fort-field, the little man dismissed Billy, bidding him to be there the next night at the same hour. Thus did they go on, night after night, shaping their course one night here, and another night there—sometimes north, and sometimes east, and sometimes south, until there was not a gentleman's wine-cellar in all Ireland they had not visited, and could tell the flavour of every wine in it as well—ay, better—than the butler himself.

One night when Billy Mac Daniel met the little man as usual in the Fort-field, and was going to the bog to fetch the horses for their journey, his master said to him, " Billy, I shall want another horse to-night, for may be we may bring back more company with us than we take." So Billy, who now knew better than to question any order given to him by his master, brought a third rush, much wondering who it might be that would travel back in their company, and whether he was about to have a fellow-servant. " If I have," thought Billy, " he shall go and fetch the horses from the bog every night; for I don't see why I am not, every inch of me, as good a gentleman as my master."

Well, away they went, Billy leading the third horse, and never stopped until they came to a snug farmer's house in the county Limerick, close under the old castle of Carrigogunniel, that was built, they say, by the great Brian Boru. Within the house there was great carousing going forward, and the little man stopped outside for some time to listen; then turning round all of a sudden, said, " Billy, I will be a thousand years old to-morrow !"

" God bless us, sir," said Billy, " will you !"

" Don't say these words again, Billy," said the little man, " or you will be my ruin for ever. Now, Billy, as I will be a thousand years in the world to-morrow, I think it is full time for me to get married."

" I think so too, without any kind of doubt at all," said Billy, " if ever you mean to marry."

" And to that purpose," said the little man, " have I come all the way to Carrigo-gunniel; for in this house, this very night, is young Darby Riley going to be married to Bridget Rooney; and as she is a tall and comely girl, and has come of decent people, I think of marrying her myself, and taking her off with me."

" And what will Darby Riley say to that ?" said Billy.

" Silence !" said the little man, putting on a mighty severe look : " I did not bring you here with me to ask questions ;" and without holding further argument, he began saying the queer words, which had the power of passing him through the key-hole as free as air, and which Billy thought himself mighty clever to be able to say after him.

In they both went; and for the better viewing the company, the little man perched himself up as nimbly as a cock-sparrow upon one of the big beams which went across the house over all their heads, and Billy did the same upon another facing him ; but not being much accustomed to roosting in such a place, his legs hung down as untidy as may be, and it was quite clear he had not taken pattern after the way in which the little man had bundled himself up together. If the little man had been a tailor all his life, he could not have sat more contentedly upon his haunches.

There they were, both master and man, looking down upon the fun that was going forward—and under them were the priest and piper—and the father of Darby Riley, with Darby's two brothers and his uncle's son—and there were both the father and the mother of Bridget Rooney, and proud enough the old couple were that night of their daughter, as good right they had—and her four sisters with bran new ribbons in their caps,

and her three brothers all looking as clean
and as clever as any three boys in Munster—
and there were uncles and aunts, and gossips
and cousins enough besides to make a full
house of it—and plenty was there to eat and
drink on the table for every one of them, if
they had been double the number.

Now it happened, just as Mrs. Rooney had
helped his reverence to the first cut of the
pig's head which was placed before her, beautifully bolstered up with white savoys, that
the bride gave a sneeze which made every one
at table start, but not a soul said " God bless
us." All thinking that the priest would have
done so, as he ought if he had done his duty,
no one wished to take the word out of his
mouth, which unfortunately was preoccupied
with pig's head and greens. And after a moment's pause, the fun and merriment of the
bridal feast went on without the pious bene-
diction.

Of this circumstance both Billy and his
master were no inattentive spectators from
their exalted stations. " Ha !" exclaimed the
little man, throwing one leg from under him
with a joyous flourish, and his eye twinkled

with a strange light, whilst his eyebrows became elevated into the curvature of Gothic arches—" Ha !" said he, leering down at the bride, and then up at Billy, " I have half of her now, surely. Let her sneeze but twice more, and she is mine, in spite of priest, mass-book, and Darby Riley."

Again the fair Bridget sneezed ; but it was so gently, and she blushed so much, that few except the little man took, or seemed to take, any notice ; and no one thought of saying " God bless us."

Billy all this time regarded the poor girl with a most rueful expression of countenance ; for he could not help thinking what a terrible thing it was for a nice young girl of nineteen, with large blue eyes, transparent skin, and dimpled cheeks, suffused with health and joy, to be obliged to marry an ugly little bit of a man, who was a thousand years old, barring a day.

At this critical moment the bride gave a third sneeze, and Billy roared out with all his might, " God save us !" Whether this exclamation resulted from his soliloquy, or from the mere force of habit, he never could tell exactly himself; but no sooner was it uttered, than the little man, his face glowing with rage and disappointment, sprung from the beam on which he had perched himself, and shrieking out in the shrill voice of a cracked bagpipe, " I discharge you my service, Billy Mac Daniel—take *that* for your wages," gave poor Billy a most furious kick in the back, which sent his unfortunate servant sprawling upon his face and hands right in the middle of the supper-table.

If Billy was astonished, how much more so was every one of the company into which he was thrown with so little ceremony: but when they heard his story, Father Cooney laid down his knife and fork, and married the young couple out of hand with all speed; and Billy Mac Daniel danced the Rinka at their wedding, and plenty did he drink at it too, which was what he thought more of than dancing.

———————

The mode of travelling through the air upon rushes is of common occurrence in fairy history;—a straw, a blade of grass, a fern, or cabbage stalk, are equally well adapted for steeds. The writer has been told of

o

many men who were obliged, like Billy Mac Daniel, to give way and keep company with the good people: to use the words of the narrator, " going far and near with them, day and night—to London one night, and to America the next; and the only horses they made use of for these great journeys were cabbage stumps in the form of natural horses."

At Dundaniel, a village two miles from Cork, in a pleasant outlet, called Blackrock, there is now (December, 1824) living a gardener, named Crowley, who is considered by his neighbours as under fairy control, and is suffering from what they term " the falling sickness;" resulting from the fatigue attendant on the journeys which he is compelled to take, being forced to travel night after night with the good people on one of his own cabbage stumps.

" The Witch of Fife" furnishes an apt illustration.

" The first leet night, quhan the new moon set,
    Quhan all was douffe and mirk,
We saddled our naigis wi' the moon-fern leif,
    And rode fra Kilmerrin kirk.

" Some horses ware of the brume-cow framit,
    And some of the greine bay tree ;
But mine was made of ane humloke schaw,
    And a stout stallion was he."

This ballad of Mr. Hogg's appears to be founded on the traditional anecdote recorded of one of the Duffus family, who by means of the phrase " Horse and Hattock," equivalent in effect to the words " Borram, Borram, Borram," joined company with the fairies on a trip, to examine the king of France's wine-cellar, where, having drunk too freely, he fell asleep, and was so found the next day, with a silver cup in his hand. The sequel informs us, that on being brought before the king, his majesty not only most graciously pardoned the offender; but dismissed him with the winecup as a present, which is said to be still preserved in the family.

A similar tradition is very common in Ireland, particularly in the county Galway, and is evidently the basis on which Billy Mac Daniel's adventure has been constructed.

To the kindness of Dr. Owen Pughe (distinguished by his standard publications on Cambrian Literature and Antiquities) the writer is indebted for the communication of some interesting particulars concerning the popular superstitions of Wales.—Relative to fairy travelling, the doctor writes—

" The word *Ellyll* may be explained as a wandering spirit or elf ;—a kind of mountain goblin, after whom the poisonous mushroom is called *Bwyd Ellyllon*, or the meat of the goblins, and the bells of the digitalis or foxglove are termed *Menyg Ellyllon*, or the goblins' gloves.

" *Yr ydeodh yn mhob gobant, Ellyllon vingeimion gant.*"

o 2

In every tiny dingle there was a hundred of wry-mouthed goblins.—So says *D. ab Gwilym*, in his Address to the Mist, 1340.

" These fairies are often inclined to play tricks with the less pure inhabitants of the mountains, who hazard to ramble in misty weather; they will seize hold of any forlorn traveller they meet with, and propose to give him a lift through the air, and they offer the choice of one out of three courses; that is, he may be carried below wind, above wind, or mid wind. Those who are used to these journeys take care to choose the middle course; for, should any one unused to such things choose to go above wind, he will be borne so high as to despair of ever alighting again on the earth; and any ignorant wight who prefers to be carried below wind is dragged through all the brambles and briers that they can find. A lawyer with a broken nose, and otherwise disfigured," continues the learned doctor, " used to relate in my hearing, when a boy, of such having been his lot, and of which he bore the marks, and was consequently called ' *Y Trwyn*,' or ' the Nosy.' This, I remember, had such an effect upon me, that if I walked in a mist, I took good care to walk on the grass, in case there should be need to catch hold of a blade of it, which the fairies had not the power to break."

Such being the pranks of Welsh fairies, it is not to be wondered at that the valiant Sir John Falstaff should feel so particularly dismayed at discovering one in company with the wickedly disposed elves of

Hernes Oak. (Merry Wives of Windsor Act V. Scene 5.) " Heavens defend me," exclaims the knight, " from that *Welsh* fairy, lest he transform me into a piece of cheese!"

The young couple, whose happiness would doubtless have been destroyed by the little man but for Billy Mac Daniel's pious exclamation, are probably the identical pair whose courtship is so particularly detailed in a popular song, of which the annexed verse may serve as a specimen.

> " Young Darby Riley,
>   He approached me slyly,
> And with a smile he
>   Unto me cried,
> Sweet Bridget Rooney,
> Here's Father Cooney,
> And very soon he
>   'll make you my bride."

The Rinka (correctly written Rinceadh) which Billy, to whom they were so much indebted, danced at their wedding, is the national dance of Ireland : for a particular account of which the reader is referred to the conclusion of Mr. Walker's Historical Essay on the Irish Bards.

Carrigogunniel Castle is an extensive ruin, five or six miles west of the city of Limerick :—it may be described by the words of the old poet, Thomas Churchyard—

" A fort of strength, a strong and stately hold,
   It was at first, though now it is full old.
   On rock alone full farre from other mount
   It stands, which shows it was of great account."

During the last siege of Limerick, this castle was
garrisoned by the adherents of James II. but was sur-
rendered by them without defence, although it was
so tenable a position that the besiegers deemed it ex-
pedient to blow it up. " The violent effect of the
explosion is still evident in the dilapidated remains of
Carrigogunniel. Massive fragments of the walls and
towers lie scattered around in a confusion not unpic-
turesque ; and it is a matter of some difficulty to trace
the original plan." A view of Carrigogunniel is given
in the second volume of Grose's Antiquities of Ireland.

THE FIELD OF BOLIAUNS.

TOM FITZPATRICK was the eldest son of a comfortable farmer who lived at Ballincollig. Tom was just turned of nine-and-twenty, when he met the following adventure, and was as clever, clean, tight, good-looking a boy as any in the whole county Cork. One fine day in harvest—it was indeed Lady-day in harvest, that every body knows to be one of the greatest holidays in the year — Tom was taking a ramble through the ground, and went sauntering along the sunny side of a hedge, thinking in himself, where would be the great harm if people, instead of idling and going about doing nothing at all, were to shake out the hay, and bind and stook the oats that was lying on the ledge, 'specially as the weather had been rather broken of late, he all of a sudden heard a clacking sort of noise a little before him, in the hedge. " Dear me," said Tom, " but isn't it surprising to hear the

stonechatters singing so late in the season?"
So Tom stole on, going on the tops of his
toes to try if he could get a sight of what
was making the noise, to see if he was right in
his guess.   The noise stopped; but as Tom
looked sharply through the bushes, what
should he see in a nook of the hedge but a
brown pitcher that might hold about a gallon
and a half of liquor; and by and by a little
wee diny dony bit of an old man, with a little
motty of a cocked hat stuck upon the top of
his head, and a deeshy daushy leather apron
hanging before him, pulled out a little wooden
stool, and stood up upon it and dipped a little piggin into the pitcher, and took out the
full of it, and put it beside the stool, and then
sat down under the pitcher, and began to
work at putting a heel-piece on a bit of a
brogue just fitting for himself.   " Well, by
the powers !" said Tom to himself, " I often
heard tell of the Cluricaune ; and, to tell God's
truth, I never rightly believed in them—but
here 's one of them in real earnest.   If I go
knowingly to work, I 'm a made man.   They
say a body must never take their eyes off
them, or they 'll escape."

Tom now stole on a little farther, with his eye fixed on the little man just as a cat does with a mouse, or, as we read in books, the rattle-snake does with the birds he wants to enchant. So when he got up quite close to him, " God bless your work, neighbour," said Tom.

The little man raised up his head, and " Thank you kindly," said he.

" I wonder you 'd be working on the holy-day ?" said Tom.

" That 's my own business, not yours," was the reply.

" Well, may be you 'd be civil enough to tell *us* what you 've got in the pitcher there ?" said Tom.

"That I will, with pleasure," said he : " it 's good beer."

" Beer !" said Tom : " Thunder and fire ! where did you get it ?"

" Where did I get it, is it ? Why, I made it. And what do you think I made it of ?"

" Devil a one of me knows," said Tom, " but of malt, I suppose ; what else ?"

" There you 're out. I made it of *heath*."

" Of heath !" said Tom, bursting out

laughing: " sure you don't think me to be such a fool as to believe that ?"

" Do as you please," said he, " but what I tell you is the truth. Did you never hear tell of the Danes ?'"

" And that I did," said Tom : " weren't *them* the fellows we gave such a *licking* when they thought to take Limerick from us ?"

" Hem !" said ·the little man drily—" is that all you know about the matter ?"

" Well, but about *them* Danes ?" said Tom.

" Why, all the about them there is, is that when they were here they taught us to make beer out of the heath, and the secret 's in my family ever since."

" Will you give a body a taste of your beer ?" said Tom.

" I 'll tell you what it is, young man—it would be fitter for you to be looking after your father's property than to be bothering decent, quiet people with your foolish questions. There now, while you 're idling away your time here, there 's the cows have broke into the oats, and are knocking the corn all about."

Tom was taken so by surprise with this,

that he was just on the very point of turning round when he recollected himself; so, afraid that the like might happen again, he made a *grab** at the Cluricaune, and caught him up in his hand; but in his hurry he overset the pitcher, and spilt all the beer, so that he could not get a taste of it to tell what sort it was. He then swore what he would not do to him if he did not show him where his money was. Tom looked so wicked and so bloody-minded, that the little man was quite frightened; so, says he, " Come along with me a couple of fields off, and I 'll show you a crock of gold."

So they went, and Tom held the Cluricaune fast in his hand, and never took his eyes from off him, though they had to cross hedges, and ditches, and a crooked bit of bog (for the Cluricaune seemed, out of pure mischief, to pick out the hardest and most contrary way), till at last they came to a great field all full of boliaun buies (ragweed), and the Cluricaune pointed to a big boliaun, and, says he, " Dig under that boliaun, and you'll get the great crock all full of guineas."

* Grab—grasp.

Tom in his hurry had never minded the bringing a spade with him, so he thought to run home and fetch one; and that he might know the place again, he took off one of his red garters, and tied it round the boliaun.

"I suppose," said the Cluricaune, very civilly, "you 've no farther occasion for me?"

"No," says Tom; "you may go away now, if you please, and God speed you, and may good luck attend you wherever you go."

"Well, good bye to you, Tom Fitzpatrick," said the Cluricaune, "and much good may do you, with what you 'll get."

So Tom ran, for the dear life, till he came home, and got a spade, and then away with him, as hard as he could go, back to the field of boliauns; but when he got there, lo, and behold! not a boliaun in the field but had a red garter, the very identical model of his own, tied about it; and as to digging up the whole field, that was all nonsense, for there was more than forty good Irish acres in it. So Tom came home again with his spade on his shoulder, a little cooler than he went; and many 's the hearty curse he gave the Cluri-

caune every time he thought of the neat turn
he had served him.

The following is the account given by Lady Morgan,
of the Cluricaune or Leprechan, in her excellent novel
of O'Donnell (Vol. II. p. 246.) which has been referred to in a preceding note.

" It would be extremely difficult," says her ladyship, " to class this supernatural agent, who holds a
distinguished place in the Irish ' fairies.' His appearance, however, is supposed to be that of a shrivelled
little old man, whose presence marks a spot where
hidden treasures lie concealed, which were buried
there in ' the troubles.'   He is therefore generally seen
in lone and dismal places, out of the common haunts
of man ; and though the night wanderer may endeavour to mark the place where he beheld the guardian
of the treasures perched, yet when he returns in the
morning with proper implements to turn up the earth,
the thistle, stone, or branch he had placed as a mark
is so multiplied, that it is no longer a distinction ; and
the disappointments occasioned by the malignity of
the little Leprechan render him a very unpopular
fairy : his name is never applied but as a term of contempt."

On this extract it should be remarked, that the word
Prechan, used in the story of the young piper at p. 51,
and explained in the note (p. 64.) as a contraction of

Leprechan, may signify a raven, and is metaphorically applied to any nonsensical chatterer;—this word is correctly written, *Prèacha'n,* or *Priàchan.*

The ancients imagined that treasures buried in the earth were guarded by spirits called Incubones, and that if you seized their cap, you compelled them to deliver this wealth. See Pomponius Sabinus, line 507. Georgics 2.

" Sed ut dicunt ego nihil scio, sed audivi, quomodo Incuboni pileum rapuisset et thesaurum invenit," are the words of Petronius, an author of whom Lady Morgan is of course ignorant.

The English reader will perhaps be surprised to see the term *boy* applied to a young man of nine-and-twenty; but in Ireland this word is commonly used as equivalent to young man, much as the word παις was employed by the Greeks, and *puer,* still more abusively, by the Romans ; as, for example, in the first Eclogue of Virgil : Tityrus, who represents Augustus as replying to his application for protection from the soldiery—" Pascite ut ante boves *pueri,*" is immediately addressed by the other shepherd—" Fortunate *senex.*" Spenser also employs it in the same sense ; for he calls Prince Arthur's squire Timias *a lusty boy ;* and Spenser, except in his finals, is good authority. Mr. Wordsworth, too, whose logical correctness in the use of words is notorious, does not scruple, among the employments which his " Old Adam" assumed on coming to London, to mention that of an " errand *boy.*" It may, perhaps, be safely

asserted, that our shoals of continental travellers do
not always find the *garçon* at a French hotel or caffé
to be an *imberbis puer*.   It is treading on tender
ground to presume to censure Miss Edgeworth, but
it might possibly be queried whether in her tale of
" Ormond" she has not o'erstepped the modesty of
nature when she makes King Corny qualify the
tough ploughman with the title of *boy*, though, indeed,
this is a point that may admit of doubt; for the devil
himself, who, all agree, is no chicken, is very commonly styled the " *Old boy.*"

It is a generally received tradition in the south of
Ireland, that the Danes manufactured a kind of in-
toxicating beer from the heath.   Dr. Smith, in his
History of Kerry (p. 173), informs us that " the
country people" of the southern part of the barony of
Corckaguiny " are possessed with an opinion that
most of the old fences in these wild mountains were
the work of the ancient Danes, and that they made a
kind of beer of the heath which grows there; but
these enclosures are more modern than the time when
that northern nation inhabited Ireland.   Many of
them," continues the doctor, " were made to secure
cattle from wolves, which animals were not entirely
extirpated until about the year 1710; as I find by
the presentments for raising money for destroying
them in some old grand jury books; and the more
ancient enclosures were made about corn fields, which
were more numerous before the importation of potatoes into Ireland than at present."

Dr. Smith may be right in his conjectures respecting the fences which he has described, though these will by no means apply to the low stone lines which are to be seen on many of the mountains in Muskerry, in the county Cork, and which were obviously never intended for enclosures, but for mere boundaries, or marks of property: the stones are placed in regular lines, and are certainly not the remains of walls, as they consist of only one layer of stones. It is also to be remarked, that the enclosures are too small and too numerous to indicate a division of land for ordinary purposes; and their use can only be explained by supposing (as we have every reason to do) that they were intended to mark out the bounds within which each man cut his portion of heath.

Gwrâch is the Welsh name for a hag or witch, and *Gwrâch y Rhibyn* signifies the hag of the dribble, a personage, according to Cambrian tradition, who caused the many *dribbles of stones* seen on the slopes of the mountains. This phrase happily expresses the boundaries just described. The legend of *Gwrâch y Rhibyn* states, that in her journeys over the hills, she was wont to carry her apron full of stones; and by chance, when the string of her apron broke, a dribble was formed.

Tom Fitzpatrick, the hero of the tale, does not seem to have been a very profound antiquary; and a case of similar ignorance in a respectable farmer may be quoted. This farmer lived within less than fifty miles of Londonderry; and yet, to a question addressed to him by a gentleman about the Danes, he replied in the very words of Tom, only substituting Derry for Limerick. In justice to the writer's countrymen, it must be, however, declared, that such ignorance is by no means common among them. They well know who the Danes were, and will tell you very gravely that a father in Denmark, when bestowing his daughter in marriage, always assigns with her, as a portion, some of the lands which his ancestors had possessed in Ireland. It would be rather curious to ascertain whether the Northumbrians and the peasants of the East Riding retain so distinct an idea of these northern invaders.

" *Dear me,*" and " *to tell God's truth,*" says Tom ; and the narrator says Tom ran for the " *dear life :*" these are odd expressions will say, perhaps, the reader. Not at all. *Dear* is almost exactly the Homeric φιλος, and is a strong expression of the possessive pronoun, and is frequently so employed by Spenser and the elder writers ; and, *by God's truth,* an Irishman means the truth, pure and unmixed as it is in the Divinity, " the whole truth, and nothing but the truth," or the truth as it should be uttered in the presence of the Divinity.

The three original diminutives are *tiny, dony,* and the Scottish *wee.* By variously combining the elements of these, the Irish make a variety of others. Thus, from the first and third they form *weeny,* and by the use of the termination *shy,* they make *deeshy, doshy,* and *weeshy.*

P

A *piggin* is a wooden vessel of a cylindrical form, made of staves hooped together, with one of the staves of double the length of the others, which serves for a handle. They are of various sizes, containing from a pint to two gallons, according to the uses for which they are intended. In Leinster there is a distinction made between those of a larger, and those of a smaller, size. The former are called *piggins*, the latter *noggins*. In the same province, the pewter measure answering to the English *gill* is called a *naggin*. Vide Gough's Arithmetic (Dublin, 1810). In the southern counties, the terms naggin and noggin are used indifferently, as before mentioned.

THE LITTLE SHOE.

" Now tell me, Molly," said Mr. Coote to
Molly Cogan, as he met her on the road one
day, close to one of the old gateways of Kilmallock, " did you ever hear of the Cluricaune?"

" Is it the Cluricaune? why, then, sure I
did, often and often; many 's the time I heard
my father, rest his soul! tell about 'em over
and over again."

" But did you ever see one, Molly—did you
ever see one yourself?"

" Och! no, I never *see* one in my life; but
my grandfather, that 's my father's father, you
know, he *see* one, one time, and caught him
too."

" Caught him! Oh! Molly, tell me how
was that?"

P 2

" Why, then, I 'll tell you.   My grandfather, you see, was out there above in the bog,
drawing home turf, and the poor old mare
was tired after her day's work, and the old
man went out to the stable to look after her,
and to see if she was eating her hay; and
when he came to the stable-door there, my
dear, he heard something hammering, hammering, hammering, just for all the world like
a shoemaker making a shoe, and whistling all
the time the prettiest tune he ever heard in
his whole life before.   Well, my grandfather,
he thought it was the Cluricaune, and he said
to himself, says he, ' I 'll catch you, if I can,
and then I 'll have money enough always.'   So
he opened the door very quietly, and didn't
make a bit of noise in the world that ever was
heard ; and he looked all about, but the never
a bit of the little man he could see any where,
but he heard him hammering and whistling,
and so he looked and looked, till at last he *see*
the little fellow ; and where was he, do you
think, but in the girth under the mare ; and
there he was with his little bit of an apron on
him, and his hammer in his hand, and a little
red nightcap on his head, and he making a

shoe; and he was so busy with his work, and he was hammering and whistling so loud, that he never minded my grandfather till he caught him fast in his hand. ' Faith, I have you now,' says he, ' and I 'll never let you go till I get your purse—that 's what I won't ; so give it here to me at once, now.' ' Stop, stop,' says the Cluricaune, ' stop, stop, says he, till I get it for you.' So my grandfather, like a fool, you see, opened his hand a little, and the little fellow jumped away laughing, and he never saw him any more, and the never a bit of the purse did he get, only the Cluricaune left his little shoe that he was making; and my grandfather was mad enough angry with himself for letting him go ; but he had the shoe all his life, and my own mother told me she often *see* it, and had it in her hand, and 'twas the prettiest little shoe she ever saw."

" And did you see it yourself, Molly ?"

" Oh ! no, my dear, it was lost long afore I was born ; but my mother told me about it often and often enough."

There is nothing very strange in the circumstance of Molly's grandfather becoming the possessor of a Cluricaune's shoe, for even in the present century, when these little people are supposed to have grown more shy and cautious of letting themselves be seen or heard, persons have been fortunate enough to get their shoes, though the purse still eludes them. In a Kilkenny paper, published not more than three years ago, there was a paragraph (which paragraph was copied into most of the Irish papers) stating that a peasant returning home in the dusk of the evening, discovered one of these little folk at work, and as the workman, as usual, contrived to make his escape, the peasant secured the shoe to bear witness of the fact, which shoe, to satisfy public curiosity, lay for inspection at the office of the said paper. It is therefore not impossible that this specimen of Cluricaune cordwainry may still exist.

The names of Cogan and Kilmallock excite ideas of rather a serious nature ; which, however little they may accord with the tone of the tales contained in the section which is now closing, serve to prepare the mind for those of a more solemn character, composing that which follows. The name Cogan cannot fail to recall to the mind of the reader versed in Irish history the celebrated Milo de Cogan, one of those early adventurers termed Strongbownians, and from whom all the Irish Cogans are probably descended ; but sadly indeed has that name declined in importance, for few who bear it now rank even in the middle classes of society. The same observation may be made concerning most of the names which occur in the history of the first invasion. Some have totally disappeared, others have sunk down into the lower orders, and but a small number retain the semblance of what they once were. Where are now the Fitz Andelms, the Fitz Hughs, the Fitz Stephens, and those numerous other families which bore the Norman patronymic of Fitz? They have vanished. Where shall we seek for the descendants of the brave Milo de Cogan, and Hugh Tyrrell, the accomplished Raymond le Gros, or the puissant Walter and Hugh de Lacy, who could venture to set at defiance even the royal authority? A few, a very few may be found among the middle ranks, but the great majority occupy no higher station than that of artizans and labourers. The Barrys, the De Courcys, the St. Laurences, the Mountmorrises, the De Burgos, the Fitz Geralds, alone appear on the rolls of nobility; but how few of these can cope in wealth and importance with some peers of far more recent creation? Of the Fitz Geralds, the Kildare branch still retains its wealth and dignity; but where are now the once potent Fitz Maurices of Desmond? Alas! with the exception of those branches bearing the romantic titles of the White Knight, the Black Knight, and the Knight of Glin (and even these are fast merging into other families), the descendants of the mighty house of Desmond are no longer distinguished by either fame or fortune; and a pang for the transitoriness of human splendour will, perhaps, be excited in a reflecting mind, on reading the following artless lines in the cathedral of Cork—

" Here lies a branch of Desmond's race,
  In Thomas Holland's burial-place."

Equally fallen with the noble race of Desmond is the former chief seat of their power, Kilmallock, distinguished by its splendid abbies, and its strong defences. It is now the abode of wretchedness and misery, interesting only by its ruins, and the associations connected with its name. What tourist, possessed of sensibility, can view Kilmallock and think of the Desmonds, their opulence and their power, without calling to mind these beautiful and pensive lines of the Italian Homer—

" Giace l'alta Cartago, appena i segni
  De l'alte sue ruine il lido serba
  Muoiono le città, muoiono i regni
  Copre i fasti e le pompe arena ed erba
  E l'uom d' esser mortal par che si sdegni ?
  O nostra mente cupida e superba !"

FAIRY LEGENDS.

THE BANSHEE.

"Who sits upon the heath forlorn
  With robe so free and tresses torn?
  Anon she pours a harrowing strain,
  And then—she sits all mute again!—
  Now peals the wild, funereal cry—
  And now—it sinks into a sigh."

                              OURAWNS.

LEGENDS

OF

THE BANSHEE.

THE Reverend Charles Bunworth was rector of Buttevant, in the county Cork, about the middle of the last century. He was a man of unaffected piety, and of sound learning; pure in heart, and benevolent in intention. By the rich he was respected, and by the poor beloved; nor did a difference of creed prevent their looking up to " *the minister*" (so was Mr. Bunworth called by them) in matters of difficulty and in seasons of distress, confident of receiving from him the advice and assistance that a father would afford to his children. He was the friend and the benefactor of the surrounding country—to him, from the neighbouring town of New-market, came both Curran and Yelverton for advice and instruction, previous to their en-trance at Dublin college.   Young, indigent, and inexperienced, these afterwards eminent men received from him, in addition to the ad-vice they sought, pecuniary aid ; and the bril-liant career which was theirs, justified the dis-crimination of the giver.

But what extended the fame of Mr. Bun-worth far beyond the limits of the parishes ad-jacent to his own, was his performance on the Irish harp, and his hospitable reception and entertainment of the poor harpers who tra-velled from house to house about the country. Grateful to their patron, these itinerant min-strels sang his praises to the tingling accom-paniment of their harps, invoking in return for his bounty abundant blessings on his white head, and celebrating in their rude verses the blooming charms of his daughters, Elizabeth and Mary.   It was all these poor fellows could do ; but who can doubt that their gratitude was sincere, when, at the time of Mr. Bunworth's death, no less than fifteen harps were deposited on the loft of his granary, bequeathed to him by the last members of a race which has now ceased to exist. Trifling, no doubt, in intrinsic value were these relics, yet there is something in gifts of the heart that merits preservation; and it is to be regretted that, when he died, these harps were broken up one after the other, and used as fire-wood by an ignorant follower of the family, who, on their removal to Cork for a temporary change of scene, was left in charge of the house.

The circumstances attending the death of Mr. Bunworth may be doubted by some; but there are still living credible witnesses who declare their authenticity, and who can be produced to attest most, if not all of the following particulars.

About a week previous to his dissolution, and early in the evening, a noise was heard at the hall-door resembling the shearing of sheep; but at the time no particular attention was paid to it. It was near eleven o'clock the same night, when Kavanagh, the herdsman, returned from Mallow, whither he had been sent in the afternoon for some medicine, and was observed by Miss Bunworth, to whom he delivered the parcel, to be much agitated. At this time, it must be observed, her father was by no means considered in danger.

" What is the matter, Kavanagh ?" asked Miss Bunworth : but the poor fellow, with a bewildered look, only uttered, " The master, Miss—the master—he is going from us ;" and, overcome with real grief, he burst into a flood of tears.

Miss Bunworth, who was a woman of strong nerve, inquired if any thing he had learned in Mallow induced him to suppose that her father was worse.

" No, Miss," said Kavanagh ; " it was not in Mallow———"

" Kavanagh," said Miss Bunworth, with that stateliness of manner for which she is said to have been remarkable, " I fear you have been drinking, which I must say I did not expect at such a time as the present, when it was your duty to have kept yourself sober ;—I thought you might have been trusted :—what should we have done if you had broken the medicine bottle, or lost it ? for the doctor said it was of the greatest con-

sequence that your master should take it to-
night. But I shall speak to you in the morning, when you are in a fitter state to understand what I say."

Kavanagh looked up with a stupidity of
aspect which did not serve to remove the impression of his being drunk, as his eyes appeared heavy and dull after the flood of tears ;
—but his voice was not that of an intoxicated
person.

" Miss," said he, " as I hope to receive
mercy hereafter, neither bit nor sup has passed
my lips since I left this house : but the master——"

" Speak softly," said Miss Bunworth ; " he
sleeps, and is going on as well as we could
expect."

" Praise be to God for that, any way," replied Kavanagh ; " but oh! miss, he is going
from us surely—we will lose him—the master
—we will lose him, we will lose him !" and he
wrung his hands together.

" What is it you mean, Kavanagh ?" asked
Miss Bunworth.

" Is it mean ?" said Kavanagh : " the Banshee has come for him, Miss ; and 'tis not I alone who have heard her."

" 'Tis an idle superstition," said Miss Bunworth.

" May be so," replied Kavanagh, as if the words ' idle superstition' only sounded upon his ear without reaching his mind—" May be so," he continued ; " but as I came through the glen of Ballybeg, she was along with me keening and screeching and clapping her hands, by my side every step of the way, with her long white hair falling all about her shoulders, and I could hear her repeat the master's name every now and then, as plain as ever I heard it. When I came to the old abbey, she parted from me there, and turned into the pigeon-field next the *berrin* ground, and folding her cloak about her, down she sat under the tree that was struck by the lightning, and began keening so bitterly, that it went through one's heart to hear it."

" Kavanagh," said Miss Bunworth, who had, however, listened attentively to this remarkable relation, " my father is, I believe, better ; and I hope will himself soon be up and able to convince you that all this is but your own fancy; nevertheless, I charge you not to mention what you have told me, for there is no occasion to frighten your fellow-servants with the story."

Mr. Bunworth gradually declined; but nothing particular occurred until the night previous to his death; that night both his daughters, exhausted from continued attendance and watching, were prevailed upon to seek some repose; and an elderly lady, a near relative and friend of the family, remained by the bedside of their father. The old gentleman then lay in the parlour, where he had been in the morning removed at his own request, fancying the change would afford him relief; and the head of his bed was placed close to the window. In a room adjoining sat some male friends, and as usual on like occasions of illness, in the kitchen many of the followers of the family had assembled.

The night was serene and moonlight— the sick man slept—and nothing broke the stillness of their melancholy watch, when the little party in the room adjoining the parlour, the door of which stood open, was suddenly

Q

roused by a sound at the window near the
bed : a rose-tree grew outside the window, so
close as to touch the glass ; this was forced
aside with some noise, and a low moaning
was heard, accompanied by clapping of hands,
as if of a female in deep affliction. It seemed as
if the sound proceeded from a person holding
her mouth close to the window. The lady who
sat by the bedside of Mr. Bunworth went
into the adjoining room, and in the tone of
alarm, inquired of the gentlemen there if they
had heard the Banshee ? Sceptical of supernatural appearances, two of them rose hastily
and went out to discover the cause of these
sounds, which they also had distinctly heard.
They walked all round the house, examining
every spot of ground, particularly near the
window from whence the voice had proceeded;
but their search was vain—they could perceive
nothing ; and an unbroken stillness reigned
without. Yet hoping to dispel the mystery,
they continued their search anxiously along
the road, from the straightness of which and
the lightness of the night, they were enabled
to see some distance around them ; but all was
silent and deserted, and they returned sur-

prised and disappointed. How much more then were they astonished at learning that the whole time of their absence, those who remained within the house had heard the moaning and clapping of hands even louder and more distinct than before they had gone out; and no sooner was the door of the room closed on them, than they again heard the same mournful sounds! Every succeeding hour the sick man became worse, and when the first glimpse of the morning appeared, Mr. Bunworth expired.

The character of Mr. Bunworth, and the particulars related of him, accord with the truth :—See Ryan's Worthies of Ireland, vol. i. p. 228, where it is stated that the harp made for him by Kelly, and which bears an inscription to that effect, is still preserved in his family. This interesting relic is in the possession of his grand-daughter, Miss Dillon of Blackrock, near Cork, to whom the musical talent of her ancestor seems also to have descended. The anecdote of the legacies bequeathed by the poor bards to Mr. Bun-worth may bring the lines of Ireland's national poet into the reader's mind.

" When the light of my song is o'er,
     Then take my harp to your ancient hall ;
Hang it up at that friendly door
     Where weary travellers love to call.
Then if some bard, who roams forsaken,
     Revive its soft note in passing along,
 Oh ! let one thought of its master waken
     Your warmest smile for the child of song."

By one of those strange coincidences which are nevertheless always occurring, the very next song in the Irish Melodies begins—

     " How oft has the Banshee cried."—

The word Banshee has been variously explained as the head of the fairies, and as the white fairy : but Dr. O'Brien, in his Irish dictionary, writes " *Bean-síghe*, plural *mná-síghe*, she-fairies, or women-fairies, credulously supposed by the common people to be so affected to certain families, that they are heard to sing mournful lamentations about their houses by night, whenever any of the family labours under a sickness which is to end in death.   But," continues the doctor, " no families which are not of an ancient and noble stock are believed to be honoured with this fairy privilege : pertinent to which notion, a very humorous quantan is set down in an Irish elegy on the death of one of the knights of Kerry, importing that when the fairy-woman of the family was heard to lament his death at Dingle (a sea-port town, the property of those knights), every one of the merchants was alarmed lest the mournful cry should be a fore-warning of his own death : but the poet assures them in a very humorous manner that they may make themselves very easy on that occasion. The Irish words will explain the rest. *An sa Daingion' nuair neartaidh an brón-ghol : do ghlac eagla ceannuidhthe an chnósaicc: 'na dtaobh féin nîr bhaoghal dòibhsin : ni chaoinid mnà-sighe an sort san."*

The Welsh Gwrâch y Rhibyn, or the hag of the dribble, mentioned in a former note, bears some re-semblance to the Irish Banshee, being regarded as an omen of death. She is said to come after dusk, and flap her leathern wings against the window where she warns of death, and in a broken, howling tone, to call on the one who is to quit mortality by his or her name several times, as thus, *A-a-a-n-ni-i-i-i! Anni.*

Keening is the Irish term for a wild song or la-mentation poured forth over a dead body, by certain mourners employed for the purpose. The reader will find a paper on this subject, with a musical notation of the Irish funeral lamentation, in the fourth volume of the Transactions of the Royal Irish Academy.

The following verses, translated from a popular keen, are given not so much because they afford a specimen of one, as because of the introduction of the Banshee. It was composed on a young man named Ryan, whose mother speaks :

Maidens, sing no more in gladness
    To your merry spinning-wheels ;
Join the keener's voice of sadness—
    Feel for what a mother feels !

See the space within my dwelling—
    'Tis the cold, blank space of death ;
'Twas the Banshee's voice came swelling
    Slowly o'er the midnight heath.

Keeners, let your song not falter—
    He was as the hawthorn fair.—
Lowly at the virgin's altar
    Will his mother kneel in prayer.

Prayer is good to calm the spirit,
    When the keen is sweetly sung.—
Death, though mortal flesh inherit,
    Why should age lament the young ?—

'Twas the Banshee's lonely wailing :—
    Well I knew the voice of death
On the night-wind slowly sailing
    O'er the bleak and gloomy heath.

        *   *   *

LEGENDS OF THE BANSHEE.

THE family of Mac Carthy have for some generations possessed a small estate in the county of Tipperary. They are the descendants of a race, once numerous and powerful in the south of Ireland; and though it is probable that the property they at present hold is no part of the large possessions of their ancestors, yet the district in which they live is so connected with the name of Mac Carthy by those associations which are never forgotten in Ireland, that they have preserved with all ranks a sort of influence much greater than that which their fortune or connexions could otherwise give them. They are, like most of this class, of the Roman Catholic persuasion, to which they adhere with somewhat of the pride of ancestry, blended with a something, call it what you will, whether bigotry,

or a sense of wrong, arising out of repeated
diminutions of their family possession, during
the more rigorous periods of the penal laws.
Being an old family, and especially being
an old Catholic family, they have of course
their Banshee; and the circumstances under
which the appearance, which I shall relate,
of this mysterious harbinger of evil took place,
were told me by an old lady, a near connexion of theirs, who knew many of the parties concerned, and who, though not deficient
in understanding or education, cannot to this
day be brought to give a decisive opinion as
to the truth or authenticity of the story.
The plain inference to be drawn from this
is, that she believes it, though she does not
own it; and as she was a contemporary of the
persons concerned—as she heard the account
from many persons about the same period, all
concurring in the important particulars—as
some of her authorities were themselves actors
in the scene—and as none of the parties were
interested in speaking what was false; I think
we have about as good evidence that the whole
is undeniably true as we have of many narra-
tives of modern history, which I could name,

and which many grave and sober-minded people would deem it very great pyrrhonism to question. This, however, is a point which it is not my province to determine. People who deal out stories of this sort must be content to act like certain young politicians, who tell very freely to their friends what they hear at a great man's table; not guilty of the impertinence of weighing the doctrines, and leaving it to their hearers to understand them in any sense, or in no sense, just as they may please.

Charles Mac Carthy was, in the year 1749, the only surviving son of a very numerous family. His father died when he was little more than twenty, leaving him the Mac Carthy estate, not much encumbered, considering that it was an Irish one. Charles was gay, handsome, unfettered either by poverty, a father, or guardians, and therefore was not, at the age of one-and-twenty, a pattern of regularity and virtue. In plain terms, he was an exceedingly dissipated—I fear I may say debauched young man. His companions were, as may be supposed, of the higher classes of the youth in his neighbourhood, and, in general, of those whose fortunes were larger than his own, whose dispositions to pleasure were therefore under still less restrictions, and in whose example he found at once an incentive and an apology for his irregularities. Besides, Ireland, a place to this day not very remarkable for the coolness and steadiness of its youth, was then one of the cheapest countries in the world in most of those articles which money supplies for the indulgence of the passions. The odious exciseman, with his portentous book in one hand, his unrelenting pen held in the other, or stuck beneath his hat-band, and the ink-bottle ('black emblem of the informer') dangling from his waistcoat-button—went not then from ale-house to ale-house, denouncing all those patriotic dealers in spirits, who preferred selling whiskey, which had nothing to do with English laws (but to elude them), to retailing that poisonous liquor, which derived its name from the British "Parliament" that compelled its circulation among a reluctant people. Or if the gauger—recording angel of the law— wrote down the peccadillo of a publican, he dropped a tear upon the word, and blotted

it out for ever! For, welcome to the tables
of their hospitable neighbours, the guardians
of the excise, where they existed at all, scrupled
to abridge those luxuries which they freely
shared; and thus the competition in the market
between the smuggler, who incurred little
hazard, and the personage ycleped fair trader,
who enjoyed little protection, made Ireland a
land flowing, not merely with milk and honey,
but with whiskey and wine. In the enjoy-
ments supplied by these, and in the many
kindred pleasures to which frail youth is but
too prone, Charles Mac Carthy indulged to
such a degree, that just about the time when
he had completed his four-and-twentieth year,
after a week of great excesses, he was seized
with a violent fever, which, from its malignity,
and the weakness of his frame, left scarcely a
hope of his recovery. His mother, who had
at first made many efforts to check his vices,
and at last had been obliged to look on at his
rapid progress to ruin in silent despair, watched
day and night at his pillow. The anguish of
parental feeling was blended with that still
deeper misery which those only know who have
striven hard to rear in virtue and piety a be-

loved and favourite child; have found him grow up all that their hearts could desire, until he reached manhood ; and then, when their pride was highest, and their hopes almost ended in the fulfilment of their fondest expectations, have seen this idol of their affections plunge headlong into a course of reckless profligacy, and, after a rapid career of vice, hang upon the verge of eternity, without the leisure or the power of repentance.   Fervently she prayed that, if his life could not be spared, at least the delirium, which continued with increasing violence from the first few hours of his disorder, might vanish before death, and leave enough of light and of calm for making his peace with offended Heaven.   After several days, however, nature seemed quite exhausted, and he sunk into a state too like death to be mistaken for the repose of sleep.   His face had that pale, glossy, marble look, which is in general so sure a symptom that life has left its tenement of clay.   His eyes were closed and sunk ; the lids having that compressed and stiffened appearance which seemed to indicate that some friendly hand had done its last office.   The lips, half-closed and perfectly

ashy, discovered just so much of the teeth as
to give to the features of death their most
ghastly, but most impressive look.   He lay
upon his back, with his hands stretched beside him, quite motionless; and his distracted
mother, after repeated trials, could discover
not the least symptom of animation.   The
medical man who attended, having tried the
usual modes for ascertaining the presence of
life, declared at last his opinion that it was
flown, and prepared to depart from the house
of mourning.   His horse was seen to come to
the door.   A crowd of people who were collected before the windows, or scattered in
groups on the lawn in front, gathered round
when the door opened.   These were tenants,
fosterers, and poor relations of the family,
with others attracted by affection, or by that
interest which partakes of curiosity, but is
something more, and which collects the lower
ranks round a house where a human being is
in his passage to another world.   They saw
the professional man come out from the hall
door and approach his horse; and while
slowly, and with a melancholy air, he pre-

pared to mount, they clustered round him
with inquiring and wishful looks. Not a word
was spoken ; but their meaning could not be
misunderstood ; and the physician, when he
had got into his saddle, and while the servant
was still holding the bridle, as if to delay him,
and was looking anxiously at his face as if expecting that he would relieve the general sus-
pense, shook his head, and said in a low voice,
" It's all over, James ;" and moved slowly
away. The moment he had spoken, the women present, who were very numerous, uttered a shrill cry, which, having been sustained for about half a minute, fell suddenly
into a full, loud, continued, and discordant
but plaintive wailing, above which occasionally were heard the deep sounds of a man's
voice, sometimes in broken sobs, sometimes in
more distinct exclamations of sorrow. This
was Charles's foster-brother, who moved about
the crowd, now clapping his hands, now rub-
bing them together in an agony of grief. The
poor fellow had been Charles's playmate and
companion when a boy, and afterwards his
servant ; had always been distinguished by

his peculiar regards, and loved his young master, as much, at least, as he did his own life.

When Mrs. Mac Carthy became convinced that the blow was indeed struck, and that her beloved son was sent to his last account, even in the blossoms of his sin, she remained for some time gazing with fixedness upon his cold features; then, as if something had suddenly touched the string of her tenderest affections, tear after tear trickled down her cheeks, pale with anxiety and watching. Still she continued looking at her son, apparently unconscious that she was weeping, without once lifting her handkerchief to her eyes, until reminded of the sad duties which the custom of the country imposed upon her, by the crowd of females belonging to the better class of the peasantry, who now, crying audibly, nearly filled the apartment. She then withdrew, to give directions for the ceremony of waking, and for supplying the numerous visitors of all ranks with the refreshments usual on these melancholy occasions. Though her voice was scarcely heard, and though no one saw her but the servants and one or two old followers

of the family, who assisted her in the necessary arrangements, every thing was conducted
with the greatest regularity; and though she
made no effort to check her sorrows, they
never once suspended her attention, now more
than ever required to preserve order in her
household, which, in this season of calamity,
but for her would have been all confusion.

The night was pretty far advanced; the
boisterous lamentations which had prevailed
during part of the day in and about the house
had given place to a solemn and mournful stillness; and Mrs. Mac Carthy, whose heart,
notwithstanding her long fatigue and watching, was yet too sore for sleep, was kneeling
in fervent prayer in a chamber adjoining that
of her son :—suddenly her devotions were disturbed by an unusual noise, proceeding from
the persons who were watching round the
body. First there was a low murmur—then
all was silent, as if the movements of those
in the chamber were checked by a sudden
panic—and then a loud cry of terror burst
from all within :—the door of the chamber
was thrown open, and all who were not over-
turned in the press rushed wildly into the

passage which led to the stairs, and into which
Mrs. Mac Carthy's room opened. Mrs. Mac
Carthy made her way through the crowd into
her son's chamber, where she found him sitting up in the bed, and looking vacantly
around, like one risen from the grave. The
glare thrown upon his sunk features and thin
lathy frame gave an unearthly horror to his
whole aspect. Mrs. Mac Carthy was a woman
of some firmness; but she was a woman, and
not quite free from the superstitions of her
country. She dropped on her knees, and,
clasping her hands, began to pray aloud.
The form before her moved only its lips, and
barely uttered " Mother;"—but though the
pale lips moved, as if there was a design to
finish the sentence, the tongue refused its office. Mrs. Mac Carthy sprung forward, and
catching the arm of her son, exclaimed,
" Speak! in the name of God and his saints,
speak! are you alive?"

He turned to her slowly, and said, speaking
still with apparent difficulty, " Yes, my mother, alive, and——But sit down and collect
yourself; I have that to tell, which will
astonish you still more than what you have

R

seen." He leaned back upon his pillow, and while his mother remained kneeling by the bedside, holding one of his hands clasped in hers, and gazing on him with the look of one who distrusted all her senses, he proceeded :— " Do not interrupt me until I have done. I wish to speak while the excitement of returning life is upon me, as I know I shall soon need much repose.—Of the commencement of my illness, I have only a confused recollection; but within the last twelve hours, I have been before the judgment-seat of God. Do not stare incredulously on me—'tis as true as have been my crimes, and as, I trust, shall be my repentance. I saw the awful Judge arrayed in all the terrors which invest him when mercy gives place to justice. The dreadful pomp of offended omnipotence, I saw,—I remember. It is fixed here; printed on my brain in characters indelible; but it passeth human language. What I *can* describe I *will*—I may speak it briefly. It is enough to say, I was weighed in the balance and found wanting. The irrevocable sentence was upon the point of being pronounced; the eye of my Almighty Judge, which had already glanced upon me, half spoke my doom; when I observed the guardian saint, to whom you so often directed my prayers when I was a child, looking at me with an expression of benevolence and compassion. I stretched forth my hands to him, and besought his interces- sion; I implored that one year, one month might be given to me on earth, to do penance and atonement for my transgressions. He threw himself at the feet of my Judge, and supplicated for mercy. Oh! never—not if I should pass through ten thousand succes- sive states of being—never, for eternity, shall I forget the horrors of that moment, when my fate hung suspended—when an instant was to decide whether torments unutterable were to be my portion for endless ages! But Justice suspended its decree, and Mercy spoke in accents of firmness, but mildness, ' Return to that world in which thou hast lived but to outrage the laws of him who made that world and thee. Three years are given thee for repentance; when these are ended, thou shalt again stand here, to be saved or lost for ever.'—I heard no more; I saw no more, until

I awoke to life, the moment before you entered."

Charles's strength continued just long enough to finish these last words, and on uttering them he closed his eyes, and lay quite exhausted. His mother, though, as was before said, somewhat disposed to give credit to supernatural visitations, yet hesitated whether or not she should believe that, although awakened from a swoon, which might have been the crisis of his disease, he was still under the influence of delirium. Repose, however, was at all events necessary, and she took immediate measures that he should enjoy it undisturbed. After some hours' sleep, he awoke refreshed, and thenceforward gradually but steadily recovered.

Still he persisted in his account of the vision, as he had at first related it; and his persuasion of its reality had an obvious and decided influence on his habits and conduct. He did not altogether abandon the society of his former associates, for his temper was not soured by his reformation; but he never joined in their excesses, and often endeavoured to reclaim them. How his pious exertions succeeded, I have never learnt; but of himself it is recorded, that he was religious without ostentation, and temperate without austerity; giving a practical proof that vice may be exchanged for virtue, without a loss of respectability, popularity, or happiness.

Time rolled on, and long before the three years were ended, the story of his vision was forgotten, or, when spoken of, was usually mentioned as an instance proving the folly of believing in such things. Charles's health, from the temperance and regularity of his habits, became more robust than ever. His friends, indeed, had often occasion to rally him upon a seriousness and abstractedness of demeanour, which grew upon him as he approached the completion of his seven-and-twentieth year, but for the most part his manner exhibited the same animation and cheerfulness for which he had always been remarkable. In company, he evaded every endeavour to draw from him a distinct opinion on the subject of the supposed prediction; but among his own family it was well known that he still firmly believed it. However, when the day had nearly arrived on which the pro-

phecy was, if at all, to be fulfilled, his whole
appearance gave such promise of a long and
healthy life, that he was persuaded by his
friends to ask a large party to an entertainment at Spring House, to celebrate his birthday.   But the occasion of this party, and the
circumstances which attended it, will be best
learned from a perusal of the following letters,
which have been carefully preserved by some
relations of his family.   The first is from Mrs.
Mac Carthy to a lady, a very near connexion
and valued friend of hers, who lived in the
county Cork, at about fifty miles distance
from Spring House.

" TO MRS. BARRY, CASTLE BARRY.

" *Spring House, Tuesday morning,*
October 15*th,* 1752.

" MY DEAREST MARY,

" I am afraid I am going to put your affection for your old friend and kinswoman to
a severe trial.   A two days' journey at this
season, over bad roads and through a troubled
country, it will indeed require friendship such
as yours to persuade a sober woman to en-
counter.   But the truth is, I have, or fancy I

have, more than usual cause for wishing you near me. You know my son's story. I can't tell how it is, but as next Sunday approaches, when the prediction of his dream or his vision will be proved false or true, I feel a sickening of the heart, which I cannot suppress, but which your presence, my dear Mary, will soften, as it has done so many of my sorrows. My nephew, James Ryan, is to be married to Jane Osborne (who, you know, is my son's ward), and the bridal entertainment will take place here on Sunday next, though Charles pleaded hard to have it postponed a day or two longer. Would to God——but no more of this till we meet. Do prevail upon yourself to leave your good man for *one* week, if his farming concerns will not admit of his accompanying you ; and come to us, with the girls, as soon before Sunday as you can.

" Ever my dear Mary's attached cousin and friend,

" ANN MAC CARTHY."

Although this letter reached Castle Barry early on Wednesday, the messenger having travelled on foot, over bog and moor, by paths impassable to horse or carriage, Mrs. Barry, who at once determined on going, had so many arrangements to make for the regulation of her domestic affairs (which, in Ireland, among the middle orders of the gentry, fall soon into confusion when the mistress of the family is away), that she and her two younger daughters were unable to leave home until late on the morning of Friday. The eldest daughter remained, to keep her father company, and superintend the concerns of the household. As the travellers were to journey in an open one-horse vehicle, called a jaunting car (still used in Ireland), and as the roads, bad at all times, were rendered still worse by the heavy rains, it was their design to make two easy stages; to stop about midway the first night, and reach Spring House early on Saturday evening. This arrangement was now altered, as they found that, from the lateness of their departure, they could proceed, at the utmost, no farther than twenty miles on the first day ; and they therefore purposed sleeping at the house of a Mr. Bourke, a friend of theirs, who lived at somewhat less than that distance from Castle Barry. They reached Mr. Bourke's in safety, after rather a disagreeable drive. What befel them on their journey the next day to Spring House, and after their arrival there, is fully recounted in a letter from the second Miss Barry to her eldest sister.

" Spring House, Sunday evening,
20th October, 1752.

" DEAR ELLEN,

" As my mother's letter, which encloses this, will announce to you briefly the sad intelligence which I shall here relate more fully, I think it better to go regularly through the recital of the extraordinary events of the last two days.

" The Bourkes kept us up so late on Friday night, that yesterday was pretty far advanced before we could begin our journey, and the day closed when we were nearly fifteen miles distant from this place. The roads were excessively deep, from the heavy rains of the last week, and we proceeded so slowly, that at last my mother resolved on passing the night at the house of Mr. Bourke's brother, (who lives about a quarter of a mile off the road), and coming here to breakfast in the morning. The day had been windy and showery, and the sky looked fitful, gloomy, and uncertain. The moon was full, and at times shone clear and bright ; at others, it was wholly concealed behind the thick, black, and ragged masses of clouds, that rolled rapidly along, and were every moment becoming larger, and collecting together, as if gathering strength for a coming storm. The wind, which blew in our faces, whistled bleakly along the low hedges of the narrow road, on which we proceeded with difficulty from the number of deep sloughs, and which afforded not the least shelter, no plantation being within some miles of us. My mother, therefore, asked Leary, who drove the jaunting car, how far we were from Mr. Bourke's. ' 'Tis about ten spades from this to the cross, and we have then only to turn to the left into the avenue, ma'am.' ' Very well, Leary : turn up to Mr. Bourke's as soon as you reach the cross roads.' My mother had scarcely spoken these words, when a shriek, that made us thrill as if our very hearts were pierced by it, burst from the hedge to the right of our way. If it resembled any thing earthly, it seemed the cry of a female, struck by a sudden and mortal blow, and giving out her life in one long deep pang of expiring agony. ' Heaven defend us !' exclaimed my mother. ' Go you over the hedge, Leary, and save that woman, if she is not yet dead, while we run back to the hut we just passed, and alarm the village near it.' ' Woman !' said Leary, beating the horse violently, while his voice trembled—' that's no woman : the sooner we get on, ma'am, the better ;' and he continued his efforts to quicken the horse's pace. We saw nothing. The moon was hid. It was quite dark, and we had been for some time expecting a heavy fall of rain. But just as Leary had spoken, and had succeeded in making the horse trot briskly forward, we distinctly heard a loud clapping of hands, followed by a succession of screams, that seemed to denote the last excess of despair and anguish, and to issue from a person running forward inside the hedge, to keep pace with our progress. Still we saw nothing ; until, when we were within about ten yards of the place where an avenue branched off to Mr. Bourke's to the left, and the road turned to

Spring House on the right, the moon started suddenly from behind a cloud, and enabled us to see, as plainly as I now see this paper, the figure of a tall thin woman, with uncovered head, and long hair that floated round her shoulders, attired in something which seemed either a loose white cloak, or a sheet thrown hastily about her. She stood on the corner hedge, where the road on which we were met that which leads to Spring House, with her face towards us, her left hand pointing to this place, and her right arm waving rapidly and violently, as if to draw us on in that direction. The horse had stopped, apparently frightened at the sudden presence of the figure, which stood, in the manner I have described, still uttering the same piercing cries, for about half a minute. It then leaped upon the road, disappeared from our view for one instant, and the next was seen standing upon a high wall a little way up the avenue on which we purposed going, still pointing towards the road to Spring House, but in an attitude of defiance and command, as if prepared to oppose our passage up the avenue. The figure was now quite silent, and its garments, which had before flowed loosely in the wind, were closely wrapped around it. ' Go on, Leary, to Spring House, in God's name,' said my mother; ' whatever world it belongs to, we will provoke it no longer.' ' 'Tis the Banshee, ma'am,' said Leary ; ' and I would not, for what my life is worth, go any where this blessed night but to Spring House. But I 'm afraid there's something bad going forward, or *she* would not send us there.' So saying, he drove forward ; and as we turned on the road to the right, the moon suddenly withdrew its light, and we saw the apparition no more ; but we heard plainly a prolonged clapping of hands, gradually dying away, as if it issued from a person rapidly retreating. We proceeded as quickly as the badness of the roads and the fatigue of the poor animal that drew us would allow, and arrived here about eleven o'clock last night. The scene which awaited us you have learned from my mother's letter. To explain it fully, I must recount to you some of the transactions which took place here during the last week.

" You are aware that Jane Osborne was to have been married this day to James Ryan, and that they and their friends have been here for the last week. On Tuesday last, the very day on the morning of which cousin Mac Carthy despatched the letter inviting us here, the whole of the company were walking about the grounds a little before dinner. It seems that an unfortunate creature, who had been seduced by James Ryan, was seen prowling in the neighbourhood in a moody, melancholy state for some days previous. He had separated from her for several months, and, they say, had provided for her rather handsomely; but she had been seduced by the promise of his marrying her; and the shame of her unhappy condition, uniting with disappointment and jealousy, had disordered her intellects. During the whole forenoon of this Tuesday, she had been walking in the plantations near Spring House, with her cloak folded tight round her, the hood nearly covering her face; and she had avoided conversing with or even meeting any of the family.

" Charles Mac Carthy, at the time I mentioned, was walking between James Ryan and another, at a little distance from the rest, on a gravel path, skirting a shrubbery. The whole

party were thrown into the utmost consterna-
tion by the report of a pistol, fired from a
thickly planted part of the shrubbery which
Charles and his companions had just passed.
He fell instantly, and it was found that he had
been wounded in the leg.   One of the party
was a medical man; his assistance was immediately given, and, on examining, he declared
that the injury was very slight, that no bone
was broken, that it was merely a flesh wound,
and that it would certainly be well in a few
days.   ' We shall know more by Sunday,'
said Charles, as he was carried to his chamber.
His wound was immediately dressed, and so
slight was the inconvenience which it gave,
that several of his friends spent a portion of
the evening in his apartment.

" On inquiry, it was found that the unlucky shot was fired by the poor girl I just
mentioned.   It was also manifest that she had
aimed, not at Charles, but at the destroyer of
her innocence and happiness, who was walking
beside him.   After a fruitless search for her
through the grounds, she walked into the
house of her own accord, laughing, and
dancing and singing wildly, and every mo-

ment exclaiming that she had at last killed Mr. Ryan.   When she heard that it was Charles, and not Mr. Ryan, who was shot, she fell into a violent fit, out of which, after working convulsively for some time, she sprung to the door, escaped from the crowd that pursued her, and could never be taken until last night, when she was brought here, perfectly frantic, a little before our arrival.

" Charles's wound was thought of such little consequence, that the preparations went forward, as usual, for the wedding entertainment on Sunday.   But on Friday night he grew restless and feverish, and on Saturday (yesterday) morning felt so ill, that it was deemed necessary to obtain additional medical advice.   Two physicians and a surgeon met in consultation about twelve o'clock in the day, and the dreadful intelligence was announced, that unless a change, hardly hoped for, took place before night, death must happen within twenty-four hours after.   The wound, it seems, had been too tightly bandaged, and otherwise injudiciously treated.   The physicians were right in their anticipations.   No favourable symptom appeared, and long before we reached Spring-House every ray of hope had vanished. The scene we witnessed on our arrival would have wrung the heart of a demon. We heard briefly at the gate that Mr. Charles was upon his deathbed. When we reached the house, the information was confirmed by the servant who opened the door. But just as we entered, we were horrified by the most appalling screams issuing from the staircase. My mother thought she heard the voice of poor Mrs. Mac Carthy, and sprung forward. We followed, and on ascending a few steps of the stairs, we found a young woman, in a state of frantic passion, struggling furiously with two men-servants, whose united strength was hardly sufficient to prevent her rushing up stairs over the body of Mrs. Mac Carthy, who was lying in strong hysterics upon the steps. This, I afterwards discovered, was the unhappy girl I before described, who was attempting to gain access to Charles's room, to ' get his forgiveness,' as she said, ' before he went away to accuse her for having killed him.' This wild idea was mingled with another, which seemed to dispute with the former possession of her

s

mind.   In one sentence she called on Charles
to forgive her, in the next she would de-
nounce James Ryan as the murderer both
of Charles and her.   At length she was torn
away; and the last words I heard her scream
were, ' James Ryan, 'twas you killed him,
and not I—'twas you killed him, and not I.'

" Mrs. Mac Carthy, on recovering, fell
into the arms of my mother, whose presence
seemed a great relief to her. She wept—the first
tears, I was told, that she had shed since the
fatal accident.   She conducted us to Charles's
room, who, she said, had desired to see us the
moment of our arrival, as he found his end
approaching, and wished to devote the last
hours of his existence to uninterrupted prayer
and meditation. We found him perfectly
calm, resigned, and even cheerful. He spoke
of the awful event which was at hand with
courage and confidence, and treated it as a
doom for which he had been preparing ever
since his former remarkable illness, and which
he never once doubted was truly foretold to
him.   He bade us farewell with the air of one
who was about to travel a short and easy
journey; and we left him with impressions

which, notwithstanding all their anguish, will,
I trust, never entirely forsake us.

" Poor Mrs. Mac Carthy——but I am just
called away.   There seems a slight stir in the
family ; perhaps——"

The above letter was never finished.   The
enclosure to which it more than once alludes
told the sequel briefly, and it is all that I have
farther learned of the family of Mac Carthy.
Before the sun had gone down upon Charles's
seven-and-twentieth birthday, his soul had
gone to render its last account to its Creator.

————————

Romantic in incident and artificial in construction
as this story may appear, it is nevertheless a narrative
of facts, if the supernatural appearance of the Banshee
be excepted ;—the names and places mentioned are, in
every instance but one, real, and that has been changed
for certain reasons which it is unnecessary to explain,
as the alteration is immaterial.   Much may even be
said in vindication of the superstition of the Banshee
on the evidence of well-informed and enlightened
persons.

Miss Lefanu, the niece of Sheridan, relates the following anecdote in the memoirs of her grandmother,
Mrs. Frances Sheridan (8vo. London, 1824), p. 32.

" Like many Irish ladies, who resided during the early part of her life in the country, Miss Elizabeth Sheridan was a firm believer in the Banshee, or female demon, attached to certain ancient Irish families : she firmly maintained that the Banshee of the Sheridan family was heard wailing beneath the windows of Quilca (the family residence) before the news arrived from France of Mrs. Frances Sheridan's death at Blois, thus affording them a preternatural intimation of the impending melancholy event. A niece of Miss Sheridan's made her very angry by observing, that as Mrs. Frances Sheridan was by birth a Chamberlaine, a family of English extraction, she had no right to the guardianship of an Irish fairy, and that therefore the Banshee must have made a mistake !"

Another account of the Banshee, although probably the reader is already acquainted with it, is yet too curious to be omitted here ;—it is given in a note on " the Lady of the Lake," where Sir Walter Scott, after describing the appearance of this mournful fairy as that of " an old woman with a blue mantle and streaming hair," thus proceeds :—" But the most remarkable instance of the kind occurs in the MS. Memoirs of Lady Fanshaw, so exemplary for her conjugal affection : her husband, Sir Richard, and she chanced, during their abode in Ireland, to visit a friend, the head of a sept, who resided in an ancient baronial castle, surrounded with a moat. At midnight she was awakened by a ghastly and supernatural scream, and looking out of bed, beheld, by the moonlight, a fe-

male face and part of the form hovering at the window.
The distance from the ground, as well as the circumstance of the moat, excluded the possibility that
what she beheld was of this world. The face was
that of a young and rather handsome woman, but
pale, and the hair, which was reddish, loose and
dishevelled. The dress, which Lady Fanshaw's terror
did not prevent her remarking accurately, was that of
the ancient Irish. This apparition continued to ex-
hibit itself for some time, and then vanished, with two
shrieks, similar to that which had first excited Lady
Fanshaw's attention. In the morning, with infinite
terror, she communicated to her host what she had
witnessed, and found him prepared not only to credit,
but to account for the apparition.—

" ' A near relation of my family,' said he, ' expired
last night in this castle. We disguised our certain
expectation of the event from you, lest it should throw
a cloud over the cheerful reception which was your
due. Now, before such an event happens in this family and castle, the female spectre whom you have
seen always is visible : she is believed to be the spirit
of a woman of inferior rank, whom one of my ancestors
degraded himself by marrying, and whom afterwards,
to expiate the dishonour done to his family, he caused
to be drowned in the Castle Moat.' "

Lady Fanshaw lived in turbulent and unsettled
times, when to the lively imagination every sight and
sound came fraught with dismal forebodings of evil.

Perhaps this reasoning will account for the Banshee being a spirit peculiar to Ireland.

A recent instance of the superstition, however, has occurred in the writer's family. A servant named Peggy Rilehan (whose father's letter is quoted at page 178) declared that some great misfortune was about to happen, as she had heard a shriek, and had seen something pass across the window. On this the writer's sister, who was present at the time, remarks—" I saw nothing, but I heard Peggy scream, and then exclaim —'There it is—there it is—what always appears when any of the Rilehans are to die.' She says she saw it before, when aunt Harriott's nurse (who was her grandmother) died at Mallow."

The poor girl's cousin was at this time in jail. He was one of the misguided followers of Captain Rock; and two or three days after was tried for being concerned in the attack on Churchtown barracks, found guilty, and executed.

In 1816, much confusion was created in the house of a gentleman, where the writer was on a visit, by the following simple circumstance.

The house was situated in a proclaimed barony of the county Tipperary, not far distant from the scene of Mr. Baker's murder, which had occurred only a short time before. Mysterious looks and whispers amongst the domestics had at that moment something in them to excite alarm ; but after strict inquiry it was found that they were caused by the voice of a Banshee, which had been heard for several nights wailing through the house. On examination, these sounds of woe were traced to the bedchamber of Miss ———, and were discovered to have proceeded from an Eolian harp, which she had placed in the window.

Since however Banshees have become amenable to vulgar laws, they have lost much of their romantic character : the particulars respecting the manner in which this important change has been effected are given on good authority.

In a retired district of the county Cork stood a solitary farm-house, where a widow lady and her sister lived, with only one maid-servant. The lawn or field before the house was covered with flax, which had been steeped, and was spread out to dry : every morning a large quantity of it was gone ; and during the night the Banshee's cry was heard sounding dismally about the grounds. The lady was satisfied the flax could not be carried away without hands, although her suspicions did not fall on any particular person ; and she determined, if possible, to discover the thief. The next night the Banshee was heard as usual, and she desired the servant-girl to find out from what part of the grounds the voice came. The servant, however, felt too much alarmed to obey the order of her mistress, when the lady, who was a woman of strong mind, notwithstanding the persuasions of her sister, determined herself on walking round the house. It was a beautiful moonlight night, and she had not advanced many steps from the

door, when she saw what appeared to be the figure of
a woman crouching in a blue cloak, singing a sweet
but most melancholy air. She walked quickly up to
the form, and laid her hand on its shoulder: it rose
slowly, and continued increasing in height: still the
lady held firm her grasp; and her sister coming up,
they seized the Banshee, under whose blue cloak a
quantity of flax was found concealed. The servant,
who had recovered her senses, on hearing the alterca-
tion which ensued, now came to their assistance, and
they contrived to secure the woman for the night.
The next day she was sent to the jail of Cork, where
at the assizes the lady prosecuted her, and she was
sentenced to seven years' transportation.

FAIRY LEGENDS.

THE PHOOKA.

" —— A dusky, melancholy sprite
  As ever sullied the fair face of light."—

  *   *   *   *

" A constant vapour o'er the palace flies;
  Strange phantoms rising, as the mists arise,
  Dreadful, as hermits' dreams in haunted shades,
  Or bright as visions of expiring maids;
  Now glaring fiends, and snakes on rolling spires,
  Pale spectres, gaping tombs, and purple fires."

POPE.

LEGENDS

OF

THE PHOOKA.

THE SPIRIT HORSE.

THE history of Morty Sullivan ought to be a warning to all young men to stay at home, and to live decently and soberly if they can, and not to go roving about the world. Morty, when he had just turned of fourteen, ran away from his father and mother, who were a mighty respectable old couple, and many and many a tear they shed on his account. It is said they both died heart-broken for his loss: all they ever learned about him was that he went on board of a ship bound to America.

Thirty years after the old couple had been laid peacefully in their graves, there came a stranger to Beerhaven inquiring after them —it was their son Morty; and to speak the truth of him, his heart did seem full of sorrow, when he heard that his parents were dead and gone;—but what else could he expect to hear? Repentance generally comes when it is too late.

Morty Sullivan, however, as an atonement for his sins, was recommended to perform a pilgrimage to the blessed chapel of St. Gobnate, which is in a wild place called Ballyvourney.

This he readily undertook; and willing to lose no time, commenced his journey the same afternoon. Morty had not proceeded many miles before the evening came on: there was no moon, and the starlight was obscured by a thick fog, which ascended from the valleys. His way was through a mountainous country, with many cross-paths and by-ways, so that it was difficult for a stranger like Morty to travel without a guide. He was anxious to reach his destination, and exerted himself to do so; but the fog grew thicker and thicker,

and at last he became doubtful if the track he
was in led to Saint Gobnate's chapel. Seeing
therefore a light which he imagined not to be
far off, he went towards it, and when he
thought himself close to it, the light suddenly
seemed at a great distance, twinkling dimly
through the fog. Though Morty felt some
surprise at this, he was not disheartened, for
he thought that it was a light which the
blessed Saint Gobnate had sent to guide his
feet through the mountains to her chapel.

Thus did he travel for many miles, continually, as he believed, approaching the light,
which would suddenly start off to a great
distance. At length he came so close as to
perceive that the light came from a fire;
seated beside which he plainly saw an old
woman:—then, indeed, his faith was a little
shaken, and much did he wonder that both
the fire and the old woman should travel before him, so many weary miles, and over such
uneven roads.

"In the pious names of Saint Gobnate,
and of her preceptor Saint Abban," said
Morty, "how can that burning fire move on

so fast before me, and who can that old
woman be sitting beside the moving fire?"

These words had no sooner passed Morty's
lips than he found himself, without taking
another step, close to this wonderful fire, beside which the old woman was sitting munch-
ing her supper. With every wag of the old
woman's jaw her eyes would roll fiercely upon
Morty, as if she was angry at being disturbed; and he saw with more astonishment
than ever that her eyes were neither black,
nor blue, nor gray, nor hazel, like the human
eye, but of a wild red colour, like the eye of a
ferret. If before he wondered at the fire,
much greater was his wonder at the old
woman's appearance; and stout-hearted as
he was, he could not but look upon her with
fear—judging, and judging rightly, that it
was for no good purpose her supping in so
unfrequented a place, and at so late an hour,
for it was near midnight. She said not one
word, but munched, and munched away,
while Morty looked at her in silence.—
" What's your name?" at last demanded the
old hag, a sulphureous puff coming out of

her mouth, her nostrils distending, and her eyes growing redder than ever, when she had finished her question.

Plucking up all his courage, " Morty Sullivan," replied he, " at your service ;" meaning the latter words only in civility.

" *Ubbubbo!*" said the old woman, " we 'll soon see that ;" and the red fire of her eyes turned into a pale green colour. Bold and fearless as Morty was, yet much did he tremble at hearing this dreadful exclamation ; he would have fallen down on his knees and prayed to Saint Gobnate, or any other saint, for he was not particular ; but he was so petrified with horror, that he could not move in the slightest way, much less go down on his knees.

" Take hold of my hand, Morty," said the old woman : " I 'll give you a horse to ride that will soon carry you to your journey's end." So saying, she led the way, the fire going before them ;—it is beyond mortal knowledge to say how, but on it went, shooting out bright tongues of flame, and flickering fiercely.

Presently they came to a natural cavern in the side of the mountain, and the old hag called aloud in a most discordant voice for her horse! In a moment a jet-black steed started from its gloomy stable, the rocky floor of which rung with a sepulchral echo to the clanging hoofs.

"Mount, Morty, mount!" cried she, seizing him with supernatural strength, and forcing him upon the back of the horse. Morty finding human power of no avail, muttered "Oh that I had spurs!" and tried to grasp the horse's mane; but he caught at a shadow, which nevertheless bore him up and bounded forward with him, now springing down a fearful precipice, now clearing the rugged bed of a torrent, and rushing like the dark midnight storm through the mountains.

The following morning Morty Sullivan was discovered by some pilgrims (who came that way after taking their rounds at Gougane Barra) lying on the flat of his back, under a steep cliff, down which he had been flung by the Phooka. Morty was severely bruised by the fall, and he is said to have sworn on the spot, by the hand of O'Sullivan (and that is no small oath), never again to take a full quart bottle of whiskey with him on a pilgrimage.

Ballyvourney, or the town of my beloved, is six or seven miles west of Macroom, and is regarded as a place of peculiar holiness. An indulgence, dated 12th July, 1601, was granted by Pope Clement the VIIIth. to pilgrims going thither, which is printed in Smith's History of Cork, from a copy in the Lambeth Library. Some other curious particulars respecting Ballyvourney may also be found in the same work.

In addition to these, a remarkable tradition concerning St. Gobnate has been communicated to the writer, which is as follows:—About eight hundred years ago, a powerful chief on the point of waging war against the head of another clan, seeing the inferiority of his troops, prayed to Saint Gobnate for assistance, in a field adjacent to the scene of the approaching battle. In this field was a bee-hive, and the good saint granted his request by turning the bees into armed soldiers, who issued forth from the hive with every appearance of military discipline, arranged themselves in ranks, and followed their leader to the contest, where they were victorious. After the battle, gratitude instigated the conquering chief to visit the spot from

T

whence he had received such miraculous aid, when he
found that the hive had likewise been metamorphosed
from straw or rushes, of which it was composed, into
brass, and that it had become not unlike a helmet in
shape.   This relic is in the possession of the O'Hier-
lyhie family, and is held by the Irish peasantry in
such profound veneration, that they will travel several
miles to procure a drop of water from it, which, if
given to a dying relative or friend, they imagine will
secure their ready admission into heaven.   Not long
since, some water from this brazen bee-hive was ad-
ministered to a dying priest by his coadjutor, in compliance with the popular superstition.   " The priest
himself who gave the water," adds the lady, to whom
the writer is indebted for the communication, " is my
authority for the story."

A pilgrimage to a place of reputed sanctity, like
that undertaken by Morty Sullivan, is the common
mode in Ireland, as in other Catholic countries, by
which the peasant endeavours to make atonement for
his sins, and to propitiate the favour of Heaven.
" The consequences of such pilgrimages," remarks
Mr. Gilly (the talented and zealous advocate of the
Vaudois), " have not unfrequently been fatal to innocence; and often have processions of pilgrims been
converted into bands of profligate voluptuaries."   Indeed this fact was so notorious, that the Catholic
clergy in the south of Ireland publicly forbade the
customary pilgrimage on the 24th June to the Lake
of Gougane Barra, as it presented an annual scene of

drunkenness, riot, and debauchery, too shocking for description.

Morty Sullivan, therefore, appears to have only followed the common practice of other devotees, when he set out on his journey, in taking the whiskey-bottle with him; and those incredulous of supernatural appearances will probably attribute his fall rather to its contents than to the terrific bound of the Spirit Horse, or Phooka.

It is difficult to explain the exact attributes of the Phooka, which have always in them something dusky and indistinct. The Welch word *Gwyll*, variously used to express gloom, darkness, a shade, a goblin, and the nightmare, is pretty nearly the Irish Phooka: thus—

" *Aeth dy enaid gàn Wyllion mynydh.*"

" Thy soul is gone with the *sprites* of the mountain."

Merdhin. A.D. 600.

And again—

" *Aed à'i câr gàn Wyllon !*"

" May such as love him go with the *glooms !*" (sprites.)

Hywel Voel. A.D. 1260.

The moving fire, or ignis fatuus, by which Morty was deluded, is termed by the peasantry in the south of Ireland " *Miscaun marry.*"

" *Ubbubbo!*" exclaims the old hag,—that is *bobo*,
an Irish interjection of wonder, like the Latin *papæ*,
and the Greek ποποι and βαβαι.

Morty swears " by the hand of O'Sullivan," an oath
not to be broken by one of the name ; for, according
to the old legend of this family—

> " Nulla manus,
>   Tam liberalis,
>   Atque generalis,
>   Atque universalis,
>   Quam Sullivanis !"

DANIEL O'ROURKE.

PEOPLE may have heard of the renowned adventures of Daniel O'Rourke, but how few are there who know that the cause of all his perils, above and below, was neither more nor less than his having slept under the walls of the Phooka's tower. I knew the man well: he lived at the bottom of Hungry Hill, just at the right hand side of the road as you go towards Bantry. An old man was he at the time that he told me the story, with gray hair, and a red nose; and it was on the 25th of June, 1813, that I heard it from his own lips, as he sat smoking his pipe under the old poplar tree, on as fine an evening as ever shone from the sky. I was going to visit the caves in Dursey Island, having spent the morning at Glengariff.

" I am often *axed* to tell it, sir," said he, " so that this is not the first time. The master's son, you see, had come from beyond foreign parts in France and Spain, as young gentlemen used to go, before Buonaparte or any such was heard of ; and sure enough there was a dinner given to all the people on the ground, gentle and simple, high and low, rich and poor. The *ould* gentlemen were the gentlemen, after all, saving your honour's presence. They'd swear at a body a little, to be sure, and, may be, give one a cut of a whip now and then, but we were no losers by it in the end ;—and they were so easy and civil, and kept such rattling houses, and thousands of welcomes ;—and there was no grinding for rent, and few agents ; and there was hardly a tenant on the estate that did not taste of his landlord's bounty often and often in the year ; —but now it's another thing : no matter for that, sir, for I'd better be telling you my story.

" Well, we had every thing of the best, and plenty of it ; and we ate, and we drank, and we danced, and the young master by the same token danced with Peggy Barry, from the Bohereen—a lovely young couple they were, though they are both low enough now. To make a long story short, I got, as a body may say, the same thing as tipsy almost, for I can't remember ever at all, no ways, how it was that I left the place: only I did leave it, that's certain. Well, I thought, for all that, in myself, I'd just step to Molly Cronahan's, the fairy woman, to speak a word about the bracket heifer what was bewitched; and so as I was crossing the stepping-stones of the ford of Ballyashenogh, and was looking up at the stars and blessing myself—for why? it was Lady-day—I missed my foot, and souse I fell into the water. ' Death alive !' thought I, ' I'll be drowned now !' However, I began swimming, swimming, swimming away for the dear life, till at last I got ashore, some-how or other, but never the one of me can tell how, upon a *dissolute* island.

" I wandered and wandered about there, without knowing where I wandered, until at last I got into a big bog. The moon was shining as bright as day, or your fair lady's eyes, sir (with your pardon for mentioning her), and I looked east and west, and north

and south, and every way, and nothing did I
see but bog, bog, bog ;—I could never find out
how I got into it ; and my heart grew cold
with fear, for sure and certain I was that it
would be my *berrin* place. So I sat down
upon a stone which, as good luck would have
it, was close by me, and I began to scratch my
head, and sing the *Ullagone*—when all of a
sudden the moon grew black, and I looked
up, and saw something for all the world as if
it was moving down between me and it, and I
could not tell what it was. Down it came
with a pounce, and looked at me full in the
face ; and what was it but an eagle? as fine a
one as ever flew from the kingdom of Kerry.
So he looked at me in the face, and says he to
me, ' Daniel O'Rourke,' says he, ' how do you
do ?' ' Very well, I thank you, sir,' says I :
' I hope you're well;' wondering out of my
senses all the time how an eagle came to speak
like a Christian. ' What brings you here,
Dan ?' says he. ' Nothing at all, sir,' says I ;
only I wish I was safe home again.' ' Is it
out of the island you want to go, Dan ?' says
he. ' 'Tis, sir,' says I : so I up and told him
how I had taken a drop too much, and fell

into the water; how I swam to the island; and how I got into the bog, and did not know my way out of it. ' Dan,' says he, after a minute's thought, ' though it was very improper for you to get drunk on Lady-day, yet as you are a decent, sober man, who 'tends mass well, and never flings stones at me or mine, nor cries out after us in the fields—my life for yours,' says he; ' so get up on my back, and grip me well for fear you'd fall off, and I'll fly you out of the bog.' ' I am afraid,' says I, ' your honour's making game of me; for who ever heard of riding a horseback on an eagle before?' ' 'Pon the honour of a gentleman,' says he, putting his right foot on his breast, ' I am quite in earnest; and so now either take my offer or starve in the bog —besides, I see that your weight is sinking the stone.'

" It was true enough as he said, for I found the stone every minute going from under me. I had no choice; so thinks I to myself, faint heart never won fair lady, and this is fair persuadance :—' I thank your honour,' says I, ' for the loan of your civility; and I'll take your kind offer.' I therefore mounted upon

the back of the eagle, and held him tight
enough by the throat, and up he flew in the
air like a lark.   Little I knew the trick he
was going to serve me.   Up—up—up—God
knows how far up he flew.   ' Why, then,'
said I to him—thinking he did not know the
right road home—very civilly, because why?—
I was in his power entirely ;—' sir,' says I,
' please your honour's glory, and with humble
submission to your better judgment, if you'd
fly down a bit, you're now just over my cabin,
and I could be put down there, and many
thanks to your worship.'

" ' *Arrah*, Dan,' said he, ' do you think me
a fool ? Look down in the next field, and don't
you see two men and a gun ? By my word it
would be no joke to be shot this way, to oblige
a drunken blackguard that I picked up off of
a *could* stone in a bog.'   ' Bother you,' said I
to myself, but I did not speak out, for where
was the use ? Well, sir, up he kept, flying,
flying, and I asking him every minute to fly
down, and all to no use.   ' Where in the
world are you going, sir ?' says I to him.
' Hold your tongue, Dan,' says he : ' mind
your own business, and don't be interfering

with the business of other people.' ' Faith, this is my business, I think,' says I. ' Be quiet, Dan,' says he: so I said no more.

"At last where should we come to, but to the moon itself. Now you can't see it from this, but there is, or there was in my time a reaping-hook sticking out of the side of the moon, this way (drawing the figure thus ⟳ on the ground with the end of his stick).

" ' Dan,' said the eagle, ' I'm tired with this long fly; I had no notion 'twas so far.' ' And my lord, sir,' said I, ' who in the world *axed* you to fly so far—was it I? did not I beg, and pray, and beseech you to stop half an hour ago?' ' There's no use talking, Dan,' said he; ' I'm tired bad enough, so you must get off, and sit down on the moon until I rest myself.' ' Is it sit down on the moon?' said I; ' is it upon that little round thing, then ? why, then, sure I'd fall off in a minute, and be *kilt* and spilt, and smashed all to bits: you are a vile deceiver-—so you are.' ' Not at all, Dan,' said he: ' you can catch fast hold of the reaping-hook that's sticking out of the side of the moon, and 'twill keep you up.' ' I won't, then,' said I. ' May be not,' said he, quite quiet. ' If you don't, my man, I shall just give you a shake, and one slap of my wing, and send you down to the ground, where every bone in your body will be smashed as small as a drop of dew on a cabbage-leaf in the morning.' ' Why, then, I'm in a fine way,' said I to myself, ' ever to have come along with the likes of you;' and so giving him a hearty curse in Irish, for fear he'd know what I said, I got off of his back with a heavy heart, took a hold of the reaping-hook, and sat down upon the moon, and a mighty cold seat it was, I can tell you that.

" When he had me there fairly landed, he turned about on me, and said, ' Good morning to you, Daniel O'Rourke,' said he: ' I think I've nicked you fairly now. You robbed my nest last year,' ('twas true enough for him, but how he found it out is hard to say), ' and in return you are freely welcome to cool your heels dangling upon the moon like a cockthrow.'

" ' Is that all, and is this the way you leave me, you brute, you?' says I. ' You ugly unnatural *baste*, and is this the way you serve me at last? Bad luck to yourself, with your

hook'd nose, and to all your breed, you black-
guard.' 'Twas all to no manner of use: he
spread out his great big wings, burst out a
laughing, and flew away like lightning. I
bawled after him to stop; but I might have
called and bawled for ever, without his minding
me. Away he went, and I never saw him
from that day to this—sorrow fly away with
him! You may be sure I was in a disconso-
late condition, and kept roaring out for the
bare grief, when all at once a door opened
right in the middle of the moon, creaking on
its hinges as if it had not been opened for a
month before. I suppose they never thought
of greasing 'em, and out there walks—who do
you think but the man in the moon? I knew
him by his bush.

"' Good morrow to you, Daniel O'Rourke,'
said he: 'How do you do?' 'Very well,
thank your honour,' said I. 'I hope your
honour's well.' 'What brought you here,
Dan?' said he. So I told him how I was a
little overtaken in liquor at the master's, and
how I was cast on a *dissolute* island, and how
I lost my way in the bog, and how the thief
of an eagle promised to fly me out of it, and

how instead of that he had fled me up to the moon.

" ' Dan,' said the man in the moon, taking a pinch of snuff when I was done, ' you must not stay here.' ' Indeed, sir,' says I, ' 'tis much against my will I 'm here at all ; but how am I to go back ?' ' That's your business,' said he, ' Dan : mine is to tell you that here you must not stay, so be off in less than no time.' ' I 'm doing no harm,' says I, ' only holding on hard by the reaping-hook, lest I fall off.' ' That's what you must not do, Dan,' says he. ' Pray, sir,' says I, ' may I ask how many you are in family, that you would not give a poor traveller lodging : I 'm sure 'tis not so often you 're troubled with strangers coming to see you, for 'tis a long way.' ' I 'm by myself, Dan,' says he ; ' but you 'd better let go the reaping-hook.' ' Faith, and with your leave,' says I, ' I 'll not let go the grip.' ' You had better, Dan,' says he again. ' Why, then, my little fellow,' says I, taking the whole weight of him with my eye from head to foot, ' there are two words to that bargain ; and I 'll not budge, but you may if you like.' ' We 'll see how that is to be,'

says he; and back he went, giving the door
such a great bang after him (for it was plain
he was huffed), that I thought the moon and
all would fall down with it.

"Well, I was preparing myself to try
strength with him, when back again he comes,
with the kitchen cleaver in his hand, and without saying a word, he gave two bangs to the
handle of the reaping-hook that was keeping
me up, and *whap!* it came in two. 'Good
morning to you, Dan,' says the spiteful little
old blackguard, when he saw me cleanly falling
down with a bit of the handle in my hand:
'I thank you for your visit, and fair weather
after you, Daniel.' I had not time to make
any answer to him, for I was tumbling over
and over, and rolling and rolling at the rate of
a fox-hunt. 'God help me,' says I, 'but this
is a pretty pickle for a decent man to be seen
in at this time of night : I am now sold fairly.'
The word was not out of my mouth, when
whiz ! what should fly by close to my ear but
a flock of wild geese ; and the *ould* gander,
who was their general, turning about his head,
cried out to me, ' Is that you, Dan ?' I was not
a bit daunted now at what he said, for I was

by this time used to all kinds of *bedevilment*, and, besides, I knew him of *ould*. 'Good morrow to you,' says he, 'Daniel O'Rourke: how are you in health this morning?' 'Very well, sir,' says I, 'I thank you kindly,' drawing my breath, for I was mightily in want of some. 'I hope your honour's the same.' 'I think 'tis falling you are, Daniel,' says he. 'You may say that, sir,' says I. 'And where are you going all the way so fast?' said the gander. So I told him how I had taken the drop, and how I came on the island, and how I lost my way in the bog, and how the thief of an eagle flew me up to the moon, and how the man in the moon turned me out. 'Dan,' said he, 'I'll save you: put out your hand and catch me by the leg, and I'll fly you home.' 'Sweet is your hand in a pitcher of honey, my jewel,' says I, though all the time I thought in myself that I don't much trust you; but there was no help, so I caught the gander by the leg, and away I and the other geese flew after him as fast as hops.

"We flew, and we flew, and we flew, until we came right over the wide ocean. I knew it well, for I saw Cape Clear to my right hand, sticking up out of the water. 'Ah! my lord,' said I to the goose, for I thought it best to keep a civil tongue in my head any way, 'fly to land if you please.' 'It is impossible, you see, Dan,' said he, 'for a while, because you see we are going to Arabia.' 'To Arabia!' said I; 'that's surely some place in foreign parts, far away. Oh! Mr. Goose: why then, to be sure, I'm a man to be pitied among you.' 'Whist, whist, you fool,' said he, 'hold your tongue; I tell you Arabia is a very decent sort of place, as like West Carbery as one egg is like another, only there is a little more sand there.'

" Just as we were talking, a ship hove in sight, scudding so beautiful before the wind: 'Ah! then, sir,' said I, 'will you drop me on the ship, if you please?' 'We are not fair over it,' said he. 'We are,' said I. 'We are not,' said he: 'If I dropped you now, you would go splash into the sea.' 'I would not,' says I; 'I know better than that, for it is just clean under us, so let me drop now at once.'

" ' If you must, you must,' said he. ' There,

take your own way ;' and he opened his claw, and faith he was right—sure enough I came down plump into the very bottom of the salt sea!   Down to the very bottom I went, and I gave myself up then for ever, when a whale walked up to me, scratching himself after his night's sleep, and looked me full in the face, and never the word did he say, but lifting up his tail, he splashed me all over again with the cold salt water, till there wasn't a dry stitch upon my whole carcass ; and I heard somebody saying—'twas a voice I knew too— ' Get up, you drunken brute, off of that :' and with that I woke up, and there was Judy with a tub full of water, which she was splashing all over me ;—for, rest her soul ! though she was a good wife, she never could bear to see me in drink, and had a bitter hand of her own.

" ' Get up,' said she again : ' and of all places in the parish, would no place *sarve* your turn to lie down upon but under the *ould* walls of Carrigaphooka ? an uneasy rest-ing I am sure you had of it.' And sure enough I had ; for I was fairly bothered out of my senses with eagles, and men of the moons, and flying ganders, and whales, driving me through bogs, and up to the moon, and down to the bottom of the green ocean. If I was in drink ten times over, long would it be before I'd lie down in the same spot again, I know that.

———

The tale of Daniel O'Rourke, the Irish Astolpho, is a very common one, and is here related according to the most authentic version. It has been pleasantly versified in six cantos of *ottava rima*, by Mr. S. Gosnell of Cork, in Blackwood's Magazine, where the localities of the gander-flight are much more copiously given :

" They bravely sped o'er Thoumuldeeshig's plain,
    And crossed the summit of Glendeeloch's mount,
Scudded along Lord Bantry's rich demesne,
    And poised a moment o'er Bosfordha's fount,
Then dash'd above the wilds of dark Drishane,
    And other grounds too numerous to recount.
For why should I such information purvey
For those who can procure H. Townsend's Survey?"
                                Canto vi. v. 12.

Every one must agree with Mr. Fogarty O'Fogarty

(under which *nom de guerre* the poem was written)
in the testimony he bears in his notes to the goodness
of the Bantry family, and the excellence of the Rev.
Mr. Townsend's Survey of the county Cork.

The catastrophe is altered a little, for some reasons
which will be found in the ingenious *Latin* verses at
the bottom of p. 432, vol. x. of Blackwood (Nov.
1821).

The following digressive extract may gratify the
reader, and affords a fair specimen of the writer's
powers :

*   *   *   *   *

" It were enough to make one's bosom bleed,
  To fancy only half the pain it were
To bound from cloud to cloud, and pant for breath ;
  No hope above—below a certain death.

" ' Oh ! then if ever I get home again,'
  He blubber'd forth, and wrung his horny hands,
' I 'll take my oath to quit *ould* Mulshinane,
  Or any other oath the priest demands :
But sure 'tis all no use.   Oh then ! oh then !
  I'll crack my neck below upon the sands,
Or ugly rocks, and wander there a ghost ;'
For he was moving fast towards the coast,

" That fringes thee, the far Atlantic sea.
  Oft have I wander'd on thy rugged shore
Ere the bright morn has bid thy vapours flee,
  And stay'd to listen to thy water's roar ;

Or wander'd on in sadness silently,
  Marking the tints the evening sunbeams wore;
Or idly musing, pick'd the pebbly sand,
Or cull'd the sea-weed on thy lovely strand.

" Oft in the bowels of some giant rock,
  That dares the storm, and scorns the tempest's
    wrath,
But cannot brave the long-continued shock
  Of calmer waters—have I chose my path,
And sometimes sat beneath the roofs that mock
  The hand of art.   Where is the man that hath
Once seen these wave-worn monuments of thee
Who loves not ocean's boundless majesty !

" Oft too has * * * * * wandered with me there ;
  And then, indeed, the caves, and strand, and sea,
And every earthly thing seem'd fresh and fair ;
  For she was every earthly thing to me ;
Yes ! she was what a love-sick swain would dare
  To dub an angel or divinity !—
She 's gone !—but think not, reader, to the tomb :
She ran off lately with her father's groom."

Canto v.

  The adventures of Daniel O'Rourke have been introduced to an English audience by that inimitable
imitator Mr. Mathews, in one of his lively entertain-
ments ; and it appears surprising that Farley, the
magic genius of Covent Garden, should have so long

overlooked a story so well calculated for pantomimic effect.

The Castle of Carrigaphooka, or the Phooka's Rock, beneath the walls of which O'Rourke was discovered by his wife, is doubtless the one of that name situated about two miles west of Macroom. Doctor Smith (History of Cork, vol. i. p. 190) seems to have written his description of this castle under the influence of Phooka power—with all the horror of being dashed to pieces staring him full in the face; for he first speaks of " dangerous and slippery footing, where no more than one person at a time can climb," and then assures us that " this rock is quite inaccessible on every other side, and hangs frightfully over the Sullane, which runs foaming at the foot of it through a craggy channel."

Those who have been so fortunate as to view Carrigaphooka free from fairy delusion will read the doctor's account with wonder—the rock on which the castle is built being neither difficult of ascent, nor situated by any means close to the water.

THE CROOKENED BACK.

PEGGY BARRETT was once tall, well-shaped, and comely. She was in her youth remarkable for two qualities, not often found together, of being the most thrifty housewife, and the best dancer in her native village of Ballyhooley. But she is now upwards of sixty years old; and during the last ten years of her life, she has never been able to stand upright. Her back is bent nearly to a level; yet she has the freest use of all her limbs that can be enjoyed in such a posture; her health is good, and her mind vigorous; and, in the family of her eldest son, with whom she has lived since the death of her husband, she performs all the domestic services which her age, and the infirmity just mentioned, allow. She washes the potatoes, makes the fire, sweeps the house (labours in which she good-

humouredly says " she finds her crooked
back mighty convenient"), plays with the
children, and tells stories to the family and
their neighbouring friends, who often collect
round her son's fireside to hear them during
the long winter evenings.   Her powers of
conversation are highly extolled, both for humour and in narration ; and anecdotes of droll
or awkward incidents, connected with the posture in which she has been so long fixed, as
well as the history of the occurrence to which
she owes that misfortune, are favourite topics
of her discourse.   Among other matters she
is fond of relating how, on a certain day, at
the close of a bad harvest, when several tenants
of the estate on which she lived concerted in
a field a petition for an abatement of rent,
they placed the paper on which they wrote
upon her back, which was found no very in-
convenient substitute for a table.

Peggy, like all experienced story-tellers,
suited her tales, both in length and subject,
to the audience and the occasion.   She knew
that, in broad daylight, when the sun shines
brightly, and the trees are budding, and
the birds singing around us, when men and

women, like ourselves, are moving and speaking, employed variously in business or amusement; she knew, in short (though certainly without knowing or much caring wherefore), that when we are engaged about the realities of life and nature, we want that spirit of credulity, without which tales of the deepest interest will lose their power. At such times Peggy was brief, very particular as to facts, and never dealt in the marvellous. But round the blazing hearth of a Christmas evening, when infidelity is banished from all companies, at least in low and simple life, as a quality, to say the least of it, out of season; when the winds of " dark December" whistled bleakly round the walls, and almost through the doors of the little mansion, reminding its inmates, that as the world is vexed by elements superior to human power, so it may be visited by beings of a superior nature;— at such times would Peggy Barrett give full scope to her memory, or her imagination, or both; and upon one of these occasions, she gave the following circumstantial account of " the crookening of her back."

" It was of all days in the year, the day

before May-day, that I went out to the garden
to weed the potatoes. I would not have gone
out that day, but I was dull in myself, and
sorrowful, and wanted to be alone; all the
boys and girls were laughing and joking in
the house, making goaling-balls and dressing
out ribbons for the mummers next day. I
couldn't bear it. 'Twas only at the Easter
that was then past (and that's ten years last
Easter—I won't forget the time), that I
buried my poor man; and I thought how gay
and joyful I was, many a long year before
that, at the May-eve before our wedding,
when with Robin by my side, I sat cutting
and sewing the ribbons for the goaling-ball
I was to give the boys on the next day, proud
to be preferred above all the other girls of the
banks of the Blackwater, by the handsomest
boy and the best hurler in the village; so I
left the house and went to the garden. I
staid there all the day, and didn't come home
to dinner. I don't know how it was, but
somehow I continued on, weeding, and thinking sorrowfully enough, and singing over
some of the old songs that I sung many and
many a time in the days that are gone, and

for them that never will come back to me to
hear them. The truth is, I hated to go and
sit silent and mournful among the people in
the house, that were merry and young, and
had the best of their days before them. 'Twas
late before I thought of returning home, and
I did not leave the garden till some time after
sunset. The moon was up; but though there
wasn't a cloud to be seen, and though a star
was winking here and there in the sky, the
day wasn't long enough gone to have it clear
moonlight; still it shone enough to make every
thing on one side of the heavens look pale and
silvery-like; and the thin white mist was just
beginning to creep along the fields. On the
other side, near where the sun was set, there
was more of daylight, and the sky looked
angry, red, and fiery through the trees, like as
if it was lighted up by a great town burning
below. Every thing was as silent as a churchyard, only now and then one could hear far
off a dog barking, or a cow lowing after being
milked. There wasn't a creature to be seen
on the road or in the fields. I wondered at
this first, but then I remembered it was May-
eve, and that many a thing, both good and

bad, would be wandering about that night, and that I ought to shun danger as well as others. So I walked on as quick as I could, and soon came to the end of the demesne wall, where the trees rise high and thick at each side of the road, and almost meet at the top. My heart misgave me when I got under the shade. There was so much light let down from the opening above, that I could see about a stone-throw before me. All of a sudden I heard a rustling among the branches, on the right side of the road, and saw something like a small black goat, only with long wide horns turned out instead of being bent backwards, standing upon its hind legs upon the top of the wall, and looking down on me. My breath was stopped, and I couldn't move for near a minute. I couldn't help, somehow, keeping my eyes fixed on it ; and it never stirred, but kept looking in the same fixed way down at me. At last I made a rush, and went on; but I didn't go ten steps, when I saw the very same sight, on the wall to the left of me, standing in exactly the same manner, but three or four times as high, and almost as tall as the tallest man. The horns

looked frightful : it gazed upon me as before ;
my legs shook, and my teeth chattered, and I
thought I would drop down dead every moment.   At last I felt as if I was obliged to
go on—and on I went ; but it was without
feeling how I moved, or whether my legs
carried me.   Just as I passed the spot where
this frightful thing was standing, I heard a
noise as if something sprung from the wall,
and felt like as if a heavy animal plumped
down upon me, and held with the fore feet
clinging to my shoulder, and the hind ones
fixed in my gown, that was folded and pinned
up behind me.   'Tis the wonder of my life
ever since how I bore the shock ; but so it
was, I neither fell, nor even staggered with
the weight, but walked on as if I had the
strength of ten men, though I felt as if I
couldn't help moving, and couldn't stand still
if I wished it.   Though I gasped with fear,
I knew as well as I do now what I was doing.
I tried to cry out, but couldn't ; I tried to
run, but wasn't able ; I tried to look back,
but my head and neck were as if they were
screwed in a vice.   I could barely roll my
eyes on each side, and then I could see, as

clearly and plainly as if it was in the broad
light of the blessed sun, a black and cloven
foot planted upon each of my shoulders.   I
heard a low breathing in my ear; I felt, at
every step I took, my leg strike back against
the feet of the creature that was on my back.
Still I could do nothing but walk straight on.
At last I came within sight of the house, and
a welcome sight it was to me, for I thought I
would be released when I reached it.   I soon
came close to the door, but it was shut; I
looked at the little window, but it was shut
too, for they were more cautious about May-
eve than I was; I saw the light inside, through
the chinks of the door; I heard 'em talking
and laughing within; I felt myself at three
yards distance from them that would die to
save me;—and may the Lord save me from
ever again feeling what I did that night, when
I found myself held by what couldn't be good
nor friendly, but without the power to help
myself, or to call to my friends, or to put out
my hand to knock, or even to lift my leg to
strike the door, and let them know that I was
outside it !   'Twas as if my hands grew to my
sides, and my feet were glued to the ground,

or had the weight of a rock fixed to them.
At last I thought of blessing myself ; and my
right hand, that would do nothing else, did
that for me.   Still the weight remained on
my back, and all was as before.   I blessed
myself again : 'twas still all the same.   I then
gave myself up for lost : but I blessed myself
a third time, and my hand no sooner finished
the sign, than all at once I felt the burthen
spring off of my back ; the door flew open as
if a clap of thunder burst it, and I was pitched
forward on my forehead, in upon the middle
of the floor.   When I got up, my back was
crookened, and I never stood straight from
that night to this blessed hour."

There was a pause when Peggy Barrett
finished.   Those who had heard the story
before had listened with a look of half satisfied interest, blended, however, with an expression of that serious and solemn feeling,
which always attends a tale of supernatural
wonders, how often soever told.   They moved
upon their seats out of the posture in which
they had remained fixed during the narrative,
and sat in an attitude which denoted that

their curiosity as to the cause of this strange occurrence had been long since allayed. Those to whom it was before unknown still retained their look and posture of strained attention, and anxious but solemn expectation. A grandson of Peggy's, about nine years old (not the child of the son with whom she lived), had never before heard the story. As it grew in interest, he was observed to cling closer and closer to the old woman's side ; and at the close he was gazing stedfastly at her, with his body bent back across her knees, and his face turned up to hers, with a look, through which a disposition to weep seemed contending with curiosity. After a moment's pause, he could no longer restrain his impatience, and catching her gray locks in one hand, while the tear of dread and wonder was just dropping from his eyelash, he cried, " Granny, what was it ?"

The old woman smiled first at the elder part of her audience, and then at her grandson, and patting him ʻon the forehead, she said, " It was the Phooka."—

Hurling, or goal, a game before alluded to, has some resemblance to the Scotch game of golf; but the ball is much larger, being in general four inches in diameter: the instruments used are larger also, and not turned angularly at the bottom, but fashioned thus:

The number of hurlers may be twenty, or even a hundred, or more. It is usually played in a large level field, by two parties of nearly balanced powers, either as to number or dexterity, and the object of each is to strike the ball over one of two opposite hedges, assigned respectively before the game begins. " *Bàire comórtais*" signifies, according to an expression quite Irish, " two sides of a country (that is, a certain number of the youth of each), who meet to goal against one another," generally on a Sunday, or holiday, after prayers. On these occasions, instead of the hedges of a field, two conspicuous landmarks (a road and a wood, for instance) are assigned, and the game is contested in the space between them with a heat and vigour which often lead to a serious and bloody conflict, especially if one of those clannish feuds, so prevalent among the peasantry of Ireland, should exist between the opposing parties; the hurley, or hurlet, being an effective and desperate weapon. The game derives one of its names from the instrument employed; the other, goal, is evidently taken from the boundary or winning-mark, which

X

must be passed by the ball before the game can be won.

Mummers, in Ireland, are clearly a family of the same race with those festive bands, termed Morrice dancers, in England. They appear at all seasons in Ireland, but May-day is their favourite and proper festival. They consist of a number, varying according to circumstances, of the girls and young men of the village or neighbourhood, usually selected for their good looks, or their proficiency,—the females in the dance, the youths in hurling and other athletic exercises. They march in procession, two abreast, and in three divisions; the young men in the van and the rear, dressed in white or other gay-coloured jackets or vests, and decorated with ribbons on their hats and sleeves; the young women are dressed also in light-coloured garments, and two of them bear each a holly bush, in which are hung several new hurling-balls, the May-day present of the girls to the youths of the village. The bush is decorated with a profusion of long ribbons, or paper cut in imitation, which adds greatly to the gay and joyous, yet strictly rural, appearance of the whole. The procession is always preceded by music; sometimes of the bagpipe, but more commonly of a military fife, with the addition of a drum or tamboureen. A clown is, of course, in attendance: he wears a frightful mask, and bears a long pole, with shreds of cloth nailed to the end of it, like a mop, which ever and anon he dips in a pool of water, or puddle, and besprinkles such of the crowd as press upon his companions, much to the delight of the younger spectators, who greet his exploits with loud and repeated shouts and laughter. The Mummers, during the day, parade the neighbouring villages, or go from one gentleman's seat to another, dancing before the mansion-house, and receiving money. The evening, of course, terminates with drinking.

May-eve is considered a time of peculiar danger. The " *good people*" are supposed then to possess the power and the inclination to do all sorts of mischief without the slightest restraint. The " *evil eye*" is then also deemed to have more than its usual vigilance and malignity ; and the nurse, who would walk in the open air with a child in her arms, would be reprobated as a monster. Youth and loveliness are thought to be especially exposed to peril. It is therefore a natural consequence, that not one woman in a thousand appears abroad : but it must not be understood that the want of beauty affords any protection. The grizzled locks of age do not always save the cheek from a *blast ;* neither is the brawny hand of the roughest ploughman exempt from a similar visitation. The *blast* is a large round tumor, which is thought to rise suddenly upon the part affected, from the baneful breath cast on it by one of the "good people" in a moment of vindictive or capricious malice. May-day is called *la na Beal tina*, and May-eve *neen na Beal tina*,—that is, day and eve of Beal's fire, from its having been, in heathen times, consecrated to the god Beal, or Belus ; whence

x 2

also the month of May is termed in Irish " *Mi na Beal-tine*." The ceremony practised on May-eve, of making the cows leap over lighted straw, or faggots, has been generally traced to the worship of that deity. It is now vulgarly used in order to save the milk from being pilfered by " the good people."

Another custom prevalent on May-eve is the painful and mischievous one of stinging with nettles. In the south of Ireland it is the common practice for school-boys, on that day, to consider themselves privileged to run wildly about with a bunch of nettles, striking at the face and hands of their companions, or of such other persons as they think they may venture to assault with impunity.

THE HAUNTED CASTLE.

The Christmas of 1820 I had promised to spend at Island Bawn Horne, in the county Tipperary, and I arrived there from Dublin on the 18th of December : I was so tired with travelling, that for two days after I remained quietly by the fireside, reading Mr. Luttrell's exquisite *jeu d'esprit*, " Advice to Julia."

The first person I met on venturing out was old Pierce Grace, the smith, one of whose sons always attends me on my shooting excursions : " Welcome to these parts," said Pierce : " I was waiting all day yesterday, expecting to see your honour."

" I am obliged to you, Piercy ; I was with the mistress."

" So I heard, your honour, which made me *delicate* of asking to see you. John is ready to attend you, and he has taken count of a power of birds."

The following morning, gun in hand, I sallied forth on a ramble through the country, attended by old Pierce's son John. After some hours' walking, we got into that winding vale, through which the Curriheen flows, and beheld the castle of Ballinatotty, whose base it washes, in the distance.

The castle is still in good preservation, and was once a place of some strength. It was the residence of a powerful and barbarous race, named O'Brian, who were the scourge and terror of the country. Tradition has preserved the names of three of the family : Phelim *lauve lauider* (with the strong hand), his son Morty *lauve ne fulle* (of the bloody hand), and grandson Donough *gontrough na thaha* (without mercy in the dark), whose atrocities threw the bloody deeds of his predecessors completely into the shade. Of him it is related, that in an incursion on a neighbouring chieftain's territories, he put all the men and children to the sword; and having ordered the women to be half buried in the earth, he had them torn in pieces by bloodhounds ! " Just to frighten his enemies," added my narrator. The deed, however, which drew down upon him the deepest execration was the murder of his wife, *Aileen na gruig buie* (Ellen with the yellow hair), celebrated throughout the country for her beauty and affability. She was the daughter of O'Kennedy of Lisnabonney Castle, and refused an offer of marriage made to her by Donough; being supported in her refusal by her brother Brian Oge, *skeul roa more* (the persuasive speaking) she was allowed to remain single by her father, and his death seemed to relieve her from the fear of compulsion; but in less than a month after, Brian Oge was murdered by an unknown hand; on which occasion Ellen composed that affecting and well-known keen, *Thaw ma cree qeen bruitha le focth* (My heart is sick and heavy with cold). As she returned from her brother's funeral, Donough waylaid the procession : her attendants were slaughtered, and she was compelled to become his wife. Ellen ultimately perished by his hand, being, it is said, thrown out of the bower window for having charged him with the murder of her brother. The spot where she fell is shown; and on the anniversary of

her death (the second Tuesday in August)
her spirit is believed to visit it.

Giving John my gun, I proceeded to examine the castle: a window on the south side
is pointed out as the one from which Ellen
was precipitated; but it appears more probable that it was from the battlement over it,
because from the circumstance of there being
corresponding holes in the masonry above and
below, it is evident that the iron-work must
have been let in at the time of building, and
that it did not open.

Having satisfied my curiosity, I was about
to quit the room, when observing an opening
in the south-east corner, I was tempted to ex-
plore it, and found a small staircase, which
led to a sleeping recess. This recess was oc-
cupied by a terrier and a litter of whelps.
Enraged at my intrusion, the dam attacked
me, and having no means of defence, I made
a hasty retreat. How far the angry animal
pursued me, I cannot say; for in my precipi-
tate flight, as I descended the second staircase, my foot slipped, and I tumbled through
a broad opening into what had probably been

the guardroom : but the evil I now encoun-
tered far exceeded that from which I fled,
for the floor of this room was in the last stage
of decay : a cat could hardly have crossed it
in safety; and the violence with which I came
on it carried me through its rotten surface
with as little opposition as I should have received from a spider's web, and down I
plunged into the gloomy depth beneath.   A
number of bats, whom my sudden entrance
disturbed, flapped their wings, and flitted
round me.

*   *   *   *   *   *   *

When my recollection returned, a confused
sound of voices struck my ears, and I then
distinguished a female, who in a tone of the
greatest sweetness and tenderness said, " It's
not wanting—it's not wanting—the life's coming into him." Opening my eyes, I found my
head resting in the lap of a peasant girl, about
eighteen, who was chafing my temples. Health
or anxiety gave a glow to her mild and ex-
pressive features, and her light-brown hair

was simply parted on her forehead. On one side stood an old man, her father, with a bunch of keys, and on the other knelt John Grace, with a cup of whiskey, which she was applying to recover me. Looking round, I perceived that we were on the rocks near the castle, and the river was flowing at our feet. Various exclamations of joy followed; and the old man desiring John to rinse the cup, insisted on my swallowing some of the " *cratur*," which having done and got up, I returned my thanks, and offered a small pecuniary recompense, which they would not accept, " For sure and certain they would have gladly done *tin* times as much for his honour without fee or reward."

I then inquired how they came to find me. " Why, as I thought your honour," said John Grace, " would be some time looking into the crooks and corners of the place, I just walked round to talk to Honny here; and so we were talking over matters, and Honny was just saying to me that the boys (meaning her brothers) were just baling the streams, and had got a can of large eels, and that if I thought the

mistress would like them, I could take as
many as I pleased, and welcome, when we
heard a great crash of a noise. ' What's
that?' says I. ' I suppose,' says Honny, ' 'tis
the *ould* gray horse that has fallen down and
is *kilt ;* or may be it's Paddy's Spanish dog
Sagur that's coursing about : there's no
thinking the plague he gives me—they're
both in the turf-house, fornent us' (meaning,
your honour, the underpart of the castle that
Cromwell made a breach into, and beside
which the cabin stands).

"In comes Tim Hagerty there, and then
we heard a screech ! ' 'Tis his honour's voice,'
says I ; ' he has fallen through the flooring !'
' Oh ! if he has,' says Tim, ' I 'm lost and
undone for ever: and didn't the Squire no
later than last Monday week bid me build up
the passage, or that somebody he said would
be *kilt*—and sure I meant to do it to-morrow.'
Well, your honour, we got a light, and we
saw the Phookas that caused your fall all
flying about, in the shape of bats, and there
we found your honour, and the turf all over
the place ; and for sure and certain, if you

hadn't first come on it, instead of the bones that Paddy and Mick have been gathering against the young master's wedding, you would have been smashed entirely. All of us were mad and distracted about the wicked Phookas that were in the place, and could not tell what to do; but Honny said to bring you out into the open air; and so we did; and there, your honour, by care and management, praise be to God, we brought you round again; but it was a desperate long time first, and myself thought it was as good as all over with you."

The reader, it is to be hoped, will not be able to form a perfect notion of the Phooka; for indistinctness, like that of an imperfectly remembered dream, seems to constitute its character, and yet Irish superstition makes the Phooka palpable to the touch. To its agency the peasantry usually ascribe accidental falls; and hence many rocky pits and caverns are called Poula Phooka, or the hole of the Phooka. A waterfall of this name, formed by the Liffey, is enumerated among " the sights" of the county Wicklow.

An odd notion connected with the Phooka is, that the country people will tell their children after Michaelmas day not to eat blackberries, and they attribute the decay in them, which about that time commences, to the operation of the Phooka.

FAIRY LEGENDS.

THIERNA NA OGE.

" On Lough-Neagh's bank, as the fisherman strays
    When the clear cold eve's declining,
    He sees the round towers of other days
    In the wave beneath him shining."

                                        MOORE.

THIERNA NA OGE.

FIOR USGA.

A LITTLE way beyond the Gallows Green
of Cork, and just outside the town, there is a
great lough of water, where people in the
winter go and skate for the sake of diversion ;
but the sport above the water is nothing to
what is under it, for at the very bottom of
this lough there are buildings and gardens,
far more beautiful than any now to be seen,
and how they came there was in this manner :

Long before Saxon foot pressed Irish ground,
there was a great king, called Corc, whose palace stood where the lough now is, in a round
green valley, that was just a mile about. In
the middle of the court-yard was a spring of

Y

fair water, so pure, and so clear, that it was
the wonder of all the world.   Much did the
king rejoice at having so great a curiosity
within his palace ; but as people came in crowds
from far and near to draw the precious water
of this spring, he was sorely afraid that in
time it might become dry ; so he caused a high
wall to be built up round it, and would allow
nobody to have the water, which was a very
great loss to the poor people living about the
palace.   Whenever he wanted any for himself, he would send his daughter to get it, not
liking to trust his servants with the key of
the well door, fearing they may give some
away.

One night the king gave a grand entertainment, and there were many great princes
present, and lords and nobles without end ;
and there were wonderful doings throughout
the palace : there were bonfires, whose blaze
reached up to the very sky ; and dancing was
there, to such sweet music, that it ought to
have waked up the dead out of their graves ;
and feasting was there in the greatest of plenty
for all who came ; nor was there one turned
away from the palace gates—but " you're

welcome—you're welcome, heartily," was the
porter's salute for all.

Now it happened that at this grand entertainment there was one young prince above
all the rest mighty comely to behold, and as
tall and as straight as ever eye would wish to
look on. Right merrily did he dance that
night with the old king's daughter, wheeling
here, and wheeling there, as light as a feather,
and footing it away to the admiration of every
one. The musicians played the better for
seeing their dancing; and they danced as if
their lives depended upon it. After all this
dancing came the supper; and the young
prince was seated at table by the side of his
beautiful partner, who smiled upon him as
often as he spoke to her; and that was by no
means so often as he wished, for he had constantly to turn to the company and thank
them for the many compliments passed upon
his fair partner and himself.

In the midst of this banquet, one of the
great lords said to King Corc, "May it please
your majesty, here is every thing in abundance
that heart can wish for, both to eat and drink,
except water."

" Water !" said the king, mightily pleased at some one calling for that of which purposely there was a want : " water shall you have, my lord, speedily, and that of such a delicious kind, that I challenge all the world to equal it. Daughter," said he, " go fetch some in the golden vessel which I caused to be made for the purpose."

The king's daughter, who was called Fior Usga, (which signifies, in English, Spring Water,) did not much like to be told to perform so menial a service before so many people ; and though she did not venture to refuse the commands of her father, yet hesitated to obey him, and looked down upon the ground. The king, who loved his daughter very much, seeing this, was sorry for what he had desired her to do, but having said the word, he was never known to recall it ; he therefore thought of a way to make his daughter go speedily and fetch the water, and it was by proposing that the young prince her partner should go along with her. Accordingly, with a loud voice, he said, " Daughter, I wonder not at your fearing to go alone so late at night ; but I doubt not the young prince at your side will go with you." The prince was not displeased at hearing this; and taking the golden vessel in one hand, with the other led the king's daughter out of the hall, while all present gazed after them with delight.

When they came to the spring of water, in the court-yard of the palace, the fair Usga unlocked the door with the greatest care, and stooping down with the golden vessel to take some of the water out of the well, found the vessel so heavy, that she lost her balance and fell in. The young prince tried in vain to save her, for the water rose and rose so fast, that the entire court-yard was speedily covered with it, and he hastened back almost in a state of distraction to the king.

The door of the well being left open, the water, which had been so long confined, rejoiced at obtaining its liberty, rushed forth incessantly, every moment rising higher and higher, and was in the hall of the entertainment as soon as the young prince himself, so that when he attempted to speak to the king he was up to his neck in water. At length the water rose to such a height, that it filled the entire of the green valley in which the king's palace stood, and so the present lough of Cork was formed.

Yet the king and his guests were not drowned, as would now happen, if such an awful inundation took place; neither was his daughter, the fair Usga, who returned to the banquet hall the very next night after this dreadful event; and every night since the same entertainment and dancing goes on in the palace at the bottom of the lough, and will last until some one has the luck to bring up out of it the golden vessel which was the cause of all this mischief.

Nobody can doubt that it was a judgment upon the king for his shutting up the well in the court-yard from the poor people: and if there are any who do not credit my story, they may go and see the lough of Cork, for there it is to be seen to this day; the road to Kinsale passes at one side of it; and when its waters are low and clear, the tops of towers and stately buildings may be plainly viewed in the bottom by those who have good eyesight, without the help of spectacles.

Stories of buildings beneath the waters have originated some in real events, as where towns have been swallowed by earthquakes, and lakes formed where they had stood; or where the sea, by gradual encroachment, has covered the land and the buildings on it; others, perhaps, from optical illusion, where the shadows of the mountains and the various and fantastic forms of the clouds are reflected from the calm and unruffled bosom of a lake. " If," said a peasant to an officer lately quartered in the west of Ireland, " if, on a fine summer's evening, when the sun is just sinking behind the mountains, you go to the lough, and get on a little bank that hangs over it on the west side, and stoop down and look into the water, you'll see the finest sight in the whole world—for you'll see under you in the water, as plain as you see me, a great city, with palaces and churches, and long streets and squares in it." There was doubtless some legend, as there always is, connected with this lake, but the peasant was not acquainted with it.

Giraldus Cambrensis takes notice of the tradition that Lough Neagh had been formerly a fountain, which overflowed the whole country, and the following passage of that writer has been frequently quoted : " Piscatores aquæ illius turres ecclesiasticas, quæ more patrio arctæ sunt et altæ, necnon et rotundæ, sub undis manifeste sereno tempore conspiciunt et extraneis transeuntibus reique causas admirantibus frequenter ostendunt."

In that most absurd book, O'Flaherty's Ogygia, we are informed, on the authority of an old Irish poem, that there were only three loughs or lakes in Ireland on the arrival of Partholan, and the dates of the appearance, overflowing, and stagnation of many others, are given with all due attention to annomundane chronology. "That we may be the more inclined to give credit to the irruptions of those lakes," writes the profound O'Flaherty (vol. ii. cap. xvii.), "Dionysius Halycarnassæus, who flourished a little before the birth of Christ, in the reign of Augustus, has recorded that the vestiges of the house of Attadius, king of the Latins, were to be seen in his time in a transparent lake."

For a city gradually covered by the sea, see the account of Mahabalipoor in that gallery of splendid poetic pictures, "The Curse of Kehama." The reader may not be displeased at being presented with the following passage from it :

" Now the ancient towers appear'd at last,
  Their golden summits in the noonday ray
  Shone o'er the dark green deep that roll'd between,
  For domes and pinnacles and spires were seen
  Peering above the sea—a mournful sight.
  Well might the sad beholder ween from thence
  What works of wonder the devouring wave
  Had swallow'd there, when monuments so brave
  Bore record of their old magnificence."

CORMAC AND MARY.

" She is not dead—she has no grave—
  But lives beneath Lough Corrib's water ;
And in the murmur of each wave
  Methinks I catch the songs I taught her."

Thus many an evening by its shore
  Sat Cormac raving wild and lowly ;
Still idly mutt'ring o'er and o'er,
  " She lives, detain'd by spells unholy.

" Death claims her not, too fair for earth,
  Her spirit lives—alien of heaven ;
Nor will it know a second birth
  When sinful mortals are forgiven !

" Cold is this rock—the wind comes chill,
  And mists the gloomy waters cover ;
But oh ! her soul is colder still—
  To lose her God —to leave her lover !"

The lake was in profound repose,
    Yet one white wave came gently curling,
And as it reach'd the shore, arose
    Dim figures—banners gay unfurling.

Onward they move, an airy crowd:
    Through each thin form a moonlight ray
        shone;
While spear and helm, in pageant proud,
    Appear in liquid undulation.

Bright barbed steeds curvetting tread
    Their trackless way with antic capers;
And curtain clouds hang overhead,
    Festoon'd by rainbow-colour'd vapours.

And when a breath of air would stir
    That drapery of Heaven's own wreathing,
Light wings of prismy gossamer
    Just moved and sparkled to the breathing.

Nor wanting was the choral song,
    Swelling in silv'ry chimes of sweetness;
To sound of which this subtile throng
    Advanced in playful grace and fleetness.

With music's strain, all came and went
    Upon poor Cormac's doubting vision;
Now rising in wild merriment,
    Now softly fading in derision.

" Christ, save her soul," he boldly cried;
    And when that blessed name was spoken,
Fierce yells and fiendish shrieks replied,
    And vanish'd all,—the spell was broken.

And now on Corrib's lonely shore,
    Freed by his word from power of faëry,
To life, to love, restored once more,
    Young Cormac welcomes back his Mary.

———————

This ballad has appeared before in a periodical
publication; but it is now reprinted, as the Legend on
which it is founded was originally collected with the
others contained in this volume, and its versification
was merely an experiment.

Gervase of Tilbury mentions, in his Otia Imperialia,
certain water spirits, called *Dracæ*, who allured young
women and children into their habitations beneath
lakes and rivers. It was supposed that any pious
exclamation had the power of breaking the charm by
which fairies detained those whom they had carried
off;—a black-hafted knife was considered as peculiarly

serviceable on such occasions, if it should be necessary to grapple with the evil ones ;—turning the coat, or cloak, was also recommended before such service. Bishop Corbet, in his Iter Boreale, thus alludes to this superstition :

" —————— William found
    A means for our deliv'rance : *turne your cloakes*,
    Quoth hee, for Pucke is busy in these oakes ;
    If ever wee at Bosworth will be found,
    Then *turne your cloakes*, for this is fairy ground."

Lough Corrib is situated in the county Galway, and is about twenty miles in length, and at the broadest part eleven. It is so contracted in the middle as to appear like two lakes.

THE LEGEND OF LOUGH GUR.

LARRY COTTER had a small farm on one side of Lough Gur, and was thriving in it, for he was an industrious proper sort of man, who would have lived quietly and soberly to the end of his days, but for the misfortune that came upon him, and you shall hear how that was. He had as nice a bit of meadowland, down by the waterside, as ever a man would wish for; but its growth was spoiled entirely on him, and no one could tell how.

One year after the other it was all ruined just in the same way: the bounds were well made up, and not a stone of them was disturbed; neither could his neighbours' cattle have been guilty of the trespass, for they were spancelled *; but however it was done, the grass of the meadow was destroyed, which was a great loss to Larry.

* Spancelled—fettered.

" What in the wide world shall I do ?"
said Larry Cotter to his neighbour Tom
Welch, who was a very decent sort of man
himself : " that bit of meadow-land, which I
am paying the great rent for, is doing nothing
at all to make it for me ; and the times are
bitter bad, without the help of that to make
them worse."

" 'Tis true for you, Larry," replied Welch :
" the times are bitter bad—no doubt of that ;
but may be if you were to watch by night,
you might make out all about it : sure there's
Mick and Terry, my two boys, will watch
with you ; for 'tis a thousand pities any honest
man like you should be ruined in such a
scheming way."

Accordingly, the following night, Larry
Cotter, with Welch's two sons, took their
station in a corner of the meadow. It was
just at the full of the moon, which was shining
beautifully down upon the lake, that was as
calm all over as the sky itself ; not a cloud
was there to be seen any where, nor a sound
to be heard, but the cry of the corncreaks
answering one another across the water.

" Boys ! boys !" said Larry, " look there !

look there ! but for your lives don't make a bit of noise, nor stir a step till I say the word."

They looked, and saw a great fat cow, followed by seven milk-white heifers, moving on the smooth surface of the lake towards the meadow.

" 'Tis not Tim Dwyer the piper's cow, any way, that danced all the flesh off her bones," whispered Mick to his brother.

" Now, boys !" said Larry Cotter, when he saw the fine cow and her seven white heifers fairly in the meadow, " get between them and the lake if you can, and, no matter who they belong to, we'll just put them into the pound."

But the cow must have overheard Larry speaking, and down she went in a great hurry to the bank of the lake, and into it with her, before all their eyes : away made the seven heifers after her, but the boys got down to the bank before them, and work enough they had to drive them up from the lake to Larry Cotter.

Larry drove the seven heifers, and beautiful beasts they were, to the pound ; but after he had them there for three days, and could hear of no owner, he took them out, and put them up in a field of his own. There he kept them, and they were thriving mighty well with him, until one night the gate of the field was left open, and in the morning the seven heifers were gone. Larry could not get any account of them after; and, beyond all doubt, it was back into the lake they went. Wherever they came from, or to whatever world they belonged, Larry Cotter never had a crop of grass off the meadow through their means. So he took to drink, fairly out of the grief; and it was the drink that killed him, they say.

There is a lake in the county Tipperary, not far from Cahir, called Lough na Bo, or the Lake of the Cow, from a Legend somewhat similar to that of Lough Gur. The horns of this cow are said to be so long, that, when the water is low, the tips of them may be plainly seen above it.

The Lake of Blarney, popular song informs us, is likewise

"———————— stored with perches
And comely eels in its verdant mud,
Besides good leeches, and groves of beeches
All ranged in order for to guard its flood."

Notwithstanding such guardianship, even out of that lake two cows have been seen to proceed, which are known to commit considerable damage in the adjacent meadow-land and corn-fields.

In addition to these subaqueous cows, every seven years " a great gentleman," to use the words of the narrator, comes out of the Lough of Blarney, and walks two or three miles from it in the hopes that some one will speak to him; but as no person dares to do so, he has always returned into the lough, and seven years elapse before he again appears.

This " great gentleman" is doubtless an Earl of Clancarthy, anxious to impart the means of discovering his plate chest, which, according to tradition, was flung into the lake to prevent its falling into the hands of the besiegers of his castle.

The name given to the present section is " Thierna na Oge," or the Country of Youth, from the belief that those who dwell in regions under the water are not affected by the movements of time. Barry, the historical painter, who was a native of Cork, used to relate to his friends an Irish fairy legend which closely resembled the Adventures of Porsenna, king of Russia, published in the sixth volume of Dodsley's Poetical Collection, and had some similarity to the subsequent tale of " The Enchanted Lake." Porsenna was carried off by Zephyr to a delightful region, with the sovereign princess of which realm (by whom he is taken for a phœnix) he remains, according to his belief, only a short time. Being anxious to return to earth,

" He ask'd how many charming hours were flown
Since on her slave her heav'n of beauty shone ?
' Should I consult my heart,' cried he, ' the rate
Were small—a week would be the utmost date :
But when my mind reflects on actions past,
And counts its joys, time must have fled more fast—
Perhaps I might have said three months are gone.'
' Three months !' replied the fair, ' three months alone :
Know that three hundred years have roll'd away
Since at my feet my lovely phœnix lay.'
' Three hundred years !' re-echoed back the prince :
' A whole three hundred years completed since
I landed here !' "—p. 219.

On his return to earth, he is overtaken by all-con-
quering Time, to whom he had so long played truant,
and becomes his victim.

The writer is indebted for this anecdote of Barry
to Mr. D'Israeli, from whose various and kind communications he has derived material assistance.

THE ENCHANTED LAKE.

In the west of Ireland there was a lake,
and no doubt it is there still, in which many
young men were at various times drowned.
What made the circumstance remarkable was,
that the bodies of the drowned persons were
never found. People naturally wondered at
this; and at length the lake came to have a
bad repute. Many dreadful stories were told
about that lake : some would affirm, that on
a dark night its waters appeared like fire—
others would speak of horrid forms which
were seen to glide over it; and every one
agreed that a strange sulphureous smell
issued from out of it.

There lived, not far distant from this lake,
a young farmer, named Roderick Keating,
who was about to be married to one of the

z 2

prettiest girls in that part of the country.
On his return from Limerick, where he had
been to purchase the wedding-ring, he came
up with two or three of his acquaintance, who
were standing on the bank, and they began to
joke with him about Peggy Honan. One said
that young Delaney, his rival, had in his absence contrived to win the affections of his
mistress ;—but Roderick's confidence in his
intended bride was too great to be disturbed
at this tale, and putting his hand in his
pocket, he produced and held up with a sig-
nificant look the wedding-ring. As he was
turning it between his fore finger and thumb,
in token of triumph, somehow or other the
ring fell from his hand, and rolled into the
lake : Roderick looked after it with the
greatest sorrow ; it was not so much for its
value, though it had cost him half-a-guinea,
as for the ill-luck of the thing ; and the water
was so deep, that there was little chance of
recovering it. His companions laughed at
him, and he in vain endeavoured to tempt any
of them by the offer of a handsome reward to
dive after the ring : they were all as little inclined to venture as Roderick Keating him-

self; for the tales which they had heard when children were strongly impressed on their memories, and a superstitious dread filled the mind of each.

" Must I then go back to Limerick to buy another ring ?" exclaimed the young farmer. " Will not ten times what the ring cost tempt any one of you to venture after it ?"

There was within hearing a man who was considered to be a poor crazy half-witted fellow, but he was as harmless as a child, and used to go wandering up and down through the country from one place to another. When he heard of so great a reward, Paddeen, for that was his name, spoke out, and said, that if Roderick Keating would give him encouragement equal to what he had offered to others, he was ready to venture after the ring into the lake ; and Paddeen, all the while he spoke, looked as covetous after the sport as the money.

" I'll take you at your word," said Keating. So Paddeen pulled off his coat, and without a single syllable more, down he plunged, head foremost, into the lake : what depth he went to, no one can tell exactly ; but he was going,

going, going down through the water, until
the water parted from him, and he came upon
the dry land : the sky, and the light, and
every thing, was there just as it is here ; and
he saw fine pleasure-grounds, with an elegant
avenue through them, and - a grand house,
with a power of steps going up to the door.
When he had recovered from his wonder at
finding the land so dry and comfortable under
the water, he looked about him, and what
should he see but all the young men that were
drowned working away in the pleasure-grounds,
as if nothing had ever happened to them.
Some of them were mowing down the grass, and
more were settling out the gravel walks, and
doing all manner of nice work, as neat and as
clever as if they had never been drowned ; and
they were singing away with high glee :

" She is fair as Cappoquin :
    Have you courage her to win ?
    And her wealth it far outshines
    Cullen's bog and Silvermines.
    She exceeds all heart can wish ;
    Not brawling like the Foherish,
    But as the brightly-flowing Lee,
    Graceful, mild, and pure is she !"

Well, Paddeen could not but look at the young men, for he knew some of them before they were lost in the lake; but he said nothing, though he thought a great deal more for that, like an oyster:—no, not the wind of a word passed his lips; so on he went towards the big house, bold enough, as if he had seen nothing to speak of; yet all the time mightily wishing to know who the young woman could be that the young men were singing the song about.

When he had nearly reached the door of the great house, out walks from the kitchen a powerful fat woman, moving along like a beer-barrel on two legs, with teeth as big as horse's teeth, and up she made towards him.

" Good morrow, Paddeen," said she.

" Good morrow, Ma'am," said he.

" What brought you here?" said she.

" 'Tis after Rory Keating's gold ring," said he, " I'm come."

" Here it is for you," said Paddeen's fat friend, with a smile on her face that moved like boiling stirabout*.

* Stirabout—gruel.

" Thank you, Ma'am," replied Paddeen, taking it from her :—" I need not say the Lord increase you, for you're fat enough already. Will you tell me, if you please, am I to go back the same way I came ?"

" Then you did not come to marry me ?" cried the corpulent woman, in a desperate fury.

" Not till I come back again, my darling," said Paddeen : " I'm to be paid for my message, and I must return with the answer, or else they'll wonder what has become of me."

" Never mind the money," said the fat woman : " If you marry me you shall live for ever and a day in that house, and want for nothing."

Paddeen saw clearly that, having got possession of the ring, the fat woman had no power to detain him ; so, without minding any thing she said, he kept moving and moving down the avenue, quite quietly, and looking about him ; for, to tell the truth, he had no particular inclination to marry a fat fairy. When he came to the gate, without ever saying good bye, out he bolted, and he found the water coming all about him again. Up he plunged through it, and wonder enough there was, when Paddeen was seen swimming away at the opposite side of the lake; but he soon made the shore, and told Roderick Keating, and the other boys that were standing there looking out for him, all that had happened. Roderick paid him the five guineas for the ring on the spot; and Paddeen thought himself so rich with such a sum of money in his pocket, that he did not go back to marry the fat lady with the fine house at the bottom of the lake, knowing she had plenty of young men to choose a husband from, if she pleased to be married.

Mankind have in all ages delighted to find their own image in all the parts of space. It is in consequence of this propensity that we find so frequently human beings, or divinities like to men in form, represented as dwelling beneath the sea, or within the waters of rivers and fountains. In Homer, the submarine cavern of Neptune at Ægæ is described in the 13th Iliad; and that in which Thetis and Eurynome concealed Vulcan, in the 18th. The only accounts given by the ancient poets of the descent of mortals into these aqueous abodes are that of Hylas, of which the best account occurs in the 13th Idyllium

of Theocritus, and of Aristæus, in the 4th book of the
Georgics of Virgil. As both these passages are remarkable, the reader will excuse the introduction of Greek
in Fairy tales, for the sake of considering them.   The
story of Hylas is well known.   Theocritus relates that
he went to fetch water for himself and his messmates
Hercules and Telamon, and that he came to a fountain
surrounded by herbage of the richest and most varied
kind.

Ὕδατι δ᾽ ἐν μέσσῳ νύμφαι χοροὸν ἀρτίζοντο,
νύμφαι ἀκοίμητοι, δεἴναι θεαὶ ἀγροιώταις.

    *   *   *   *   *   *

ἤτοι ὁ κοῦρος ἐπεῖχε ποτῳ πολυχάνδεα κροσσόν,
βάψαι ἐπειγόμενος, ται δ᾽ ἐν χερὶ πᾶσαι ἔφυσαν,
πασάων γὰρ ἔρως ἁπαλὰς φρενὰς ἀμφικάλυψεν
Ἀργείῳ ἐπὶ παιδὶ· κατήριπε δ᾽ ἐς μέλαν ὕδωρ.

        *   *   *   *

νύμφαι μὲν σφετέροις ἐπὶ γούνασι κοῦρον ἔχοισαι
δακρυόεντ᾽, ἀγανοῖσι παρεψύχοντ᾽ ἐπέεσσιν.

Hercules missing him, goes in search of him.

τρὶς μὲν Ὕλαν ἄϋσεν ὅσον βαθυς ἤρυγε λαιμὸς,
τρὶς δ᾽ ἄρ᾽ ὁ παῖς ὑπάκουσεν· ἀραιὰ δ᾽ ἵκετο φωνὴ
ἐξ ὕδατος· παρεὼν δὲ μάλα σχεδὸν εἶδετο πόρρω.

" Within the fount the nymphs perform'd their
        dance ;
The sleepless nymphs, aye rev'renced by the swains."

* * * * *

" The youth his spacious urn held o'er the fount,
Hastening to plunge it in, when all the nymphs
Caught on his arm, for love had clouded o'er
The tender minds of all, love for the charms
Of th' Argian boy, and Hylas headlong fell
Into the clear dark water."

* * * * * *

" The nymphs the weeping boy upon their laps
Holding, did soothe with gentle coaxing words."

* * * * * *

" Thrice he called Hylas, loud as his deep throat
Could shout, and thrice did Hylas hear him call :
A slender sound came from within the fount,
And though at hand, the voice seem'd far remote."

In Virgil, Aristæus, after the loss of his bees, stood
lamenting at the head of the Peneus, and is heard by
his mother from her cavern beneath the stream, who
directs Arethusa to bring him in :

" Duc, age, duc ad nos ; fas illi limina Divûm
    Tangere, ait ; simul alta jubet discedere late
    Flumina qua juvenis gressus inferret.   At illum
    Curvata in montis faciem circumstetit unda,
    Accepitque sinu vasto, misitque sub amnem."

The water thus forming a vault, yields an open
passage, and Aristæus arrives at the subterranean region, wherein are the caverns and sources of all the

rivers of the earth, and is received and entertained by
his mother after the fashion of the heroic age :

> " Manibus liquidos dant ordine fontes
> Germanæ, tonsisque ferunt mantilia villis.
> Pars epulis onerant menses, et plena reponunt
> Pocula ; Panchæis adolescunt ignibus aræ."

On comparing these passages of the classics, it will
appear that the idea the ancients had of the habitations
of the gods and nymphs beneath the water was, that
their caves were dry and impenetrable to the surrounding fluid, through which they could ascend and
descend at pleasure.   But the oriental conception of
the rational inhabitants of the aqueous realms is very
different, and of a more pleasing and philosophical
cast, and it is curious to compare the account of the
inhabitants of the sea given by Gulnare to the king
of Persia, in the story of King Bedir in the Arabian
Nights, with the philosophical Mythus in the Phædon
of Plato.   According to the former, the people of the
sea walk on the bottom of it with as much ease as
men do upon land, and the water answers to them
all the purposes that the air does to the inhabitants of
the earth : they have a succession of day and night,
and the moon, stars, and planets are visible to them.
Their palaces and other buildings are framed of the
most precious materials, far more splendid than any
thing upon earth ; and the sea-people have the power
of transporting themselves with incredible velocity

from place to place: in short, in every thing they have the advantage over the dwellers on earth. Now the sublime conception of Plato is, that what we call earth is not the true earth, but merely the bottom of one of the chasms of it; that the true earth is of prodigious extent, far excelling in every respect the spot on which we dwell, and which we dignify with the name of the earth; that the æther is its atmosphere, and the air is to it what the water is to this; that we, as has been said, dwell at the bottom of one of its seas, and consequently see all the heavenly bodies and the colours and forms of natural ones dimly and indistinctly through a dense medium. The chief difference between the Grecian philosopher and the eastern storyteller is, that the former more justly gives the advantage to those who respire the purer and rarer element, and are nearer in situation to the celestial regions.

In the romances of the middle ages, we meet, as might be expected, splendid dwellings beneath the surface of lakes. Of the romance-writers' mode of managing them, the reader may form a tolerable conception from that part of Don Quixote where the gallant Hidalgo frames a tale of adventure in strict accordance with what he had read in his books of chivalry; or perhaps better from the following extracts from the Orlando Innamorato, which the reader must take in the original Italian, as those parts of that poem have not been versified by Mr. Rose: had that been the case, or had they occurred in the first

eighteen cantos of the Furioso, it had been inex-
cusable not to quote from the most faithful, elegant,
and spirited translation that the English language can
boast of.

In l. 2, c. 8, of that most romantic of all poems,
Orlando, travelling in company with the enchantress
Falerina, after he had destroyed her magic garden,
comes to a lake, near which, in a meadow, stood a
gigantic Saracen. Orlando, in compliance with the
advice of his companion, was about to avoid the lake,
till, seeing the arms of his cousin Rinaldo suspended
as a trophy in the meadow, and thinking that Rinaldo
had been slain, he, though he had been latterly on bad
terms with him, determines to avenge his death. Accordingly, in spite of the entreaties of Falerina, he
defies the Saracen. After a long and fierce combat,
the latter, finding he could not vanquish the brave
Paladin, caught him up in his arms and jumped into
the water with him.

" Cadon egli ed il gigante dalla cima
    Del lago e l' un con l' altro al fondo viene
    Di quel lago crudel.

" Sen' andavano per luoghi oscuri e bui
    E già erano andati quasi un miglio.
    Essendo presso al fondo, dopo lui
    Vide il ciel chiaro Orlando alzando il ciglio,
    E l' aria tutta asserenarsi intorno,
    E trova un altro Sole, un altro giorno.

" Come se nato fosse un altro mondo
   All' asciutto trovarsi in mezzo a un prato,
   E sopra se videan del lago il fondo,
   Ch' era dal nostro Sole alluminato,
   E fea parer il luogo più giocondo,
   Il qual era poi tutto circondato
   D' una bella grotta cristallina,
   Anzi pareva pure adamantina.

" Era la bella grotta appiè d' un monte,
   Tre miglia circondava il vivo ghiaccio."

The other passage is in the last canto of the same
book. The same Orlando is led by the magic of
Atlantes into a laurel grove, and comes to a fountain:

      " Il fiume di Riso
   Ch' era l' Inferno e pare il Paradiso."

The poet thus relates the adventure:

" Entrato (nel bosco) scavalcò di Brigliadoro,
   Desideroso la seta saziare,
   Poichè legato l'ebbe ad un alloro
   Chinossi in su la ripa all' onde chiare.
   Dentro a quell' acqua vide un bel lavoro,
   Che tutto attento lo trasse a guardare.
   Là dentro di cristallo era una stanza
   Piena di donne, e chi suona e chi danza.

" Danzavan quelle belle donne intorno,
   Cantando insieme con voci amorosi

Nel bel palagio di cristallo adorno,
Smaltato d' oro e pietre preziose.
Già si chinava all' occidente il giorno,
Il Conte Orlando al tutto si dispose
Vedere il fin di questa maraviglia,
Nè più vi pensa, nè più si consiglia.

" Dentro a quell' acque, siccome era armato,
Gittossi e presto andò nel basso fondo.
Il fondo era un aperto e verde prato,
Il più fiorito mai non fu nel mondo.
Verso il palagio il Conte s' è avviato,
Ed era nel suo euor tanto giocondo
Che per letizia si ricorda poco
Perchè quivi sia giunto e di che loco.

" Vedesi avanti una porta patente,
Che d' oro è fabbricata e di zaffiro ;
Come il Conte fu dentro incontanente
Fur le donne a danzarli intorno a giro."

The circumstance of losing a ring in a lake is a
common preface to Irish tales of enchantment ;—see,
for instance, The Chase, in Miss Brooke's Relics of
Irish Poetry, p. 100.

THE LEGEND OF O'DONOGHUE.

In an age so distant that the precise period is unknown, a chieftain named O'Donoghue ruled over the country which surrounds the romantic Lough Lean, now called the lake of Killarney. Wisdom, beneficence, and justice distinguished his reign, and the prosperity and happiness of his subjects were their natural results. He is said to have been as renowned for his warlike exploits as for his pacific virtues; and as a proof that his domestic administration was not the less rigorous because it was mild, a rocky island is pointed out to strangers, called " O'Donoghue's Prison," in which this prince once confined his own son for some act of disorder and disobedience.

His end—for it cannot correctly be called his death—was singular and mysterious. At

A A

one of those splendid feasts for which his
court was celebrated, surrounded by the most
distinguished of his subjects, he was engaged
in a prophetic relation of the events which
were to happen in ages yet to come. His
auditors listened, now wrapt in wonder, now
fired with indignation, burning with shame,
or melted into sorrow, as he faithfully detailed
the heroism, the injuries, the crimes, and the
miseries of their descendants. In the midst
of his predictions he rose slowly from his
seat, advanced with a solemn, measured, and
majestic tread to the shore of the lake, and
walked forward composedly upon its unyield-
ing surface. When he had nearly reached
the centre, he paused for a moment, then
turning slowly round, looked towards his
friends, and waving his arms to them with
the cheerful air of one taking a short farewell,
disappeared from their view.

The memory of the good O'Donoghue has
been cherished by successive generations with
affectionate reverence; and it is believed that
at sunrise, on every May-day morning, the
anniversary of his departure, he revisits his
ancient domains: a favoured few only are in

general permitted to see him, and this distinction is always an omen of good fortune
to the beholders : when it is granted to many,
it is a sure token of an abundant harvest,—
a blessing, the want of which during this
prince's reign was never felt by his people.

Some years have elapsed since the last appearance of O'Donoghue.   The April of that
year had been remarkably wild and stormy ;
but on May morning the fury of the elements
had altogether subsided. The air was hushed
and still ; and the sky, which was reflected in
the serene lake, resembled a beautiful but de-
ceitful countenance, whose smiles after the
most tempestuous emotions tempt the stranger
to believe that it belongs to a soul which no
passion has ever ruffled.

The first beams of the rising sun were just
gilding the lofty summit of Glenaa, when
the waters near the eastern shore of the lake
became suddenly and violently agitated,
though all the rest of its surface lay smooth
and still as a tomb of polished marble. The
next moment a foaming wave darted forward,
and, like a proud high-crested war-horse, ex-
ulting in his strength, rushed across the lake

towards Toomies mountain.   Behind this
wave appeared a stately warrior fully armed,
mounted upon a milk-white steed; his snowy
plume waved gracefully from a helmet of
polished steel, and at his back fluttered a
light blue scarf. The horse, apparently exult-
ing in his noble burthen, sprung after the
wave along the water, which bore him up
like firm earth, while showers of spray that
glittered brightly in the morning sun were
dashed up at every bound.

   The warrior was O'Donoghue; he was
followed by numberless youths and maidens,
who moved light and unconstrained over the
watery plain, as the moonlight fairies glide
through the fields of air; they were linked
together by garlands of delicious spring
flowers, and they timed their movements to
strains of enchanting melody.   When O'Donoghue had nearly reached the western side of
the lake, he suddenly turned his steed, and
directed his course along the wood-fringed
shore of Glenaa, preceded by the huge wave
that curled and foamed up as high as the
horse's neck, whose fiery nostrils snorted above
it.   The long train of attendants followed

with playful deviations the track of their leader, and moved on with unabated fleetness to their celestial music, till gradually, as they entered the narrow strait between Glenaa and Dinis, they became involved in the mists which still partially floated over the lakes, and faded from the view of the wondering beholders : but the sound of their music still fell upon the ear, and echo catching up the harmonious strains, fondly repeated and prolonged them in soft and softer tones, till the last faint repetition died away, and the hearers awoke as from a dream of bliss.

Every person who has visited Killarney must be familiar with the Legend of O'Donoghue and his white horse. It is related in Mr. Weld's account of these lakes, in Derrick's Letters, and in numerous poems of which Killarney is the subject. Mr. Moore has made it the subject of a song in his Irish Melodies ; and the pencil of Mr. Martin, distinguished by his unbounded imagination, has been employed to illustrate it. This elaborate drawing is in the possession of Mr. Power, the spirited publisher of Mr. Moore's work.

That particular mortals have been permitted, as a
reward for their virtues, or condemned as a punish-
ment for their crimes, to revisit, at certain seasons,
their favourite haunts on earth, is a belief to be found
in most countries.   In Ireland, the princely O'Donoghue gallops his white charger over the waters of
Killarney at early dawn on May morning; and on a
certain night in August, one of the ancient Earls of
Kildare, cased in armour, and mounted on a stately
war-horse, reviews his shadowy troops on the extensive plain called the Curragh of Kildare, for

" ——————— Quæ gratia curruum
    Armorumque fuit vivis, quæ cura nitentes
    Pascere equos, eadem sequitur tellure repostos."

In Hindoostan, the virtuous and beneficent giant
Bali, whose pride when on earth brought down from
heaven the mighty Vishnoo to quell it, is, as a reward
for his virtues, permitted once in each year to revisit
earth, to feast his soul on the praises which the grateful
inhabitants of the land bestow on the memory of the
generous Bali.   The legends of the Germanic nations
are of a darker character, and in them we usually
meet the dead who " revisit the glimpses of the moon"
in the character of " wild huntsmen," sentenced, for
their tyranny or disregard of the rights of property, to
pursue the chase through the air and along the earth.
The north of England peasant stops and listens with
awe—

" For overhead are sweeping Gabriel's hounds,
    Doomed, with their impious lord, the flying hart
    To chase for ever on aërial grounds."

And the German *Bauer*, when benighted, often hears
howlings and shoutings in the air:

> " *Das ist des wilden Heeres Jogd*
>   *Die bis zum jüngsten Tage währt*
>   *Und oft dem Wüstling noch bei Nacht*
>   *Zu Schreck und Graus vorüber fährt*
>   *Das könnte, müst' er sonst nicht schweigen*
>   *Wohl manches Jägers Mund bezeugen.*"

It was a happy idea, and does credit to the imagination of the Irish peasantry, to assign May morn,
that most delicious of all days, that season so universally consecrated to the festive adoration of fresh and
youthful nature, as the period of the appearance of
the " good O'Donoghue," whose presence is the harbinger of plenty ; a sight like the Arabian " Gardens
of Irem" vouchsafed to but a favoured few.   The
Legend may remind the reader of the following beautiful passage in " The Flower and the Leaf :"

" ————————————— Know
That what you saw was all a fairy show,
And all these airy shapes you now behold
Were human bodies once, and clothed with earthly
    mold :

Our souls, not yet prepared for upper light,
Till Doomsday wander in the shades of night ;
This only holiday of all the year
We, privileged in sunshine, may appear :
With songs and dance we celebrate the day,
And with due honours usher in the May.
At other times we reign by night alone,
And, posting through the skies, pursue the moon."

It has been attempted, in the preceding notes, to
point out the circumstances from which the belief of
the existence of buildings and inhabitants beneath the
surface of lakes may have originated ; and it shall now
be attempted to explain the appearance of the " departed" at certain seasons. The human imagination
delights in bestowing the attributes of the animated
portion of nature on mere matter, particularly when
in motion : this was the source of ancient mythology,
and of the splendid system of polytheism formed by
the brilliant imagination of the Greeks. Thus At-
traction and Repulsion became animated, and were
Love and Strife ; these latter were personified ; behold Venus and Mars, whose offspring are Harmonia,
and Eros or Cupid, who rules over gods and men. The
savage or the unlettered hind stands on the shore of the
sea, or the border of a lake, and beholds waves dashing,
foaming, and chasing each other, and his fancy recalls
the speed, the emulation, and the foam of a set of spright-
ly coursers, and he terms the waves "white horses ;" by
the Welsh, in whose mythology *Gwenidw* is a female

who presides over the sea, the white breakers on the
shore are called *Devaid Gwenidw*, or the sheep of
Gwenidw. In the northern parts of Ireland, when the
wind blows softly from the east, and the snow slowly
descends in broad flakes, the children say the Scotch-
men are plucking their geese ; and towards the south
of the island they assign this action to the Welsh of
the opposite coast.   Herodotus gave the same solution
long since of the wonderful story which circulated in
Greece of a region far to the north where showers of
feathers continually filled the sky.   Optical illusions
may also contribute to cheat the imagination; and
the magic shows of the Mirage and of La Fata Morgana are well-known examples.   In one of the Spanish
histories of South America, we read that the inhabitants
of a certain district long resisted the attempts of the
missionaries to convert them, alleging as a proof of the
truth of their own religion, that at certain seasons their
gods used to appear to them, surrounded by troops of
worshippers, on the opposite side of a lake, in a consecrated valley.   An intelligent missionary examined the
story accurately ; he found that they had erected sta-
tues of their gods on the eastern side of the lake, and
that in particular states of the atmosphere, and at a certain elevation of the sun, as in the parallel case of the
" aërial Morgana," the figures of the idols and those of
their worshippers were reflected on the dense vapour
beyond the lake.   He explained the phenomenon, removed the idols, and his sagacity was rewarded by the
speedy conversion of the entire district.   If these two

B B

circumstances are combined with the *additive* power
of the imagination, the phenomenon of O'Donoghue
and his white horse will not be of difficult solution.
The stories of " Wild huntsmen" probably originated
in the distant baying of dogs, or other sounds heard
by the " lated peasant," when passing in the night
over the tracts where those mighty hunters had pursued the chase ; and imagination quickly conjured up
the rider and the steed, the hounds and the horns.

----

*The Shefro, the Banshee, and the other
creatures of imagination who bear them company, now take their farewell of the reader.
As knowledge advances, they recede and vanish,
as the mists of the valley melt into air beneath
the beams of the morning sun.*

*When rational education shall be diffused
among the misguided peasantry of Ireland,
the belief in such supernatural beings must
disappear in that country, as it has done in
England, and these " shadowy tribes" will
live only in books. The Compiler is therefore
not without hope that his little Volume,
which delivers the legends faithfully as they
have been collected from the mouths of the*

peasantry, may be regarded with feelings of interest.

And now, gentle reader, permit the " tiny folk," at parting, to address thee in the words of their British kindred, after their revels through " the Midsummer Night's Dream :"

> " If we shadows have offended,
>   Think but this (and all is mended),
>   That you have but slumber'd here
>   While these visions did appear : -
>   And this weak and idle theme
>   No more yielding but a dream,
>   Gentles, do not reprehend ;
>   If you pardon, we will mend."